SCORCHING LIES

C.M NYX

COVEN AND CO PUBLISHING

SCORCHING LIES

Book One

C.M Nyx

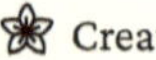 Created with Vellum

AUTHOR NOTES

Scorching Lies began as a co-write that soon turned into a story that I couldn't put down. Kenna Kingston and Ryker Stone have been pushing me to write their story as soon as I knew their names.

I thank Harper Ray for releasing this book to me to serve as my debut Dark Romance book! Thank you so much Harper for being such an amazing friend, author, teammate. This book wouldn't have been thought of if not for you.

I hope Kenna and Ryker are exactly who you pictured. To my readers, I pray that even in your darkest hour, you rise. Because you can be found even in the ashes. Rise.

DEDICATION

This is for the ones who show loyalty without question. The ride or die people who make water thicker than blood. Stand tall and bleed for me. Because you bleed, I bleed.

RYKER

TWO YEARS EARLIER

Smoke fills my lungs with each inhale. The open warehouse floods with the rancid smell of flesh burning, blending with the stench of death. Heat creeps up my spine, making my way through the open doorway, eyes stinging from the smoke, I struggle to see in front of me.

"Kenna!"

Coughing, my hand shoots up to my face in an attempt to block out the thick cloud of smoke. Fuck, I'm glad my boy G has been keeping an eye on the warehouse for me. Dad and Mr. Kingston have been meeting up here more often than normal, so I decided to keep my eyes on the lookout for intel. Being blindsided is the last thing we can afford right now.

The Kingston family has been in business with us for years, hell, ever since I could walk, and Kenna Kingston has been our little toy for longer. My brothers took the time to build a friendship where I decided to watch just in case. After all, she's set to be the princess of her daddy's empire.

"Dad!"

Shouting through the roaring flames my gaze finally falls on a shadow slumped against the corner wall. The size is too small for my father or Mr. Kingston, but Kenna has a thinner frame so I'm instantly on alert. Pulling in air through my nose under my lifted shirt, in an attempt to block out the soot, my knees drop to the ground.

Each move forward heats my skin under the orange glow. The concrete flooring scorches my skin as I crawl to the figure.

Long black hair covers a rounded face behind the raven dark curtain. Paige. What the hell is Kenna's best friend doing here?

"Paige?"

Brushing the wisps of hair from her sweat soaked face my body jolts back at the sight in front of me. Wide pale blue eyes stare blankly ahead focusing on the darkness behind me. Stumbling to the side my ass slams down on the floor, squeezing my eyes closed, I try to shake off the urge to vomit. What the hell happened? Rolling my shoulders my eyes pop back open scanning over Paige's body to see if there's any sign of foul play but come across nothing.

Bringing my hand up to her face, my fingertips gently brush her eyes closed. Swallowing down rage at the sight of my brother's first love dead in front of me I keep moving the need to find my dad and Kenna urging me forward. Pressing my body lower to the ground praying the ceiling holds long enough for me to find them. My gaze shifts to the left where a small room is. I hope that they made it there.

"Dad! Kenna!"

Clearing my throat, I try to shout their names again but the sound of creaking wood clashing with the roar of flames licking up the walls drowns me out. My palms blister against the sweltering floor, the pain biting into my skin until it sinks deeper, digging into my bones.

I mentally kick my own ass for not calling anyone, but my gut tells me this wasn't a planned meet up. None of this shit screams accident.

A small whimper pulls me closer to the room.

"Kenna?" My words scratch at the back of my throat.

"Rye?" A soft voice croaks.

My pulse kicks up when that name falls from her lips.

Speeding up, my shoulder presses into the wood opening the door more, causing blazing heat to rush from the room. Flames spread up the walls to cover the ceiling scathing everything in its path. I need to get to Kenna. My need to protect her spurs me forward through the biting heat that burns up my arms.

"Kenna?"

Two dark figures huddle together on the floor in the center of the room, with each step closer my stomach churns, knowing that one figure is far too fucking still. Kenna's usual blonde hair normally bright with a shine is now matted a dirty brown stuck to her sweat soaked body. Charring flesh fills my nose flooding my mouth with acid, but I keep my eyes on Kenna hoping she's still breathing.

Kneeling beside her, my eyes fall to the tall, lean, form next to her clutching her hand in his. My father.

"Dad?"

Gripping his shirt, I force him on his back bringing his eyes to mine, the slow blink making my heart pinch in my chest.

"Come on, I need to get you both out of here."

My words are gritted through clenched teeth. Hauling him closer my body screams under the new pressure of his weight. There's no way in hell I'm going to drag them both out at the same time. Slapping my dad's cheek, I force him to look at me begging him to see how hard this is for me.

"Dad, we have to go. Come on, please get up!"

Dragging him by his shirt my hands avoid the blisters covering his arms not wanting to cause him more pain. The smell of burnt hair fills my nose gagging me from the over-whelming aroma surrounding me. A hand grabs my wrist halting my forward movement with one touch.

"Take her first son."

His words are garbled but they ring in my ears, each word louder than the one before, he wants me to save her first. Shuddering breaths wrack his body, the rattling in his chest shattering the organ in mine. Shaking my head back and forth I'm forced to pull my mask down, blocking out all emotions until ice seeps into my veins. Ryker fucking Stone.

Licking my dry cracked lips, with a grunt I shove off the floor coming to a stand, the fear of being burned cast out of my thoughts. Reaching down, my hands wrap around

Kenna's blistering skin pulling a piercing scream from her lungs.

"Shhh baby girl, I've got you."

Her weight slams into me, tossing her over my shoulder, I call back behind me to the man who made me who I am.

"I'm coming back for you. I fucking promise."

It's that promise that haunts my nightmares. The same nightmares that house a scarred blonde princess, dragging me out of the fire by her teeth, snarling like the wolf she is.

She may have escaped with a few scars but when I'm finished with her, she'll wish the scorching flames engulfed her. I won't stop until she answers our questions starting with where the hell her dad went.

That night changed everything. The phoenix rose from the ashes more sinister than before and now I have the pleasure of plucking her wings, making sure she never flies again.

Saving Kenna killed my dad but that's not why she's going to suffer. No, the princess must pay for her fathers' sins and my dick twitches at the prospect of making her bleed.

CHAPTER ONE

KENNA

Reality. It was never as simple as being normal. For instance, college wasn't just college here in Del Mar. It didn't serve as a place to further education like the ads and letters in the mail explained. Instead, it was an egotistical place for frat boys and sorority girls to fuck and get drunk on any given day of the week. It's where money bought you a place on the social status train. Where elitist families fork out money to secure their little shits place here. It's also the place that bred my family, where my mom met my dad, where we built our name. It belongs to me.

Only, it doesn't belong to only me. Acid fills my mouth at the name sitting on the edge of my tongue. The Stone family and mine mixed in a liquid fire mess of status quo and power. This town wasn't home to me for the past few years. Yet, here I was going to school and contemplating my life choices. Was I throwing myself a pity party because things didn't go my way? *Fuck no.* That certainly didn't mean I wasn't void of emotions. I heard the whispers behind my back when people thought I couldn't. I saw the look of disgust from the people who were supposed to be my friends. This was all because of what went down that night, a night I would do *anything* to forget about.

Small fingers snapped in front of my face. "Kenna, are you listening?"

I blink, doing my best to revert back to the version of myself everyone wanted to see. The girl who was flawless and had no scars running down the side of her body hideous enough for people to run away screaming. The girl who wasn't hated by the three people she needed most. Nah, I was suppose to remain the rich girl who had everything handed to her. I was suppose to be the one who turned the Stone brothers lives upside down. That was my identity here at Hawthorne but I knew the truth and I plan on making sure everyone else does as well. I plaster a fake grin on my face.

"I'm listening."

Ally raises an eyebrow. "Oh really? And what did I say? Hmm?"

I scramble my brain to remember what she was talking about before I zoned out. I open my mouth to say something, but decide against it. All I'd come up with was a smartass retort she probably didn't want to hear. All I knew was it involved a guy, one I'd rather not think about, not yet at least. How had I ended up gaining a roommate that not only knew who the Stone brothers were, but happened to have fuck buddy status with West Stone himself.

She rolls her eyes. "As I was saying, a certain someone really knows how to rock my world if you know what I mean."

I scrunch my face and throw a fry at her. "Gross."

She wiggles her eyebrows, "You're just mad you didn't get any last night."

Hardly. I also wasn't in the mood to hear about how great she thought West was in bed. As far as I was concerned, he was dead to me. The *three* of them were dead to me. Of course, the three assholes were always around. It's been impossible to avoid them with the whole school kissing their asses. The people on campus *bowed* to them as if they were royalty anytime they came near. *It was bullshit.* They walk around campus like their shit doesn't stink and expect everyone to do their bidding. People fear them. God knows I should, but somewhere deep in my bones that little girl with cotton colored hair remembers how special and safe they made her feel.

"What are you thinking about?" Ally was always the inquisitive one, bringing me back to the tainted world around me.

On nights when the memories flood my dreams, a small part of me wishes it was me that died in the fire. Then the pain would fade away, the *torture* would be non-existent, and my scars would be gone. I'd managed to escape death twice and I wasn't sure how many more times I could escape it before meeting a fatal end. Hell, if Ryker had it his way, I *would* be dead.

I place my hand over my face in an attempt to wipe away the negativity I had running through my brain. "Everything, I'm having a hard time getting my head to shut up."

Understanding crosses her features and for a moment it seemed like concern shines bright in her hazel eyes, but it vanishes quickly after. "Have you run into them since they arrived?"

Rolling my eyes I laugh, "Like they would let me walk around campus without the constant reminder that they're here for me. West could have gone to a D1 school yet here he is, at a college built to breed businessmen and compliant women."

I mentally scoff. There was a lot I could've done. I could've done more to save my best friend. The boys' father would be alive, Ryker would still be my dirty little secret, and my dad would be here instead of where he is. Most importantly, Paige would be alive, here with me like we always planned. Nothing could ever be that simple though. I was destined to live life suffering through this loop of degrading torture.

Yeah, life was a fucked up world of what ifs. All because of that one night, my previous best friends, and family hated my guts. They want nothing more than to torture me until I burn in hell. I knew for a fact that Ryker, the oldest, was the one who wanted to see me perish. He blamed me. *They* blamed me for everything. I just wish I could remember the details of that night. I had to know if I truly was to blame. If my father really was the cause of everything that's happened since that day.

"Kenna, girl. I love you and all but you need to snap out of it. I said I had a brilliant idea and you're ignoring me. Again."

This was the one reason I loved this girl. She tended to call me out on my bullshit and not take any crap. I shake my head and clear my never-ending thoughts to focus on my best friend. "What's your idea?"

Her eyes lit up like a Christmas tree and a grin spreads over her face. "Milkshakes at The Yard?"

A laugh bubbled out of me. After everything, ice cream was the least of my worries. Ally had a weird obsession with ice cream. Really anything sweet, but ice cream was her weakness. The girl was obsessed to the extent of having it for breakfast some days. Rocky road would soon sell out if she kept up the pace. I had no room to talk because my obsession with chocolate went just as deep as hers.

"Alright, we can go," I paus, wrapping my fingers quietly around my keys. Her excitement bubbles over, but she has no idea who she is up against. "Last one to the car is buying!"

I bolt from the chair at the table and run as quickly as I can out of the room.

"Hey! Hold up you sly little shit!"

I laugh all the way out to the parking lot and slide in my red Mazda CX-3, waiting for her slow as molasses ass to show up. She huffs and glares as she climbs into the passenger side. "Not cool, Kenna."

A teasing grin plays on my lips as I start the ignition. "It's not my fault you're slow."

"You won this round bitch, but you're paying for the next one."

I put the car in reverse and begin to pull away from the spot when I hear a hissing outside. "Shit." I throw the car in park and swing the door open to see what was going on. My eyes immediately slide to the back tire on the driver's side when I see the evidence of what I heard. "Fuck!"

Ally rushes to get out the car, gripping her fingers around the door frame, "What's wrong?"

I purse my lips, breathing out a long exhale "Flat tire." My body moved around to check to make sure my other tires are good and my stomach drops when I realized not one, but all four of my tires are flat. "God dammit!"

A whistle comes from behind me and I quickly turn around. My gaze landing on Ryker leaning against the light pole watching. "Didn't your parents ever teach you to watch your language, princess?"

I grit my teeth. "What the fuck is your problem?"

His eyes darken with my words as he shoves off the post, stepping towards me.

"I'd watch that sharp tongue of yours princess, I'd hate for someone to cut it out." His smirk turns into a full smile filled with wicked intent.

My stomach bottoms out, his white teeth on display, the smile more of a snarl to those who really know him. This may be the smile he gives most people but I know the real one is hidden behind the mask. No, this one is saved for those who are on the outside looking in. Built for traitors and murderers. At least that's what he sees when he looks at me.

Ryker is gorgeous at first glance but he's rotten on the inside. Hell, at one point I was a girl that used to fall for his bright wide smile and sharp jawline. But it's his eyes that captivate you. It used to hurt looking into those deep pools of honey. Not anymore. I know better. His short midnight hair, thick tribal tattoos twist and swirl down the length of his arms. A large moth with its wings spread fan across his knuckles. Every inch of him pulls me in, not to mention the abs on his lean body, the man was designed for fighting. Power poured from him in droves. Every guy wants to be in his circle and every girl wants to fuck him.

"Just back off Ryker." Ally's trying her best to stick up for me, but I honestly wish she would just kept her mouth shut.

Ryker's smile is replaced with a sneer. "Stay in your place, pet." His gaze runs up and down the length of my body, holding a promise that my suffering would continue.

Ally clamps her mouth shut, not wanting to be added to his shit list, and I don't blame her. No one would. Becoming my friend may just cost her more than she bargained for when she became my roommate. Maybe I should have just rented out my own place so I don't drag anyone down with me but my need to be normal took over. If they're right about my father the last thing I want is to spend a dime of blood money. Fuck no.

A shudder escapes me, but I take a deep breath to try and keep myself from punching him in the face. "What do you want?"

He pulls out a cigarette and lighter, placing the cigarette between his lips. He takes his time bringing the flame towards the cancer stick, his eyes roll to the back of his head as he inhales a large drag through his lips, flicking the ash into the wind.

"Let's start with you leaving. Now. You came back for nothing princess. There's nothing left here for you."

"You don't run shit around here anymore. Hawthorne has always been Kingston territory, don't get it twisted."

Ally kicks me in the shin and gives me a *what the fuck* look. Tempting the devil must be a fucking skill.

If you can't beat them, join them. My dad's words ring through my head. If only he'd known the dangerous situation he'd put me in. Should I really be following the advice of a possible murderer?

Ryker's lips briefly tilt up at the corners. "Cute, killer. Really fucking cute."

He takes a few steps until he's standing directly in front of me. The sun beats down on us, and the heat, god, it's hot enough to make me sweat in places I didn't know I could sweat.

In the amount of time we've been standing here we've gained bystanders hanging around, gossiping, waiting to see what the infamous Ryker Stone plans on doing to the pathetic Kingston today. They are so fake. Always looking for a handout. I'm a princess, an heiress, until the Stone brothers come around. Then I'm nothing but trash they love to watch get tossed around. Like I said, fake. It's just a reminder that no one here can be trusted.

Suddenly, I want nothing more than to grab ice cream with Ally and forget about the shit show that is my life. I want to escape into a sea of ice-cold bliss for a few minutes, letting go of the stress and pain, saving it for a later day.

Ryker's brown eyes sparkle with malice as he makes his next move. Before I can blink, his lips are on mine, the sudden movement is overshadowed by the pain that flares against the flesh of my neck. That familiar burning heat that I know so well sears into my skin. Pure adrenaline and fear build in the pit of my stomach. A scream erupts from my mouth, pulling on my hair to deepen the kiss, and silence my screams. He shoves his tongue down my throat instantly making me forget the pain. Metal clicks against my teeth with the force of his kiss. It's brutal and bruising but my mind hazes over from the numbing fear.

Heat sears into my flesh, the smell of burning skin bringing back everything from that night. My muscles lock with fear. The force of his mouth on mine almost drowns out the horror of my skin on fire all over again. It's like I'm back in that fiery building, every nerve ending exposed, my skin melting off. Ryker sinks his teeth into my lip dragging me back to my body, that's in his arms, plastered to his chest.

For a moment, a brief moment, I forgot about where we were and the dick he'd turned into and lose myself in his kiss. With the mixture of cigarettes and mint invading my senses, he, once again, has me caught in his trap. A trap full of lies and deceit, and unrequited love. Like a snake coiling around his prey, squeezing the very breath from my lungs. Deep down, the boy I loved was trapped in the devil's body. The boy from my past would have never hurt me. Now that's the only thing that gives him pleasure. He tortured me. Made a mockery of his jokes. He used my pain and guilt to get ahead in life.

A throat clears in the background, snapping me back to the six foot tall boulder that inhabits every inch of my skin. Pressing my hands against his solid chest, I attempt to shove him away from me. I can't breathe. Can't think when he's that fucking close. His lips leave a searing hot pain in their wake, cracking my traitorous heart wide open once again for him. Our eyes connect and for a split second I swear the boy that I remember ages ago glimmers back at me. But just as quickly as it appeared, it's gone, leaving me longing for the Ryker I want, but can't have.

With a grin plastered on his face he steps back. He got exactly what he wanted. *Humiliation. Control. Taking what isn't his. Possession.*

The small wound on my neck was scalding, but not to the extent of something I couldn't handle. *No, I had been there before.* What Ryker did wasn't just to humiliate me, but to prove his ownership to any guy that may have shown any interest in me. I was a fucking toy to him. A plaything that he wanted to use and throw away whenever he damn well pleased. He wanted to make me rot for everything that I apparently did, and to do that, he was going to make me suffer.

CHAPTER TWO

RYKER

The taste of cherry chapstick still lingers on my lips, her wide doe eyes filled with shock still branding my thoughts. Kenna fucking Kingston. Shoving the fridge door shut, the beer in my hand chills my skin. Walking into the living room of our apartment a block away from Hawthorne Elite where all the rich pricks go to school. My brothers and I included, but we didn't feed into their bullshit there. No, we had bigger plans to worry about, ones that included the princess herself.

"Yo, man." West says, plopping down on the black leather couch.

Handing him and Cole the two beers in my left hand, I pop open mine before sitting on the other side of the couch. Cole ignores West, keeping his eyes trained on the baseball game on our large 62-inch T.V. hanging above the glass gaming system we have set up.

"What plans have you made now?" I ask, knowing he's gearing up to ask us to go out tonight.

West has never been able to sit around and keep his nose clean. Causing trouble and getting his dick wet has always been the goal for him. Cole keeps his business to himself but we all know where he goes every Sunday morning before he hits the gym. It's not spoken out loud and it won't be until he's ready to talk about it. We have one rule and that's *family*, always.

Smirking, West looks at me from the other end of the sectional, "Ally said there's a Hawks party tonight. Why don't we take a break from all the planning you have going on and get out of this damn apartment?"

Cole doesn't respond, he'd rather I handle the childish shit our middle brother pulls, but his shoulders tense at the mention of Ally. Or it could be the fact that Ally brings around Kenna, the one female none of us would touch, unless it's to cause the pain she's earned. My thoughts drift back to her mouth on mine curling my lip at the memory. Fuck.

A pillow smacks into my arm.

"What the hell?"

Chuckling, West yanks it back toward him when I reach for the soft weapon, "Come on. I won't get into anything that's not someone's pussy. Scouts honor."

"You were never a boy scout." Cole quips, a smile barely pulling at the corner of his mouth.

"What the hell ever. Are you in or not? It's not like I won't go by myself, more warm mouths for me and all that."

"Stop thinking with your dick. We have a meeting with the foundation tomorrow morning before school." I say, annoyed with this conversation.

Flexing my fingers, the itch to pound into flesh starts to creep back in. Hunger to spill blood twists my stomach, needing to get my hands on someone and fast. Maybe this party is exactly what I need. Hell, Cole could use a girl under him for one night with the way he's been lately. West, on the other hand, never has a shortage of women falling at his feet ready to blow him, fuck him, or share him all in the name of climbing the ladder.

Del Mar belongs to the Stone and Kingston family but not for long. As soon as we bring the princess to her knees, her perfect little kingdom will come falling down and there's fuck all she can do about it. The little killer has no idea what's coming for her. The image of her tear stained face begging for mercy makes my dick hard. I can taste her fear on the tip of my tongue.

"Rye."

Sighing, all I give him is a nod before standing up to go take a shower. He yells over the back of the couch making sure I can hear him.

"She'll be there."

My knuckles crack under the pressure of my fist clenching.

"I'm betting on it."

* * *

COLE SITS BEHIND me tapping away on his security app, running different codes on whatever the hell he works on for the foundation, while West scans Pandora for a song to blare on the radio. My grip on the wheel tightens with each turn we take that brings us closer to the Kappa house where the party is held.

Football punks always have to throw the biggest parties to fill the void of not being the prized possession of Hawthorne. That falls to the baseball team and with West as their pitcher we are set to go all the way to the championships. If it's not money pulling in women, it's his status as the school pitcher that does the trick.

Music floods from the speakers blasting Post Malone's new single *Mourning* blocking out the thoughts that try to take over. Tinted windows obscure our faces but everyone in Del Mar knows who drives the blacked out Chevy Tahoe with white rims. Spotting my boy standing at the edge of the lawn I swerve the SUV to the side, pulling partially on the sidewalk and putting it in park.

Rolling down the window, "G man." I call out, nodding my head at the approaching figure, waiting for him to give me the breakdown.

"He's here with her. They're inside dancing, but she hasn't had anything to drink yet."

He keeps his brown eyes level with mine, his mask in place not showing any emotion to the girl who used to hold all of our hearts in her hands. Until she bled us all dry.

Licking my lips I motion for him to hop in. Walking to the passenger side, he slides in behind West. Never one to feel uneasy around us, G falls into conversation with Cole and

West about bullshit while I think over my plan for tonight. He was warned to stay away from the princess but it looks like Romero never learned to follow the rules.

"Romero's getting handsy with what doesn't belong to him."

"And she belongs to you, brother?" Cole says, voice void of any inflection.

My grip on the wheel tightens, "She belongs to us until I fucking say otherwise. I have plans for the little princess but for now, we need to put Romero in his place."

West turns toward me, "Don't we have bigger fish to fry than some bitch boy on the football team? We may be going to this school for the foundation's benefit but that doesn't mean we have to act like them."

"West is right. Bringing the Kingstons down is the only reason we came to this school, not to run off any dick that tries to enter her rancid cunt. Kenna is our target, not Romero."

G looks between all of us but his stare lands on mine. He's been my right hand since we met in grade school and that was solidified the night of the fire. I can still hear him screaming my name over the roar of the flames outside the building. It took him an hour to calm me down after we saw them drag out my dad's charred body. His skin bubbled and blistered. I trust him almost as much as I trust my brothers.

"Handle him so I don't have to but leave the princess to me."

Jumping out of the SUV we head inside. West splits from us the moment he spots Ally in the doorway to the kitchen,

Cole's gaze following him the whole way. Grumbling something about needing a drink, Cole slinks off to the backyard where a keg is parked outside the door. Catching the back of G's head my eyes track him all the way to Romero where Kenna stands off to the side with a smile covering her face, her long blonde hair falling in waves down her back.

Dark blue jeans hug her thighs and hips like they were painted on. Paired with a deep red tank top, revealing the tan skin of her stomach when she laughs at something he says. I watch his hand reach up to brush a strand of hair from her face, his knuckles grazing her skin pulling her eyes to his. He fucking touched what I own.

Venom fills my veins at the sight of her joy. The urge to snuff out her freedom and drag her back to hell with me almost takes over, but I stand back to watch the show. She sees G a split second before he snatches the punk off his feet. G is a good foot taller than him, drags him away from Kenna in one swift move.

"Gio!" She screams, her voice grates against my skin.

G ignores her, continuing to haul him out to the front lawn. With all the partiers watching, he tosses Romero on his ass. Jumping to his feet they come nose to nose but before Romero thinks to take a swing he sees me from the corner of his eye. Leaning against the frame of the house my eyes stay on his. I can feel the heat of her stare glaring into the side of my face but I don't look away from the fucker in front of me.

"Looks like Romeo here doesn't know how to follow the rules." I announce.

No one moves. No one speaks or takes a drink of their alcohol. I have everyone's attention on us. Not only are we going to humiliate her but I'm going to make sure she never forgets her place here. Hawthorne belongs to the Stone family now.

"He's all yours G." I nod, giving him what he craves.

My finger twitches with the sound of fist hitting flesh, wishing it was my hands beating the shit out of Romero but I have my sights set on punishing a killer. Pushing off the frame my legs eat up the distance between us bringing her mere inches from me.

"What, are you following me now?"

Without a word, my fist closes over her hair dragging her into me, I grip her thigh with my free hand lifting her over my right shoulder. No one stops me from hauling her back in the house and up the stairs to an empty room.

"Put me the hell down asshole!"

Screaming and punching my lower back, I wince when she hits a sore spot in the center of my spine. Kicking the door shut behind me, I drop her to the ground not concerned with how hard her ass slams into the hardwood flooring. She cries out in agony, but I don't give a single fuck. I yank her from the floor, slamming her chest into mine.

"Let me go!"

My hand closes around her throat, cutting off her next breath. My blood boils with the feel of controlling her, having power over the princess. The killer who ruined my fucking life. I promised him that I'd make her pay. This was my chance to taint her, just a little taste, before we bring her castle crumbling down.

Leaning in, my breath fans across her skin, "I promise to fuck your foul pussy while I watch you burn. I can see the way your body begs for my dick just like when we were kids."

Squeezing tighter, I force her back against the door, tears springing to life at the edge of her eyes, her chest heaving with the attempt to breathe.

"I bet your cunt is dripping." I grit, my teeth clenched.

"Fuck. You." She manages to get out.

"Oh I will. As I carve my name into your skin."

We are chest to chest now, her face red and tear stained. I just need to know. Sliding my fingers down her stomach, I watch her as they slip into her jeans, gliding past her thong. Her eyes widen.

"You sick fuck." She growls out.

Licking the side of her neck, I bite down hard forcing a deep groan from the back of her throat. The little bitch is getting off on it.

"You're a fucking slut for my hands, aren't you? I bet this pussy is soaked from the thought of me touching you. Let's see how wet you really are."

My fingers inch lower, brushing the tips along the seam of her wet cunt. I look her dead in the eyes, my gaze turning feral. Moving the fabric to the side, I plunge two fingers inside her without warning. My eyes never leave hers, examining her features, but she slams a mask into place.

Twisting my fingers inside her I pump them in and out while watching her struggle to breathe.

"That's right princess you're going to fucking come all over my hand knowing I'm the only one that will ever touch your pussy before you're ruined. No one will want you when I'm done."

Biting her bottom lip to hold in her moans, not willing to give me the sounds I force from her lips, I press my thumb against her clit. My dick strains against the zipper of my pants. My hold on her throat sends visions of her choking on my dick into my head. Until they are replaced with the smell of burning flesh.

Repulsion fills me. I'm letting her fuck my hand when all I really want is to make her hurt. Make her *suffer*. Sneering at her, my body tenses when I feel her cunt start to quiver around my fingers. Pulling out right before she comes down my hand, I shove her to her knees and pull out my dick. Pumping myself with the hand that was just inside her, I spread her wetness around my dick.

Tilting her head back with her hair wrapped in my fist, I growl, "You're going to watch me come knowing that you don't get that fucking privilege."

Pumping my hand faster, I watch her eyes take in my length, the curious look on her face fueling my wicked pace. Her tongue peeks out to wet her lips and I'm tempted to shove it in her mouth but I refrain. Fucking my hand faster, I snake my other one around her head, pulling her hair harder until she's crying out in pain. The music bellowing from her throat pulls the orgasm out of me, white hot ropes of cum decorating her face.

I keep pumping until I have control over myself again. Tucking myself away I lean down looking at the beautiful mess I made. My smile drops as I see the moment it clicks for her. I don't get off on what she makes me feel. My dick is only hard at the thought of her suffering.

"That's it princess, now you see. You'll never be anything more than a place for my cum to land and a warm hole for my dick. Let another man touch what belongs to me and I'll fuck you on his dead body as we watch the life drain from his eyes. The last thing he'll see is your pussy choking my dick."

Her eyes widen in shock but lust swirls in her irises. "We both know I'll do it so don't test me again, killer."

Gripping her around the throat, I shove her onto her ass and storm out the door. With a stiff dick and a craving for blood, I head to the one place that will take care of both.

CHAPTER THREE

KENNA

*O*range flashes with each blink of my lashes bringing the bright glow closer. Heat crawls across my skin until I'm fully covered in sweat mixing with the damp tears that roll down my cheeks. It's so hot. Scorching. My hands struggle to find something, anything, to grip in an attempt to drag me from my spot on the concrete. Everything is on fire, flames engulfing everything in its path. A choked sob catches in the back of my throat at the thought of my best friend, Paige, laying on the other side of the burning wall.

Knowing she's gone and processing the loss of her isn't the same but I don't have time to focus on that. Not when Mr. Stone is lying across from me bleeding and blistering from the fire licking its way up his body. Dead, we're all going to be fucking dead, and my father is missing with no trace of where the hell he went. The ache in my bones is nothing compared to the chill my nerves feel being torched down to bare flesh.

"Kenna!"

A deep voice screams my name from somewhere in the clouds of smoke but I can feel my chest getting heavier with each breath.

"Kenna!"

That voice reaches me again only it's closer and more frantic. I beg my eyes to open, my lashes fanning across my cheeks, the smell of singed hair and vomit pungnet around me. The fire reaches me before the voice does, the flames climbing my leg. My mouth falls open on a scream, the pain overtaking every inch of me, wide eyes watching the orange spread up my left side, my vision blurs.

"Oh god! Oh god!" My voice is hoarse.

Thrashing in an attempt to put out the fire melting my flesh, sweat pools around the top of my lip. Before blacking out, all I see is a dark figure running towards me and my screams cutting off.

Jolting awake from the nightmare from that night I roll over to check the time on the clock next to my bed.

"Shit."

Cursing myself for being up an hour before my alarm is set to go off I swing my legs off the bed to sit up. My grey sheets are soaked down to the mattress with sweat, the Nirvana shirt I wore to bed sticking to my back. Fuck it, I needed a shower anyway. I only give myself a second to breathe through the terror of my memories. Memories that fade once I wake, before jumping up to take a cool shower. My dorm room is a decent size, considering the money we poured into this place, so I got lucky when I was able to pick from the best ones.

Stepping into the living room from my doorway I head down the hall towards the shared bathroom between mine and Ally's rooms. We fought over the color scheme for the shared space since she's all pinks, purples, and girly while I'm more grey, black, and beach bum. Combining the two styles was hard enough, but once you add her need for all things beauty products the bathroom is kind of a fucked up place. Slowly opening the door to avoid the creak it makes, my toes scrunch into the fuzzy grey rug I bought after winning that one fight.

It was a win so that's all that matters, because aside from the rug, everything else in here is covered in pinks and blacks. One thing we could come to an agreement on, is that black and pink go together. I get what I want and so does she, even if we bickered the entire shopping trip. Tugging back the black cloth shower curtain covered in pink lilies to turn the water on, I step back to let it warm while my eyes trace over my reflection. Trailing my fingers over the dark circles under my eyes, my inner bitch drags me for letting a nightmare ruin my sleep. As if I had a choice.

Stripping down and stepping under the warm water, my muscles release with a long exhale. Why did I have to relive that night before the first day of school? As if I didn't have enough shit to worry about this semester. The Stone brothers have turned my life upside down since they arrived a few weeks ago. They'll never forgive me for something I can't remember and the other night at the party is just a reminder that Ryker just wants to watch me break.

Avoiding my left side, my loofa scrubs my skin until it's bright red. My eyes never stray to the burns that start at my ankle and spread to the top of my thigh, ending just below my ass cheek. Unable to stomach the constant reminder of despair that haunts my flesh, I keep my gaze away. The carnage of losing my best friend and my father, permanently etched into my skin. I finish my shower with my thoughts on Rykers hands around my throat, my core clenching with the reminder.

Wrapping my favorite fluffy black towel around me, I head back to my room to get dressed for the day. The only plus side to being up before the sun is being able to shower without Ally banging on the door rushing me. That girl lives in front of the mirror but I love her anyway.

Meeting her on the first day of orientation was a blessing I didn't know I needed, but it was her bubbly personality that covered the fact that I hated being here at all. My mother being an Alumni was the only driving force for me coming to this prim and proper snob fest.

Spending months in the hospital with countless skin grafts changes a girl's look on money and status, even when I'm the richest of them all. Not that it stops them from fucking with me every chance they get now that the Stone brothers are here to sik their dogs on me. Little bitches. Once upon a time, I thought college would be the place where I could be myself. Maybe join a sorority, or live off campus and party it up with the Stone's, but now? I know that was just a fantasy that went up in flames along with my life.

Dressing in dark skinny jeans and my white long sleeve crop top, I decided to leave my damp hair hanging down my back. Not in the mood to put anything on my face to cover the dark rings under my eyes. My bare feet slap against the wood floor on my way to the kitchen, I flip on the light and make my way to the coffee pot, going through the motions to get ready for the day.

Coffee, check.

Cereal, check.

To go cup for Ally and myself, double check.

I'm sitting at the small marble countertop, my spoon clinking against the bowl, when a groan meets my ears.

"Why does the first day back have to be right after a party?" Ally's sleep filled voice comes up from behind me.

Chuckling, I slide her cup of coffee to the edge of the counter, "I think it's the other way around. Why is a party thrown the night before school starts?"

Her dainty hands grip both sides of the cup, tilting it to her lips, her eyes drifting closed with the first sip.

"Hardy har har. You're just pissed because psycho number one ruined your fun with the jock." Her smirk slides into place.

Closing my mouth over the last bite of chocolate cereal, I make an effort to ignore her snarky remarks but her next one makes it impossible.

"Too bad too because I've heard he's good in bed. Lucky for you I got laid last night by Mr. Playboy himself so you can live through me now that they all but declared you off limits."

My spine snaps straight, "What the hell do you mean off limits?"

Looking at me from the corner of her eye while she preps her breakfast she must see the look on my face because her smile drops instantly.

Letting out a breath, "Ryker dropped that little bomb last night after you rushed back here. Apparently he's naming your pussy his and no one is allowed to touch."

Shrugging my shoulders I let it roll off me.

"Not like I give a shit anyway."

Dumping my bowl out in the sink I wash it and put it away before turning back around.

"I'm going out tonight after classes so don't wait up but if you decide on dinner let me know and I can Venmo you for my half."

With that I leave behind my roomie to get herself all dolled up for the day. It takes me ten minutes to reach the south side building for my first course. The lawns on campus are maintained with perfection. Each bush trimmed, every tree perfectly pruned, and the sidewalks lined with flowers. Coming up to the entryway, the two giant hawk statues on each side of the massive double door entrance stare back at me. The crest of Hawthorne Elite mocks me with each step closer, my fingers close over the brass handle, but before I can tug it open the door flies at me.

"Shoot, I'm sorry!" A deep voice fills my ears.

My eyes shoot up, connecting with deep blues matching the color of the sea. One is darker than the other, pairing perfectly with the black and blue covering one half of his face. My mouth opens but snaps shut once my brain finally connects the dots. Holy shit.

"They did this to you?" I snap, my voice is an octave too high.

He checks over his shoulder, looking around as if someone will see him speaking to me. Never making eye contact.

"Look, you're a fun time but I can't afford to be seen with you. No pussy is worth losing my place on the team and your boy Ryker has made it clear that if I touch you again, or so much as breathed on you, I'd be dead."

"You don't honestly think he'd kill you Romero." My eyes roll.

That's when he finally meets my glare, "Yes, I do. Him and his brothers are fucked in the head and when it comes to their little toy? Yeah, it's not worth it."

Storming past me his long legs carry him further away until there's nothing left of him visible. What the hell was that?

CHAPTER FOUR

RYKER

The tapping of my thumb on the leather steering wheel of our Tahoe mimics the beat of Cole's music.

"How long are we going to sit here watching her walk through campus?" Cole asks, his eyes not lifting from his iPad.

He never goes anywhere without at least one of his toys. His need to be in control of everything. He has gotten us out of serious shit, the way he can move around inside networks, decoding, it's a brilliant skill to have for our particular family business. It's even better when he can track a certain blonde haired princess that's out late tonight.

"Until I figure out where the little killjoy goes every night."

West scoffs from the passenger seat, phone in hand, scrolling whatever app he has pulled up. It's a surprise that he's with us tonight instead of in the pants of one of the cheerleaders. Hell, our little killer's roommate, Ally, is always riding his jockstrap. Ignoring my brother's complaints, my gaze finds the back of her head. Long blonde hair is piled high on her head. She uses an oversized black hoodie to cover her body, but what catches my eyes is the long expanse of leg visible under that hoodie.

What the fuck? Her toned tan legs are bare all the way up to the hem. My fingers tighten around the wheel, knuckles turning white, just looking at her shuffling into her dorm hall. It takes me several minutes to process what I saw before my attention is pulled to Cole.

"What the hell was she wearing walking across campus at night?" My voice is hard.

"Well, she wasn't with Romeo because a little bird just posted a photo of him and Cassie with his tongue down her throat. So, the question is who didn't listen to the hands off order."

Looking up from his iPad the light shines on his hollow green eyes, the dark circles under them staring back at me. Reminding me that we need to keep an eye on him. West pockets his phone beside me, our eyes connecting for a split second before he breaks the silence. My attempt to tune him out about getting his dick wet is useless. Coming to Hawthorne was supposed to serve a purpose, to make sure she suffered for what her dad did.

"Yo, let's go. I've had enough of this undercover cop bullshit take me by the baller's house. I have a cream pie sandwich to fill." West says, propping his elbow against the window.

Slugging him in the shoulder, I pop the SUV into reverse and pull out the parking lot. We only make it a block away before G is calling my phone. Running the metal ring across the back of my teeth my finger taps the green button on the screen.

"Hey man." I answer, keeping one hand on the wheel.

"My man, we have movement from Kingston's lackey Hank. We've been keeping tabs on Kingston's calls and who he meets with and this time we have someone that's pulling on the list you gave us. Want us to follow him?"

Hank was one of my dad's old colleagues that was brought into the business by Kingston himself. He hasn't been seen since that night and now we have him spotted close to town. My phone creaks under the pressure of my fingers and the taste of rage seeps into my tastebuds. If he and Kingston are working on something together we'll be the first to know about it, that I'll make sure of. This isn't their town anymore. The Stone family no longer holds a partnership with the Kingstons and never will again.

"Follow him but lay low. The last thing we need is him aware of us watching Kingston's every move."

Hanging up, my phone slides across the dash after I toss it. It takes a deep breath and Cole's voice to yank me back to the road.

"Hank Harlow?" Cole asks.

I give him a curt nod, keeping my focus out the windshield, "He's back in town it seems. Which means we need someone with eyes on Princess Kingston every second. If she so much as breaths near her dad's building I want to know about it. West, get a team together to snuff her out, we need her to think she's back in your good graces. Use her girl Ally if you have to, fuck her, turn her out, I don't care."

He pulls out his phone with a smirk, "I'd fuck her for the hell of it, but the motivation makes it more fun. Cole, let's see if we can get the little killjoy's phone for a tracker. If Hank is close and visiting her dad then that means they are planning something."

"Hmm."

Cole adjust his legs again, getting restless with the constant reminder of what her family did to ours. What we lost because of greed and money hungry men. The air around us shifts into revenge driven rage and now we all have a job to do, but I'll take joy in mine. She thinks the fire burned her perfect bronze skin? I'll make sure she's nothing but embers drifting into nothing when I'm done with her, but not before I fuck the happiness from her eyes.

West steps out into the dark night, shutting the door without saying anything. He'll be home later, either tonight or tomorrow, after he's finished having his fill of the pussy sandwich he plans to indulge in tonight. Cole stays in his spot, unmoving, eyes still cast down at whatever he sees on the screen. Driving the three blocks back to our place we ride with the radio off, both of us lost in our own thoughts. Where Cole goes when he's thinking of her we don't know, but the danger is always there buried deep in the ground. We almost lost him to the deepest depths of his mind after the fire. After we lost her. Thankfully our focus on making the princess pay has given him something to fixate on.

Sunday is tomorrow though and Cole will be gone all day just like every other Sunday before. It's all he can do to keep his head on straight. West on the other hand would rather bury his dick into anything that walks to drown out what it meant to lose everything we thought we had. Using warm bodies.

I use other things.

Things that could ruin us.

Pain. Blood. Money. They all have one thing in common. Control. It's what makes us the most powerful college students at Hawthorne Elite.

Money brings us anything we want. Everything.

Blood spilling, well that brings us fear. Drinking it in like the devils we are.

Pain. Causing it and living in it. They go hand in hand and my addiction to it will be my greatest downfall. When they all bring me back to my little killer I know it will be me who does her in but what they don't know is I'll follow her down to hell. The hellfire of what we are, what we've become, will bring us both to our end but she'll be at my feet when she falls.

When we were kids my brothers pampered her with love, gifts, and adoration. Her hold on them, my family, even her father was unmatched. I can still see her wide smokey eyes looking up at me with curiosity. Short blonde hair bouncing with each laugh escaping her pink lips. My hands twist the leather of the wheel remembering the way my hands would sweat whenever she came near me. It's like my body knew she was the burning sun, forbidden to look at, a burning star forever out of reach. The singe on the tips of my fingers is a sign that we've orbited too close to each other but what's an inch closer?

A taste.

A drop of blood.

I need to feel her skin under mine. Heated. Flushed. *Searing.*

CHAPTER FIVE

KENNA

It's been three days of nightmares. Three days of me waking up to a soaked bed. Sweat and tears mix into my skin through the terrors that take over my body. Each night I wake to the same thing. A dark voice in my memories, sobs rattling my chest, and exhaustion have been my constant this week. It's what led me to the same place each night for over a week, my muscles spent, and my energy so low I could barely manage to force my legs to make the distance back to my dorm.

Ally texted me earlier asking if I wanted her to grab me something for dinner, but my stomach groaned at the thought immediately. My body couldn't handle as much fast food as she ate, but I stopped at Murphys to grab a few things the other day, so I knew there was something in the fridge for me to make. Making it back to the dorm was the only thing keeping me from stuffing my face and it damn sure wasn't getting easier to walk. Crossing into the court-yard only two buildings from my dorm, I spot a large SUV sitting off to the side of our parking area just under the broken street lamp.

Keeping my head forward while I peeped over my shoulder, my gaze rolls over the dark tinted windows where the heat of someone's stare meets mine. Chills run down my spine with the feel of someone's eyes boring into me. Gripping my hoodie sleeves, pulling them over my hands, I pick up my pace attempting to make it into the lit space just ahead. The dorm building appears in front of me after a couple seconds of power walking, the strain on my legs screaming at me, but I can finally see the large glass double doors.

My building is tall and wide with three stories of decent sized apartment shaped dorms. The outside is old style Victorian with flower baskets on the outside of each window. Our campus keeps the lawn well kept with flowers, bushes, and greenery. Our headmaster has a green thumb. Our entire campus has massive rod iron fences surrounding the grounds that stretch to just over six feet tall, but it's the sharp diamond shape points on each post that grabs people's attention. Our families poured money into this school, making damn sure that it had the appearance of a castle, built perfectly for their little royalty elite brats. Money has never been a problem for me, but after losing everything it's the least important thing in my life right now.

The Stone brothers don't think I belong here, after all I don't flash my wealth around like most of these spoiled shits, and well, I killed their dad. At least that's what they want me to think. The problem is I can't seem to make myself believe I didn't, other than the voice in my ear when my eyes close. It tells me that they're there to help me and they make promises that, from what I can tell, have not been kept. A door shutting has me jumping back into the here and now, my head whipping around to see a tall lean figure standing in the shadows near the SUV.

"Fuckkkk." I breathe.

I'm only a full yard away from the door handle, but footsteps behind me almost have my body locking into place out of fear. That SUV? Yeah, I've seen it around campus before, it's one of theirs. It's one of the Stone brothers or their right hand man, G. Scoffing at his one letter name seems to snap me out of my fear induced shock. My steps pick up until I'm almost sprinting the short distance.

Why am I running from them?

Reaching out for the door, my fingers close over the cold metal when a heavy body slams me into the glass, cracking my head on the hard surface.

"Because your body is smarter than your head. It knows a viper when it sees one."

His voice is muffled by my ear pressing against the glass. My head swims from the force of his weight throwing me against the door. It takes me a few seconds to come back to the present, my eyes blurring for a moment. He must feel my muscles bunch, preparing to struggle, because his laugh is low and deadly, prompting me to pause.

"Come on killer, you think I'd let you get away so soon? Don't tell me you don't enjoy my body being on top of yours." His voice is still too low.

"Get- get off!"

Bucking against his heavy arms that are holding me in place, I begin to heave from struggling against him. Heated fingers brush the fallen hair from my face, revealing a lethal Ryker looking like a snake ready to strike. The way his eyes roam over me with disgust has me biting into my cheek until blood spills into my mouth.

"Get the fuck off me!" My palms shove against the glass.

Only moving an inch, his chuckle is low and dangerous. The scent of musk, danger, and fire lingers on his skin, assaulting my senses as he pinches the sides of my face with one hand. His thumb and pointer finger digging into my face, pressing my skin against my teeth.

"Looks like the little killjoy found herself out all alone in the middle of the night. Don't you know better than to walk the campus after dark princess?"

Shaking my face so hard the skin on the inside of my cheek split against my teeth. Growling under my breath, I refuse to give him anything other than indifference. Two more steps and his heated body is flush against me digging me into the door even more. Rolling his gaze down my frame they stop on my legs. *The* leg. The one place I hate having attention. He sees it and that's enough to make my stomach recoil. It's not the blood, or the forceful way he controls my body, or even the fear drowning me from the inside out. No, it's antici-pating the look of horrified disgust that I know is coming.

"Hmmm, look at that."

Using his free hand, he traces the space between the back of my knee and thigh on my left leg Brushing his fingers over the jagged skin and scars that spread down, down, down. I tear my eyes from his hand, from the reminder of what happened. The tips of his fingers drag my eyes to his, but what I see isn't what I expected. I expected horror and disgust to stare back at me. I'm caught off guard when I see pure, raw hatred shining back at me.

"Looks like we're not the only ones who carry that night around with them. Mine comes with the last name of the person we lost, but you? You, killjoy, carry the mark of a fucking murderer."

He twists me until I'm no longer sideways on the door, instead my back is pressed into the handles, forcing a grimace on my face. Sliding his grip from my face to my throat, he drags me up with no effort. My toes scrape the ground and my heart is punching out of my chest. My hands grip around his, clawing at his skin as my breathing becomes ragged.

Leaning closer his nose brushes mine, lips millimeters away, his words hit somewhere buried deep in my soul. A place I refused to go.

"You were his princess. Our fucking ride or die." His tongue slips out to wet his lips. "It'll taste so sweet when I'm the one who gets to set you on fire."

"I didn't-"

Slamming his mouth down on mine, he bites my bottom lip, yanking it so hard my scream shoots out of me. By now my mouth is filled with cuts, each one caused by the viper striking his prey, taking and taking until there's nothing left. Kissing me, biting me, stealing my air. My legs shake, fear turning and twisting into need and I fucking hate myself for it. My mind battles my body in a war of will. He pulls away from the kiss just as quickly.

"I don't want to hear your lies. Because that's all they are. Fucking *lies*. You wear the mask well, but when I'm done with you, there'll be nothing left but a shell. A corpse. Ashes. You are nothing to us. You don't belong here anymore princess and it's time you learn your place."

He leans down, grazing his lips up the length of my neck. Goosebumps prickle my flesh from his touch. I hate that he makes me feel like this. Loathe the fact he causes me to have a reaction at all. A grunt is pulled from his throat, waves of vibration replacing his touch.

"I can't wait to fuck you. It'll be the last thing you remember when I destroy you. My dick buried so far in your wet cunt that it's the only feeling you have left before I snuff the life out of you."

His tongue flattens against my skin, sweat starts to bead and my legs shake from his words. The worst part? Battling my inner demons at the thought of him inside me. My core clenches with images of him over me, fucking me, choking me, dragging my body close, only to lose everything. Because I will lose everything after he leaves me for dead.

"That's it baby, you can't wait to feel me sinking into you. Taking everything from you."

"Fuck you." I spit between clenched teeth.

Tisking, dark eyes peer at me through long lashes.

"Don't let me see these again." Fingers drag across my leg.

Tears build, but I hold them back refusing to let them spill.

Releasing me, I'm finally able to pull in a deep breath. My hands fall to my knees, my body sagging.

"Next time I catch you out after dark walking around dressed like that, I'll make sure your knees are bruised for weeks."

Squeezing my eyes closed, his footsteps drift until all I hear is my heart pounding in my chest. Anger, hurt, disgust, they all war within me, beating against my ribs. Yet still I hold the tears. I don't let them fall, not while I'm walking into the building. They don't fall when I step into the small metal elevator, or even when my hand closes around the small silver doorknob to my dorm. Inhaling a large breath, the door swings open to our dimly lit living room, Ally long gone to bed.

Still the tears don't fall. Passing the sectional couch pressed along the far wall, I step past the end tables filled with family photos from Ally. I walk by the kitchen with marble counters and stainless steel appliances and pass by the bathroom with Ally's night time skin care scattered over the counter. Yet the tears hold. I finally reach my bedroom door and fling it open, revealing my partly made bed and last nights pajamas littering the floor. Not attempting to shower or change, I decide that stripping off my hoodie and sleeping in a sports bra and shorts is fine, as long as I don't have to move, I climb into bed and burrow under the blankets.

Memories of hide and seek, family BBQ's, shared Fathers Days, and so many other family events flash behind my eyelids. The dam breaks. Finally fucking breaks causing a tsunami of to wreck through my body.

It's always the silent cries that hurt the worst, that drain everything from you, the silent pain that you carry on your shoulders because you have no one else to give it to. When you lose someone, someone so close to you that it's like losing a limb. There is no healing that pain. So I cry. I scream into my pillows. The unknown of why this happened fades into anger. The questions drift into demands. And all it really leaves me with is a cold resolve that if I can't remember what really happened then I'll ask the one other person left alive that does.

Tonight I don't dream of fires and screams. I don't see flames and bodies. My skin isn't melting from the heat. There is no deep voice of soft words and kindness. No. I see the boys from my childhood playing tag and letting me win. Cole rushing to me with flowers freshly snatched from his mom's garden. My memories drag West from the bushes scaring us so bad I cry, but not for long. No, Ryker comes from around the back of the house when he hears me, only to stop when he sees his brothers are already calming me.

Standing off to the side watching us. Watching me. Heated stares comfort me into a deep sleep and I don't stop feeling them even when I wake up to my phone alarm the next morning.

CHAPTER SIX

KENNA

Migraines are the bane of my existence. Waking up with one after a night of no nightmares? Ironic. Even when I'm awake my brain has to fuck with me. Groaning, I roll off my bed, my energy already drained before my feet even hits the floor. This calls for hot coffee and my favorite oversized navy blue sweater. It's my comfort item. My eyes adjust to the dim light in my room, thank fuck for blackout curtains. I end up tossing on the sweatshirt over my sports bra opting out of an actual shirt and pairing it with loose fitted joggers.

Ignoring the rumble coming from my stomach I head to my door, but pause when I hear a deep baritone coming from the living room. Only pausing for a nanosecond I swing the door open and head for the kitchen, my eyes squinting from the bright light assaulting my eyes, but my steps falter when I spot Ally from the corner of my eye.

Who the hell...

Turning her direction slowly it takes a minute for my aching brain to process what I'm seeing. Ally is straddling thick tanned thighs, her black tank and white jean shorts straining to cover her curves, with a large hand gripping her hair while they kiss. I start to roll my eyes at the sight, but stop short when a stabbing pain shoots through my head. Medicine, that's what I need. I spin on my heels, my socks gliding over the floor, but my eyes catch on something that has my heart pounding as hard as my head.

The Cobra tattoo winding down one arm catches my attention, the head of the snake peeking around the man's wrist, West. West fucking Stone is in my dorm and Ally is dry humping him a few short feet from me. Balling my fist, I refuse to acknowledge him being here, so I keep moving into the kitchen to fix my coffee and make some food. My stomach grumbles, reminding me that I never made it into the kitchen last night for food. Not after my little run in with fuck boys brother. Ryker sure knows how to ruin my plans.

"Kens! I didn't see you come out of your room. What are your plans today?"

Ally's already talking a mile a minute, not knowing that each high pitched word she says slams into me like a freight train.

Turning away from the coffee pot, I eye her and she must see the pain on my face because she winces and sends me an apologetic look.

"Another migraine?" She asks.

Nodding, "Yeah, but don't worry about it. I'm probably going to hang around here today. I need to get some work done before classes pick back up tomorrow. Sundays suck."

"You used to love Sundays." A low voice says.

Whipping my gaze to his, my heart stutters behind my ribs. His caramel brown eyes, so much lighter than his older brother, study me. Searching for a sign that he hit a sore spot. He did, but I refuse to let him know that.

My upper lip curls in a snarl as I bite back, "Like you know anything about me."

Snapping at the beast of a jock isn't the best move, but with my roomie's pussy pressing against him the way it is, I doubt he'd toss her off his lap. Going back to the coffee pot, I can feel the heat from his eyes seer into the back of my head. Adding to the pain that is already a consistent throb in the back of my skull. Opening the cabinet to grab my favorite mug, a small smile lifts at the corners of my mouth as the words *Book crazy over boy crazy* stare back at me with a stack of books resting on the other side.

When I'm done fixing myself a breakfast bowl from the freezer, I step into the living room, not bothering to hide from West. It's too late for that now, plus it's my dorm I'll eat wherever the hell I want. Hiding from the big bad wolf doesn't help anything in the end. Opting to sit in the small recliner next to the one window in the decent sized room, my seat facing both the T.V and the couch. Having a sectional leaves little to no space.

"We were thinking about watching a few movies today and chilling here. You okay with that?" Ally speaks up, her focus finally pulled from West.

I can feel his stare on the side of my face. Shrugging my shoulders, letting her know that it's fine with me. I can't help but notice the surprise behind his eyes, but he hides it almost immediately.

"This is going to be so fun!" She squeals.

Huffing out a laugh, I finish off my breakfast while an old friend and new enemy tracks my every move. It's not long before Ally is planted on her ass next to West while she hounds me about last night, throwing out the fact that I didn't get in until past midnight. She only knows that because I was still gone when she went to bed.

"I went out to clear my head."

I can't stop myself from glancing at West.

A wide smile spreads across Ally's face, "Oh my gooooddd! Who was it? Did you go back to his place?" She's practically bouncing in place.

West raises his eyebrows in question, waiting for my response, both of them watching me like I'm prey.

Wetting my lips, my mouth opens but snaps shut.

"I knew it! You were with a guy last night."

My eyes bounced from her to West several times, but no words came out. I can see it click in his head. The wheels turning behind her giddy squeaks and squeals. I'm sneaking around with someone even with a no touch ban on me. That's what he sees, but a small part of me laughs at the fact he'll never find out the truth. I owe him nothing. Not after they abandoned me.

"Are you going to spill the beans?" Ally says, her eyes wide with excitement, such a girl.

West watches me, "Yeah, princess share with the class. Who is it you're going to see so late?"

His question sounds innocent. The way he worded it to seem like he's joking around, playing with me, teaming up with Ally. I know the truth. He can't wait to run off to Ryker with whatever he came here to learn. They promised I'd suffer. He warned me that I'd never fully be out of sight but I thought my dorm was safe. Off limits. Oh how wrong I was. They owned Hawthorne but then again so did I and it's about time they got a taste of that.

"If you really wanna know who I was with, why don't you ask your brother."

Planting a seed, I wait to see if he bites. Not mentioning one by name only goes so far because we both know Cole wouldn't touch me, not after everything he lost. But Ryker? He'd touch me if only to break me and I'm going to make sure he shatters right there with me.

"Bullshit."

Pressing my lips to the side, my eyes widened mockingly, reaching up to pull down my sweatshirt to reveal my neck, "Looks like he wanted a taste last night. So much for me being off limits. He sure doesn't follow the rules he puts in place. Does this mean you and Cole can play too? Or is he the only one allowed to play with his food?"

Sick of this conversation and the headache pressing into my skull, I jump to my feet abandoning my cold coffee and the movie Ally selected. Ignoring West and Ally calling after me

I head to the door, slipping on my Nike slides and make my way into the courtyard. She may be confused but he knows exactly what he's doing.

Our fathers were brothers in their own right. They met in college, this college. Even back then it was prestigious, but not in the same way it is now. Now there's rules, families that run the school, students that control the staff, money that buys grades. Placements. Scholars. Back then it was built on fear, loyalty, hard work, and of course money.

Walking through campus, I let myself remember my dad. Both of them because the truth is Alec Stone is just as much my father as my real one. I think that's what makes this so much harder for me. They met before my dad met my mom, both freshmen coming in wild and fighting every single rule given. The part that always made me smile was neither of them came from the kind of money our mothers did. No, they came from dirty money, but my mom was an heiress and so was Mrs. Stone.

Walking past the Opulent Mess Hall building that *should* feed thousands, but chooses to only supply food to the ones that line their pockets. Deciding against going inside, my pace doesn't slow. Instead I turn right, heading towards the on campus gym. My mother's family hated my father and what he stood for, so he decided to prove them all wrong. He and Alec came together to build an empire that grew into billions. Millions weren't enough for them; they had to make sure my moms father knew what they were capable of.

My mom was beautiful, smart, strong, but she was deadly in her own way. She held so much power over the staff, the students, anyone who walked the halls of this place. Her charm and power extended past the campus and into her fathers company. That's how she was able to take over for him at such a young age. Because she didn't wait for things to come to her, she took them. Without question or moral. I was bred into a family of vicious intent. Alec and his wife were no different, they just hid it better. Showering the people around them with gifts instead of fear. That's where my father went wrong.

Forcing the knee to bend will soon break the bones of those who kneel. He didn't change until he married my mother and had me, but it was always there under the surface. The strength to take down the town they all held in their hands. Stores, shipping, warehouses, weapons, you name it and they owned it. What no one knew, what I wasn't supposed to know, was that they owned banks strictly to launder money. That's what I learned a week before the fire. The one secret I've kept since finding out.

Two families, four powerful and feared people, gave birth to four children who were destined to be intertwined in their families business. Now I'm left with blood money and jaded memories, while the brothers are left with all consuming power. But if my mom taught me anything, it's that the Kingston women are unstoppable. I just hope we don't find something that should have burned in that warehouse, left to die with the men who left us in this mess.

Snapping out of my thoughts, I spot a tall lean figure leaning against one of the many art buildings. Irritation creeps under my skin. I'm sick of being followed. So, instead of keeping on the path that heads to the gym, I find myself walking towards the asshole in front of me. When I come closer I notice how slender he is, more so than both of his older brothers. Cole's head swings in my direction when my shoe crushes a twig beneath my foot. It's instant, the way his form tightens, tensing with each step closer.

"Princess." His voice sounds softer than the other two, but the vitriol is falling off his tongue in waves.

No one despises me more than Cole. His hatred is carved into his bones, buried under his skin, imprinted in the muscle of his heart.

Stuffing my hands in my jogger pockets, my shoulders tense under his stare. I stop walking when the toe of my shoes are only an inch from his.

My mouth opens with a smart remark, but before I'm able to speak he lunges off the wall. He grips my upper arms, spinning us both until my back is pressed into the brick.

"I don't know what led you here and I care even less, but let me give you a little advice princess. Stay. The. Fuck. Away. From. Me." Pushing me roughly, my head swims with the force.

I'll never shake this migraine if they keep putting my head into walls. Watching him disappear between two buildings, I wait for my heart to slow back down before I head into the gym. Even with a headache I could use a way to clear my thoughts. Unload all things Stone brothers and family secrets. They may not see it, but I'd never betray them. They're dead set on forcing my hand. The question is, when the time comes am I going to pick them or my dad? Or will I sacrifice myself to the devil instead.

CHAPTER SEVEN

KENNA

$\mathcal{M}$y ass slams into the chair next to Ally, the legs screeching against the tile floor in our physics class. She flashed me a quick "what the fuck" look before turning back to the professor. Unable to focus on the lecture, I zone out while pretending to take notes. Dragging my pen around the white paper, the black ink jagged and angry. Each curve, swirl, and sharp edge meeting the tip of my pen loosens my muscles. Sweat builds at the base of my neck, trickling down my spine.

There's a dull ache around my fingers from the tight grip. Shaking my wrist and bending my fingers back and forth to make the pain dissipate, the feel of someone's eyes on me makes my movements halt.

. It's been like this all week. It started with a lighter that was left in the door of my car a few days ago. Yesterday, I found a burning incense hanging from my dorm door when I got home from class. But it's the feeling of a heated gaze that makes my skin crawl. I gradually lean back against my chair. Trying to look around the room without moving, attempting to spot one of the Stone brothers.

"What's been up with you?" Ally whisper shouts.

Flinching from the sudden sound my head whips towards her, "What?"

"You've been acting weird as shit lately. What's going on with you?"

I shake my head, keeping my lips pressed together. I don't have an answer to give her anyway, not with West being the main dick she sees lately. Not with him coming over every. Single. Night. Tonight was no different.

"Kens." Her big hazel eyes bore into mine.

Looking down, my gaze catches on the scar peeking out the cuff of my joggers. I run my fingers through my hair, flipping it over my shoulders to hide their view, snapping my gaze back to her.

"I feel sick. I'm going to head back to the house." I take a deep breath, "I'll see you later."

"Wait Kens-"

I don't hear the rest of what she had to say due to the door swinging closed behind me. My Converse squeak across the floor with each hurried step. A laugh startles me. My head snaps up searching out the sound, landing on a shadowed figure that lingers in the alcove where the fountain used to stand. The laugh tapered off as I stopped dead in my tracks. The hairs on my arms stood tall, but it wasn't from the ominous figure in front of me.

I could still feel the gaze of someone behind me. My eyes strain to see through the dark to make out the figure in front of me but all I see is black.

"Princessa."

My knees lock when I notice it's a voice that doesn't belong to one of the brothers. Then... Who the fuck?

"Don't look so scared, sweetness. I don't bite."

My laugh is forced, but not out of fear. The only ones who have the power to hurt me are apparently absent, so I relax, giving the facade of trust.

Mistake number one.

Stepping to the side, my stare stays on his dark one. No light touching his frame from where he stands, still shrouded in shadows. His voice is deep for a student, but then again most of the students are more man than most. Inching my foot up the ashen grey brick wall, the ball of my foot presses into the brick. I make sure my back is leaning against the wall because the last thing I'll do is give him an opening. I assess the man hidden in the shadows in front of me. It's the need for him to hide his face that has me on edge, but I ignore it in place of curiosity. You know what they say, curiosity killed the pussy, or cat. *Whatever.*

"And you are?" I raise a brow.

Heat skates down the right side of my body, awareness of another pair of eyes on me, coming from the direction I just left. So, our little friend is still there watching and waiting. For what I don't know, but I plan on finding out. No one can be trusted here at Hawthorne. Rolling my lips between my teeth, my head dips to the side in question.

"Let's just say I'm a friend. From the looks of it you could use one." His voice scratches on the last word giving him away.

A small laugh slips out, "I think I have enough friends but thanks."

Twisting the edge of my *Coheed and Cambria* shirt between my fingers my tongue wets my lips. Bending forward, my foot still propped against the wall, I zero in on his form.

"I don't need friends who are too pussy to show themselves. So, tell me. What exactly can I do for you since there's fuck all you can do for me."

A big fake ass smile paints along my lips, my back straightens but my gaze never leaves the spot where his should be. Movement from the darkness grabs my attention and a low laugh leaves me. I guess my shadow doesn't like being called out on his bullshit. Putting my foot back on the tile floor I listen for the bell that's about to go off and time it just right. The long ring startles my little shadow here so I use that as a distraction for me to slip behind the door to my left but not before I spot tattooed arms and brown hair.

I slam the door behind me, darkness engulfs me because fuck I walked right into a closet trying to make the slip from whoever that was. Using the band on my wrist I pile my hair on my head to let my neck get air. All this hair has sweat building around the collar of my shirt.

Like it has nothing to do with not one but two different sneaky fucks following me around?

My eyes roll to the top of my head, with that thought my hand closes over the doorknob when the door swings open. My whole body is slammed backwards at the same time. My shoulder jars against metal, forcing a cry from my lips but it's hushed with a hand over my mouth. Panic immediately shoots through me. Warm fingers close over my throat while the other hand keeps my screams quiet.

"Always making noise killer."

Ryker.

"That's it. Your body already knows my touch so well."

Shaking my head against his hand trying to break his hold I bring my knee up but miss his junk, instead hitting his thigh. He grunts from the force only to laugh at the attempt. Spinning us around my back is forced into the door, my eyes barely adjusting to the dark, only able to see his silhouette. Leaning closer his lips skim my earlobe, his words hot on my flesh.

"Who were you talking to killjoy?"

His words are soft against my skin but the edge behind them is still there. He's fuming at the thought of me breaking his little rule so I decide to fuck with him. I'm sick of him touching what he doesn't own. My tongue presses into his fingers against my mouth so he removes it letting me speak.

I wipe my mouth, a small smirk presses along my lips, letting him see just how much I love it, "Oh him? He's just someone who wanted to see what I taste like. You know, since no one on campus is allowed to, I thought I'd find someone who is. I guess since he's a real man, he isn't scared of little boys who think they run the school."

I'm pushing it. I know it because his entire body tenses with each word that leaves my mouth but I can't seem to stop. I fucking crave it. He doesn't own me and he never will. The hand around my throat tightens from a soft touch to a bruising hold so fast a choking cough sputters out. He steps into my space, his knee slips between my thighs, pressing into me.

"Oh princess, I thought you were smarter than that." He tisks, rage barely suppressed.

Turning my head roughly against the wood he exposes my neck. Dropping his mouth to the skin between my jaw and collarbone, biting until my skin tears under his teeth.

"Fuck!" I cry out.

"Yeah baby, scream for me. Let everyone know exactly who fucking owns you. I'm going to brand this pretty pink pussy with my name before I ruin you. Did you know my dick fucking aches when I mark your skin?"

Sucking, biting, sucking, biting. He repeats the same pattern up and down my neck. Blood dripping down my throat in small drops from the cuts his teeth caused. Frustration builds, my stomach filling with acid, but my panties are drenched through it all. A fact he reminds me of.

Trailing his tongue from my jaw to my ear his next words have my heart in my throat, "I can't wait to feel how wet you are."

"Go to hell." I grit.

I try to move but it's a fight I can't win. Panic starts to really set in when my lungs struggle to drag in oxygen. I gasp for air. I start to feel dizzy from the overwhelming emotions drowning me in such a small space. I can't fucking breathe.

"Stop." I gasp out. Too low. My voice is too low.

Thighs hit the back of mine, pressing my front deeper into the door. There's no space left for me to move. I can't move. His body heats mine, bringing my blood to a boil under my skin. If the lights were on I'd see flames. I can feel the heat from fire licking up my legs. Hell, it's fucking hell.

"Don't fucking touch me." Louder. My words were louder.

Ryker can hear the panic in my voice moving back an inch. Only an inch and I think I can breathe until I feel his fingers trailing up the backside of my thigh, crawling their way between them, until the tips of his fingers are drawing circles on the thin cotton of my red thong. Red. The color of fire. I almost laugh at that comparison because why the fuck is my mind there right now?

"How wet is this tight little cunt?"

Whimpering with each touch, my core clenches and it's like a bomb to my heart. Traitor. My body betrays me by enjoying, craving, and loving his touch. I beg him for more, my ass moves on its own, pressing deeper into him.

"That's it killer. Open those thighs for me."

My entire body is covered in sweat but my legs obey their master. His demand lost on me, they hear him loud and clear. He controls me now. Slipping a finger past my thong to caress my lips, he groans at the feel of how wet I am. And I am so fucking wet for him.

"Fuck, I knew you were a fucking slut princess. I knew your pussy would be drenched for me." He pauses, the heat of his breath against my skin, "Killer, I want to see you on your knees begging for me to be down your throat, but we don't have time for that, so ride my hand and fucking scream for me."

For a split second, I wish I had died in that fire. Burning here for him is so much worse because he'll forever be seared into my skin now. My next inhale gets stuck in my throat, his thick finger plunges into me, and I scream. Not his name. I just scream. Tears pool in my eyes but my pussy pulls him in deeper with each tear that slides down my face. My body wars with my mind until all I can see or feel is Ryker. And then my hips move.

His hand presses into my throat, cutting off my next scream. "Fuck my hand. Ride it hard, I know you love the feel of me inside you. Stretching your cunt." He growls deeper, "Show me just how fucking much you crave being my little slut. Soak my fingers."

I groan with pleasure, my legs shake when he adds a second finger. The third has me crying out. It's too much. His thighs against mine. His breath fanning the hairs on my neck. His fingers pumping and twisting inside me. My core clenching around him. It's all too much and my mouth falls open on a silent scream.

"That's it baby, chase it. Beg for it princess. Only I can give you this. Only me. You're mine."

Shaking my head I agree. My body agrees. Fuck, my pussy cries in agreement.

"Yes." I whisper.

"Say it louder."

"Yes."

"Killer." He snarls.

Twisting my hips and dropping them down on his fingers my toes curl.

"Fuck! Yes, I'm yours. Fuck please. Please."

Curling his fingers he adds his thumb, pressing it into my clit sending stars behind my eyelids. My eyes closing to watch the show of sparks and little dippers shine.

"So fucking filthy. I knew you were a slut for me."

His thick hands squeeze my throat, my air is completely cut off, my face turning hot, tears spilling faster, fear spiking, but my pussy? She purrs to the feel of him controlling her. My legs give out, his thighs catching me until my whole body is leaning on him, my orgasm making me tremble.

"God damn, killjoy. Your pussy is gripping my fingers so tight." Grunting he twist his fingers dragging out my orgasm. "Fuck, I need to taste you on my tongue."

Slipping his fingers from below my skirt, my thong slaps against my skin with a wet plop. His chest heaves with his excitement while my mind fogs with overwhelming emotion. I can hear his mouth close over his fingers, sucking them and the sound drives me insane. Tears spill faster, my breathing ragged, but still I stand there leaning on Ryker. Listening to him swallow me down.

Finishing, he bends his head down to nip at my earlobe, "You taste like brimstone and heaven dripping down my throat, princess. Such a dirty feeling drinking you down, my pretty little killer." His breath tickles my skin, wanting more, "Now we're both stained with your orgasm. Forever. Now we can both be scarred, baby."

Kissing my neck he moves me off him, my knees smacking into the tile when my legs refuse to stand, and that's where he leaves me. In the darkness, tainted by him, spent and stained. The feel of his fingers still inside me, the touch of his hand around my throat, and fuck, if I don't ride my own hand before leaving the closet. Gaining some control back while fighting the images of him filling me to the brim.

For as much as I hate him, I crave him even more. And for that I'd gladly let myself fall to his feet. Because I'll bring him with me in the end.

The sound of bone meeting flesh fuels me forward, my body ignoring the pain, adrenaline masking each blow from my opponent. Swinging my right arm around, the edge of my knuckles splits his skin open just below his eye, and the crowd fucking roars. We side-step each other for a few seconds, his chest rising faster from exhaustion, but my blood sings in my veins. Each blow brings me higher. I live for this. The pain is nothing compared to how I feel when I control my opponent's life.

"Put him down!"

"Let's go!"

"Drop his ass!"

"Come on Rye, get 'em!"

Ignoring the bullshit the crowd spews, I pick up my brother's voices in the mix, but I don't let it stop me from slamming my knee into his ribs. I'll give him credit where it's due, this fucker can take a hit, and I've been landing them for a solid three rounds. No matter how many times I put him down, he jumps right back up like a damn rabbit. Bouncy fucker. Two steps to the left and he sees it. Smiling, I let him see the blood smeared over the front of my teeth from the one hit he landed on my face. Not that he's been able to do it again.

Twisting my head to loosen my strained muscles, I roll my shoulders, watching the way he rolls on the balls of his feet, my gaze tracks every hesitant move. Anticipating my next hit coming from my right hand, because he assumes it's my dominant one, I lash forward with my left fist hitting him on the edge of his temple. Being sure to clear the distance before he swings back, twisting my hips, my right leg juts forward jamming my shin into his side knocking the wind from his lungs.

Bouncing backwards on my toes the crowd loses it. Drinks and food are thrown at the mat, screaming echoing against the stone walls of the basement, but my eyes don't leave his form. Tattoos stretch across every inch of his torso in different swirling patterns, but it's his purple hair that makes him stand out against everyone else. He's a drifter that decided he needed to prove himself, but instead he caught me in a rare mood. Ready to end this, my knee drops into his lower back, releasing a gust of air from his chest.

"Stone!"

And the chants begin.

"Stone! Stone! Stone!"

Grunting, "Tap out." I ordered.

Giving him a chance to back out before my rage took over. He laughs, hollow eyes staring back at me over his shoulder, he wants this. Another blow to his face sprays blood across my mine but he still refuses to tap out. Hands slap the mat fueling our barbaric bullshit. Flipping him on his back my fist lands blow after blow into his torso, head, face, over and over. I no longer see purple hair instead blonde hair fans out against the blood stained white mat. Throbbing shoots from my knuckles, split open from the abuse, the skin of a princess flashes in and out of my vision.

"Rye!"

Not sure if that was Cole or West, my arms shake with the next blow even with the numbness crawling up my spine. The drifter is out cold by now, his face almost unrecognizable, but still my hits keep coming. My body screaming from relief it almost gives out and I might have if Cole and West didn't grip my arms hauling me from the ring.

Rolling my eyes to the side, a flash of tan skin with a massive wolf biting a sheep's head tattooed on his spine. *Fuck, they're here.* With my head swimming, there's no time to worry about our guests. Cole and West drag me towards the door, someone shouts off to the side, "Clean this shit up!".

We don't trust anyone outside of G, but I don't remember seeing him arrive so I'm not sure who that order was for. All I know is my entire body is shaking from adrenaline and built up rage. Coming to the ring helps me blow off steam when it becomes unmanageable. I've only let myself get that far once before and it almost ruined everything we built here.

We end up in a bathroom upstairs, Cole turning the cold water on, while West shoves me under the spray without stripping me of my shorts. Not that any of us give a shit.

Cole gets in my face, my hands on my knees, the only thing holding my weight up, looking me in my eyes.

"Get it out ya system this time? Huh? Cause we could have been looking at something real fucking bad if we didn't haul your ass off him."

Closing my eyes to avoid the hardness in his all I see are bright grey looking back at me. Growling out a curse, my eyes pop open, shoving Cole backward into West who takes up the back wall of the walk in shower.

Standing, my height brings me taller than both of my brothers, "Well I guess it's a good thing you did. Not that it's a concern since we run Del Mar. You really think the foundation is going to let anyone here touch us while they use us?"

West shifts forward, "Watch what you say outside of the house, Rye." His head turns towards the open doorway.

Shaking my head, snickering at how worried they are, "Look at you, watching your back as if we don't run a business full of-"

Cole steps into my chest, his fingernail digging into my skin, "Close your fucking mouth. I don't know what the hell has gotten into you, but you need to take some time away from Hawthorne. She's in your head and one slip up could cost us more than just the power over the Kingstons."

Looking over his shoulder to West, "Take his ass home I'll clean this shit up. G should have Dane out of here by now."

Dane. That's his name. West says something in response, but I've already checked out of their conversation. They will never understand the way I feel because it was my choice to leave dad in the warehouse dying while Kenna was in my arms. He made me choose her and I'll regret that until the day I die. Kane Kingston left us a mess to clean up with not only the family business, but the foundation as well. It's hard as fuck to wash money when there's an active investigation of two deaths involving arson.

Mom's been useless since dad died, but who can blame her? He was the love of her life and when she lost him we lost a part of her. Leaving the foundation with no one else to make the calls means it's us on the chopping block when shit goes down. With Hank sniffing around Kingston they have been on high alert, which brings me back to why I was in the ring tonight. Getting a call about a rival family from Seattle causing waves in town wasn't how I wanted to spend my night.

The Lawless and Savage families are making noise with their feud pulling too much attention on our side of town. Coughing, my ribs twinge with the motion.

"Fuck." I grunt.

West chuckles from the driver's side of our SUV, "That's what you get for getting in your head instead of coming to us. We always bring shit to the table, but lately you're going off on your own. Should we be worried about her being at Hawthorne? If I knew you couldn't handle being around her, we wouldn't have enrolled."

I can hear the concern in his words, but it pisses me off all the same.

"We have the foundation breathing down our necks, Kane sitting pretty just out of reach, his daughter living the perfect heiress life under our noses, and I'm supposed to sit back and smile?" My fist hits the dashboard.

His stare meets mine before it moves back to the dark road ahead, "We have a plan, Ryker. Stick to it."

"Our plan or their plan?"

"Stone. Don't forget what name is stamped on everything in Del Mar, Rye. It's time we start taking back control over what is rightfully ours." His hands tighten around the leather wheel.

I don't respond at first, my thoughts running wild in my head, but then I'm reminded of something G said earlier today.

Rubbing my hands to ease the ache, "The Lawless brothers are in town." Is all I say.

It's not a question. It's a statement neither of us respond to, instead the rest of the ride to our home is silent. Blonde hair and grey eyes taunt me well into the night.

CHAPTER NINE

KENNA

"Rocky Road again?" I laugh, watching Ally shovel a spoonful of ice cream into her mouth.

"Mhmhh" Her words are lost behind the sugary treat.

We both burst into laughter at her attempt to speak around the spoonful. We decided to spend our Friday night in, watching movies, and eating junk food. After last week's run in with Ryker I've avoided going out, unless it's to class or my late night appointments. Rubbing my thigh to ease the itch where my scar is, I'm reminded of how sensitive the area is after a tattoo. Getting ink over healed skin grafts and burns is equivalent to setting your skin on fire after letting it heal. It's not the tattoo itself that brings back the pain, it's the healing process afterwards, though it's worth everything that comes with it in the end.

Ally hangs her head over the armrest of the couch, purple hair dangling on the edge. Smiling, she winks at me.

"Let's watch *Twilight*."

Scrunching my nose, "Really?" My brows dip.

"Yeah!" Her small fist shoots into the air.

Shaking my head at her antics I agree, secretly loving the series, and of course the books. We're halfway into the spider monkey scene when my phone vibrates in my lap. Glancing down, my muscles tense, spotting an unknown number on the screen. Looking over at Ally, who is way too into the movie, my finger swipes over the number to pull up the message.

Where have you been Princessa?

Nerves sink into my stomach at the name used by the shadowed man in the hallway.

Who is this?

My fingers fly over the screen typing as fast as I can but a message comes through before I can set it down.

You don't belong to them. You were mine the day your father betrayed theirs.

Air rushes past my lips exhaling in shock. If this isn't Ryker or one of the Stone brothers who the hell is it? And how did they get my number?

I'm not finished typing out the next message before his final text comes in, my fingers releasing the phone, letting it fall into the crack of the couch.

I'll be collecting what's mine. See you soon Princessa.

Now on edge, it takes effort to focus on the movie, and Ally must sense it because once the credits roll she sits up to look at me. There is worry shining in her eyes, but something deeper reflects back at me. It's gone all too soon when her mouth opens to speak.

"What's-"

A knock at the door stops her next words, both of us looking in that direction, yet neither of us move from our spots.

Looking my way, "You expecting anyone?" She asks.

Not taking my eyes off the doorway, my head shakes. Normally I wouldn't feel dread in the pit of my stomach when someone knocks on the door on a Friday night but right after that message? Yeah, fuck that.

"Yo Ally!" Is shouted from the other side of the door followed by two more loud bangs.

"Fuck." She mumbles, "I forgot he asked to stop by. I'm sorry Kens, I can make him leave if you want." Her hazel eyes roam over my face, looking for the answer she doesn't want to find.

We both know she wants him here, even if they are only fuck buddies. They have a weird relationship, one I used to have, minus the sex. Jealousy spikes like acid bubbling in my throat, but Ally's shy smile and excited hip shimmy has me swallowing it down.

Rolling my eyes, "It's fine Ally, I promise."

Jumping from the couch, her smooth caramel legs are on full display in her black shorts paired with stockings that have the most beautiful rose pattern, and the smile on her face. Bouncing on her toes, she bends down to wrap me in a quick hug before dashing to the door. This girl. West steps inside the door, his eyes meeting mine instantly. Choosing to look away first, leaning to the right, my arm stretches across the couch to snag the remote.

"I call next pick." I say, my gaze trained on the T.V.

Focusing on selecting the next movie, my body is aware of his large presence in our space, the warmth from him radiating around us, it's what Ally likes about him. He's warm, welcoming, flirty, and he works hard to make you smile. At least he did. Now, I'm a stain in his life that he can't seem to remove. Not that I give a fuck since he's in my space.

Choosing to sit off to the left side of the couch, he now has the perfect angle to keep his eyes on me. Ally sits with her back against the arm rest, legs stretching across his lap, completely unable to see the screen at all. Selecting a scary movie, I lean back against the couch trying to ignore the itch to check my phone. That's how I spend the rest of the movie, unfocused, and full of anxiety about who this random stranger is. He knows my name, my number, and has access to me at school. So, the first thing that comes to mind is either the foundation or... My father.

If he's found out where I am, then he could be getting closer to us. Even if that's through the shadowed man. Blindly picking at my nails, I jump when West's voice directs a question at me.

"What has you all wound up?" He studies me.

Looking away, my gaze falls on a photo of the beach with colorful shells and bright blue water. The wave distracting me from the questioning looks coming from the other side of the room.

"Kens." He says.

Snapping my head in his direction, my lip curls, "You don't get to call me that. Not now, not after everything. Don't pretend like you give a shit about anything other than your brothers and getting your dick wet."

Leaning forward, he keeps his dark eyes on me, "I know everything there is to know about you, princess. There isn't a step you take that we don't know about, so I'll ask again, What the fuck is your problem?"

Large hands grip Ally's legs, dragging her ass onto his lap. Her eyes widen before a small smirk plants on her face. Guess I'm not the only one hiding something tonight. Picking at the skin under my nails, we stare each other down, neither willing to break.

"Well.... This is awkward. Just give it a rest for tonight, babe." Ally whines, winking at me before kissing the side of his neck.

One. Two. Three. Three seconds is all it takes for him to pull his attention from me and focus on the pussy sitting on his stiff dick. She can handle him tonight because I don't have time to stroke his ego or give him more than I'm willing to. Scooting to the edge of the couch to slip on my running shoes, Ally pulls away from their kiss.

"It's a little late for a trip out don't you think?" Her perfectly plucked eyebrows raise.

Giving her a *shut the fuck up* look I quip, "Isn't it too early to fuck the team captain?"

Jerking back from my comment, she rolls her eyes when she sees the joke in mine, but it's the harsh glare from West that has ice filling my veins.

"Is this about the text you got earlier?" Ally presses, far too observant.

Pausing behind the couch on my way to the door, my back ramrod straight. Silence.

Laughing, "What text?" Play dumb. That's the plan.

It's not their business to know anything that's going on, but I know Ally and she'll push until I give her what she wants. She's been far too nosey lately. First it's questions about my dad, where my mom is, and why I left town two years ago. Then it was my history with the Stone's. Why they felt the need to fuck with me. So many questions and yet she never asked the one that needed to be answered. I won't give her anything for free. Trust is earned, being my roommate and best friend doesn't give her a free pass. No one gets one anymore. I learned the hard way that even family can't be trusted. Loyalty is earned, forged in pain, but maintained with respect and love.

Curiosity comes naturally to her it seems. Now she has West looking at me expectantly, but he lost my trust a long time ago. Rolling my shoulder, turning back to the door, I leave them there to watch me walk away.

"You can have the apartment for the night, just don't fuck him on the couch." I throw over my shoulder.

I can imagine how red her cheeks are when West's deep laugh rattles behind my rib cage. How long has it been since I've been the one behind the cause of his laughter?

"Where are you going this late Princess? Late night fuck?" Mocking words hit my ears when I reach the door.

Slowly turning to face him, "I don't know, ask your brother if it's too late, he loves to fuck me." I jab, my taunt left to hang in the air.

With that I slam the door behind me and head out into the cool spring night, heading to the one place that gives me peace. It's almost enough to make me forget the eyes that track my moves the whole way. Feeling the piercing gaze observing each step I take. Each rustle of wind, snap of a twig, it all sets me on edge. Until the door of the tattoo shop opens, casting a bright red light onto the sidewalk. Time to erase tonight with ink therapy.

"Back already?" A low gruff voice says, startling me.

Jerking my head to the left, I spot Jax sitting at the counter smoking a cigarette.

"Shit Jax, I didn't see you so I figured you had a client. Scared the hell out of me!" I laugh, stepping further into the tattoo shop.

Artwork covers the walls expanding in both directions and a long hallway. Tattoo rooms lining both sides each dimly lit with a casting blue hue. Being here has a way of calming my nerves, so I come here often to take back something that was stolen from me.

Standing from the desk, Jax steps around it, crossing his arm and eyes me closely.

"What brings you back so soon? I thought I told you, your leg needs time to heal before we do anymore work."

I know he's only worried about me, but I'm sick of men thinking they can tell me what to do. Yeah, it's his job and his craft, but if I want another tattoo I'll get one here or somewhere else. I just so happen to like this place. It's expensive as fuck but if I'm going to spend a dime of that blood money it'll be on this. On the one thing that gives me something back from that night. My fresh ink itches at the reminder of the artwork that I had done two days ago.

"Plenty of people get tattoos more than once a week. Hell, sometimes more than once a day. You turning away my business?" Resting my hands on my hip I give him an annoyed look.

Tossing his head back on a sigh, he breathes out his nose before looking back at me.

"No more leg work this week. Pick somewhere else, but I won't touch that piece until it's healed up more. Tattooing on scars is hard enough, the last thing we need is to fuck up your skin grafts with an infection. Stop trying to push it, sweetness."

Flashing him a soft smile, my chest aches with the nickname he gave me a few weeks back. Jax has become a safe place for me to find comfort in and I don't have to worry about him wanting anything from me other than his money when the work is done. He isn't hitting on me when he calls me sweetness, instead he's giving me a reason not to hate what I see when I look in the mirror. He understands how it is to be different. To have nightmares. He's lived his own.

Jax has a scar stretched across his throat from his past that affects his voice, giving it a gruff, low rasp sound. Standing over me like a mountain man I chuckle under my breath at the fact that this huge muscled up man is such a softie. Thank god he isn't heavy handed when it comes to ink, because his are massive. Covered in his own form of art, not an inch of skin left untouched, his muscles tighten under his tight grey shirt.

"Pick your poison. I don't have time for a large piece, but I'll give you two hours tonight." He says, heading to the back where his station is.

Most of the guys, and girls, are gone for the night. Jax is the only one who has seen me fully and that's only for the purpose to work on me. I make sure to come when everyone's gone for the night, and for that reason, I pay him good money. He's always here when I need him, even if he isn't expecting me. When the sun falls, and the moon rises, the open sign blinking at me; shining down on me like a beacon of hope. On nights like tonight, when my head is a mess, and the only thing that can numb the pain is his needle piercing my flesh.

The sound of metal clinking against each other echoes from the back room. I head towards the couch and sit, scrolling through Pinterest, trying to land on inspiration while he prepares his station. With only two hours I have to be smart, I won't waste my next appointment with finishing up a last minute edition. No, I need to finish what I started on my leg. It's been a week and he's only giving me one appointment, so I have a feeling that project is going to take time. My other tattoos are smaller and hidden, but this one will be on display for everyone.

Spreading from my ankle up and around my leg where it ends at my hip. Taking over the entirety of my scarred flesh. My fingertips trace over the pattern over the top of my sweatpants lost in thought while I scan through the books, looking for something to soothe my need for the needle.

"Find something you like?" Jax says, walking up behind me.

My hand flies to my chest, a squeal breaking free from my lips.

"Fuck! You need a bell on your big ass."

Grunting out a reply, he steps past me to grab a large blue binder with his name scribbled across the top.

Holding it out for me he says, "Page 73, take a look and let me know if it's what you want."

Grabbing the book our gaze connects for a second before he's gone again to the back room. Flipping through the pages, I stop when I see a small scribbled 73 in the bottom corner. Chills spread over my arms, my next breath frozen in my lungs, my entire being in agreement. This tattoo was made for me and I know just where to put it.

"This will take longer than two hours, Jax." I say, loud enough for him to hear me.

When I don't hear his response I stand, heading down the hallway, peeking through the blue light trying to see Jax.

"You spying on me, sweetness?" His whisper echoes behind me, bouncing off the surrounding walls. My body instantly pinches forward, my hands flying to my bent knees while my chest heaves from fear. .

"Fucking christ! That's the third time tonight Jax!"

"Hmmm." He grunts. "You decide on the tattoo?" He questions, leaning on the doorframe.

He assesses me with a heated gaze, crystal eyes cutting into me, trailing over my face.

Standing, I flip him off before letting him know where I want the placement of the tattoo he recommended. We go over everything before he gets the stencil ready to go, leading me to the back where his table is set. Motioning for me to strip off my shirt before laying on the white film that covers the table, his head turns to the side while I get the rubber pasties to cover my nipples.

Laying on my back, I keep my stare on the ceiling, the anticipation making my legs shake.

"Easy, sweetness. You're safe here."

With those words and the feel of the needle, my body relaxes until I feel my eyelids start to drift. That's all I remember for drifting off to a dreamless sleep.

CHAPTER TEN

KENNA

"*D*amn girl."

Hazel eyes meet mine in the bathroom mirror. Ally stands in the doorway, fully put together in a cropped black and gold shirt, paired with a leather mini skirt and her signature fishnet stockings. This pair has snakes slithering up the side of her thighs and for a small moment that has me pausing. Ignoring the tug at my mind, I look over her make-up, from the winged eyeliner to the ruby red lipstick covering her lips.

"Damn yourself." I wink, turning back to my reflection.

I peel off the clear film that's covering my newest addition, using cool water and antibacterial soap to clean it. Ally's stare lingers on my freshly painted skin.

"That's some badass ink, Kens."

Her words are soft as they reach my ears. Memories turn over in my mind, causing my chest to pull tight, gripping my anxiety in an unrelenting hold. The meaning permanently etched on my chest, the reminder forever staring back at me. Squeezing my eyes shut for a split moment until a ding on my phone has them shooting open. That sound has become a smoking gun ever since those texts came in. They haven't stopped either. Pulling my sports bra over my head to cover my tits, not that Ally cares, I turn to step around her when she stops me.

"You sure you're up for tonight?" Her question has me pulling back.

My brows dip, "Why wouldn't I be?"

I never told her about the text from 'Shadow fucker' and she's never cared about how the Stone brothers treated me since she hasn't been around for the handsy parts. Not that West shows her his true colors anyway. So, my reaction is solely based on her concern when there should be none. Holding her hands up in mock surrender she smiles, a coy look on her face.

"I just thought with Romero being there you wouldn't want to go."

Scoffing I step past her, "He's not even on my radar of things to worry about. Not tonight or any other night." I throw over my shoulder.

"I'm leaving in ten with or without you!" She yells after me.

I can't help the laugh that leaves me. I'm the one with the car since hers has been in the shop since the semester started. Another thing she has yet to have fixed, even though she could buy the entire dealership with just her allowance. Rolling my eyes, making my way to the decent sized closet to the far left wall, my phone burns a hole in my pocket with the need to check it. Even when I know better I find myself pulling the sleek iPhone from my back pocket. Flipping it over the screen lights up with two texts. The first one is from Ryker.

Stay away from him tonight, Killer.

But it's the second one that has my blood running cold.

I can't wait to see if you taste as good as you look tonight. Do me a favor, Princessa. Turn around so I can see you.

Dropping the phone on my bed, shaky hands fumble with the blinds on my window, shutting out anyone who might be attempting to see into the two-story window. It's my fear that keeps the text coming through, ding after ding, each one more chilling than the next.

Spread your wings, little Phoenix. They'll clip your wings and leave you bare for me.

You'll burn for him, but would he burn for you?

Slamming my phone down on the dresser, my fingers press down on the side button until it shuts off, my chest heaving the entire time. Who the fuck is this psycho? Knocking at my bedroom door causes me to jump.

"Fuck." I mumble to myself. "Coming!" I shout at Ally.

"Come on Kens, we're going to be late." She whines from the other side of my door.

Sighing, I skip on changing out of my skinny jeans and just grab a clean shirt from a hanger in my closet. Pulling it over my messy bun, a chuckle leaves me when I see what shirt I grabbed. The red rolling stones ribbed T-shirt hugs my frame with cut outs showing the perfect amount of skin on my sides. The neckline is low cut but keeps the goods hidden enough to keep them guessing.

Snatching my keys, phone, and wallet from the dresser I swing open my door, but my mouth clamps shut when it's not Ally's hazel eyes I'm staring into. No, it's the deep brown ones that I've been avoiding. West. Flashing me a bright smile his muscles strain under the black fitted tee he paired with dark wash jeans and white Nike shoes. Fuck, he is breathtaking too. All of the Stone brothers are.

"There you are, Princess." He says.

The nickname makes me flinch backwards, a fresh reminder of my Shadow's text messages. Slipping my phone in my back pocket I shuffle past him, eyeing Ally over his shoulder. She just shrugs. She can act like she didn't know he was coming, but I call bullshit. Friend or not, she can't seem to keep her legs closed long enough to turn away fresh dick, and West seems to be her pick of the month. She loves using him to make a statement. Trying to catch the attention of someone who is never around to witness it. Tonight that will all change, which is why she hangs on his arm all the way out the dorm.

"I'm driving." I call over my shoulder.

"Duh." Ally says.

Inhaling a deep breath, I slip into the driver's side and start the car. Thankful to have my car back from the shop after Ryker slashed my tires. Gripping the leather, my body relaxes under the purr of her engine. Fuck, I love this car. Ally and West slide into the back seat, not that they can fit well, but that's not really their concern right now. I avoid using my rearview mirror, trying to save myself from having that image burned into my brain. Keeping my gaze ahead of me, I. moving through traffic to Cambridge College where the away game for the football team is. I almost make it to the parking lot without using my mirror, but right before my turn, my gaze flicks up to the small mirror, spotting the large blacked out SUV following way too close.

"Fuck." I groan, sinking deeper in my seat.

Deep laughter comes from behind me, "Come on, Princess. You didn't think I'd come here alone did you? Not that Ryker would let you have any fun anyway."

They slap the back of my seat, causing a grunt to pull from my throat with each hit. . Fucking assholes. For whatever reason, Ally decides now is the best time to ask the obvious.

"What's your deal with Kenna? Did her family do something to yours? I know you guys used to be close."

Her questions sends a shock through my chest. My eyes straining through the mirror at West. We both clamp our mouths shut, letting the words linger in the air around us, going unanswered. I pull into a parking spot on the other side of the school's stadium, hoping to avoid the crowd. Shutting the car off, I wait for them to climb out before pulling my phone from my pocket and powering it back on. I'd rather deal with the devil on my phone than the one making his way to my door right now. Before the last text can load on the screen, my door is pulled open and the scent of my nightmares flood into the small space. Cigarettes and mint mix together wreaking havoc on my nerves.

He kneels down, our eyes connect, dark to light, night meeting day. Milk chocolate eyes darken when they take in my outfit. Moving in closer, he crowds me against the seat, sucking the oxygen from the car.

"What the fuck is this?" His fingers pinch the fabric of my shirt pulling it towards him.

Tugging me towards him, dropping the thin material, he moves his fingers to my face squeezing my cheeks together in a bruising hold.

"I thought you were only a slut for me." He raises an eyebrow, watching, waiting.

Biting the inside of my lip, I decide quickly, "You're not the one I want between my legs tonight." I quip.

Squeezing harder, my teeth dig into the inside of my cheeks drawing blood. The taste of copper fills my mouth, but I don't move. I don't breathe. Not with the viper ready to strike. Leaning in, Ryker takes my bottom lip in his mouth, sucking it hard before sinking his teeth into it. Tearing it open and flooding both of our mouths with the crimson liquid.

"Bleed for me, Killer. It's the only taste you'll have on your tongue tonight."

Licking the red drop from the corner of my mouth, he kisses me deep. Cleaning up every drop of blood and swallowing it down. Taking from me. Squeezing out more while sucking up all I have to offer and I chase it with my own tongue. Fighting for what belongs to me. Unwilling to let him win, but knowing all the same that he will.

"That's it, baby. Fight me, you're so beautiful when you fight. A beautiful mess made just for me to ruin."

Pulling away, I see West and Cole standing near the SUV, blocking Ally from coming this way. Ryker moves into my line of sight with a wicked grin on his face.

"If you forget who you belong to again, come find me. I'll remind you over and over just how much of you is mine. And, Killer? If anyone touches your pussy other than me, his death is on your hands."

Before my next breath he's off his knees and back with his brothers, while Ally makes her way to me. Eyes wide with worry and questions. I waive her off, needing a second to come down from whatever the hell that was. Stepping out of the car with shaky legs and drenched thighs, I keep my stare trained ahead. Almost forgetting what I was doing before he pulled that stunt, I grab my phone and open it to the last text.

He won't be able to touch you like that for long, Princessa. Don't worry, I'll take care of them for you.

Swallowing, I thumb out of that conversation and pull up a different one. It's time to do some digging of my own. I refuse to be in the dark any longer. Not with the Stone brothers, and not with my Shadow Stalker. It's time for me to take back the Kingston name. Blood and all. Shooting off a text that will put some of the puzzle pieces together, I meet Ally halfway to the SUV when we both turn towards the football field.

"Let's go." She says, grabbing my arm and dragging me with her.

With the boys following behind us, we make our way to the bleachers where our school is crowded in a sea of gold and black; Hawthorne students. Ally drags me to the top of the metal steps until we reach the very top middle section. She plops her ass down, squealing when her bare ass hits cold metal.

"Holy shit!" She wiggles and laughs.

"Looks like you'll have a frosty ass." I joke, elbowing her in the ribs.

"Ha Ha." She mocks rolling her eyes.

Ryker, Cole, and West keep walking heading to where G is sitting near the field, watching the players warm up. G stands saying something only to Ryker before addressing all of them, nodding his head to the field, where our team is.

"I wonder what that was about." Ally says.

Shrugging, I take in the large field covered in players from each team. Propping my feet up on the empty space below us, my legs stretch out. Ally does the same, crossing her leg over the other. Gold and red cover the field. Two teams. Two rivals. And a stadium filled to the brim with wild drinking college students. We sit there in the cold crisp air, watching the teams battle it out on the field for the first two quarters, before Ryker's eyes meet mine again. This time I was waiting for it. Searching him out in the crowd and his dark smile lets me know he is well aware.

"Kenna?" A low voice says to my right.

Ally and I turn to see a tall dark-haired man that looks a little too old for a college football game.

"Yeah?" I question, curious who this stranger is.

Looking both ways he hands me a small package before walking back down the stairs without so much as another word.

"What is this?" I shout over the noise of the game, but it's too late.

He's gone and now I have a small brown box sitting in my lap with a big red satin bow holding it together.

Leaning in closer Ally eyes it, "Who was that?"

"Mmhm." Is all I can manage.

My throat feels dry, my tongue heavy in my mouth. The name scribbled in sloppy writing on the top has my heart pounding in my chest. *Princessa.*

It's from him. The Shadow. Unbridled fear grips me like a vise. Picking the box up as I stand, my feet move on their own accord. . Rushing down the bleachers, I almost stumble making my way to the bottom row. Once my feet hit concrete, I'm sprinting. Running to my car to get the hell away from whoever he is. But that's what he wants right? Why else would a Shadowed figure be standing next to my car in the middle of the dark parking lot while everyone is in the stadium.

"Fuck." I breathe.

My chest rises and falls faster after running here. I slow when I spot him standing closer. Stopping in the middle of the parking lot, I beg my eyes to adjust to the darkness so I can see him. Something. Anything that will tell me who he is, but all I see is a silhouette. The box in my hand starts to slip from my fingers, so I grab it with my other hand when I hear my name being yelled behind me. Not taking my eyes off him, I step backwards towards the voice.

"Kenna!" Ally shouts.

The dark figure matches me step for step, my blood turns to ice. He'll reach me before she does and what if she gets in the way? I can't risk Ally.

"What do you want?" I whisper, afraid of what he might say.

Tilting his head to the side as if I'm a frightened animal, fuck I might be, he steps forward again. Stumbling over my next step, he pauses watching and waiting.

"Kenna! What the fuck?" Ally yells, closer this time.

Shadow man steps forward, closer to the light, my palms sweating the closer he gets to showing his face.

"Princess." West calls out.

That stops him. Wests' voice has him pausing to look over my shoulder. Moving back a step while he's distracted, I can hear them getting closer, so I chance a glance behind me, but when I look back to the Shadowed figure he's gone. Hidden in the darkness.

"Kenna what the hell?" Ally says, grabbing my arm and spinning me to face her.

Shaking my head I laugh, "I thought I saw someone I knew. I guess I was just seeing shit."

Pulling my arm free from hers, I take the small brown box and slip it into my back pocket on our way back to the bleachers. For the rest of the night my heart skips a beat every time a dark figure flashes behind my eyelids. Looking down towards the field, Ryker looks up at me with a questioning stare as if he isn't the devil in my story. I may have a Shadowed stalker, but the real monster I fear is the one I can see.

After our team secures the win, everyone files out of the stadium, heading to Seaside Bar. It's tradition to go to the offshore club after games. At least that's where the football team goes. They worry more about partying than anything else, while the baseball team has bigger concerns. Being the top earning team at our school has its perks, but the Hawthorne foundation has their claws sunk deep into the wires of their program. Something I learned after taking over for my father two years ago.

There's a lot that happens at this school that they try to hide behind fancy new programs, buildings, dorms, and even cafes on campus. Even the replacement of the Dean was planned and pushed by the foundation. Dean Addington was hand picked from their circle a year ago after the last one signed his resignation. I've been looking into everything Hawthorne has done since the fire that night. With our money being the founding factor of the Elite College I want to make sure I look into everything.

Pulling the car into the small parking space off the main road, I shut the headlights off and close my eyes for a second. Ally rode up front this time since West decided to hop inside the SUV, complaining about backseat space in my tiny car.

Fucking prick.

"You need a drink."

Ally's words have my eyes popping back open, only to see Ryker standing at the hood of my car with a sneer on his face. Bastard. Curling my lip at him I turn to Ally.

"I need more than one and tonight you get to take my car for a spin. Tossing her my keys, I step from the car with a new attitude.

CHAPTER ELEVEN

RYKER

Watching the way those jeans hug her hips has my dick twitching in my pants. She is a true vixen. A Phoenix that burns too bright for those around her. Pink lips tip up in a smile as she sips her fruity drink. The third one. Fuck, I'm counting. A small drip of liquid slips from the corner of her mouth, making me itch to taste it. Hatred and lust wars inside me, but anger wins over. Fury for the way she controls everyone around her. Men bending to her demands, women wishing they were her, and my brother second guessing her motives.

West has been spending too much time with his dick buried deep in her roommates cunt to see past her smoke show. Kenna is playing us and I'm sick of waiting around for more information. Spotting purple hair mixed in the crowd of dancing men, Ally grinds her ass on a tall lean body. His hands slide up her thighs, close enough to touch bare ass a few inches away.

"Well shit." Cole says beside me with a beer in his hand.

Shaking my head, my eyes find Kenna's long blonde hair piled high on her head, exposing the sleek skin on the back of her neck. My teeth ache to bite into her perfect flesh, ready to mark it as mine. My hands ball into fists at my side, fists curl when a man twice her age slips behind her. His hands grip her waist, moving her in slow deliberate motions against his cock. Her body tenses, sensing his hands on her skin. Her gaze flies over her shoulder, but stops on me. Something passes between us, just a flicker when time stops. It ends just as quickly as it started. Instead of pulling away, she shoots me a smirk, a gleam shining in her eye, before bending lower, lower, lower. The hem of her shirt starts to rise, bunching together at her waist, leaving the soft skin of her lower back on full display.

"Shit." Cole grunts.

Our eyes stay connected as she rubs her ass on his dick. I know damn well he's rock hard for her, how could he not be? I'm fighting the urge to adjust myself and she's not even touching me. Pale eyes darken, her pupils blown wide with excitement at watching me watch her. She knows exactly what effect she's having on me. It's not like I can easily hide the raging hard on that's straining against my zipper.

Slowly rising, she brushes her hair to one side, giving him the opening he wanted. I'm already pushing through the crowd. Before his lips graze the sensitive spot right below her ear, my fist is flying at his face, snapping his nose with one blow.

She doesn't scream. She doesn't flinch. Instead, she watches as I land hit after hit to the stranger who touched what doesn't belong to him. He may be missing a few body parts tomorrow, but right now I have a brat to punish.

Standing over the bloodied man, I look over to see Cole and West watching with blank expressions.

"Basement."

With that one word, they both give me a nod, before finishing off their drinks and heading our way. Lashing out to snatch up my little killer, I pluck her off her feet in one move. No amount of kicking and screaming will have anyone here moving a muscle. They know exactly who has her and they won't do a damn thing to stop me. Keeping the princess firmly pressed into my chest, I step out into the cold brisk night air. Ally rushes out, not far behind me, following the sounds of Kenna's protests all the way to the SUV.

"Ryker stop!" She calls behind me.

I toss Kenna in the backseat, slamming the door before she can try anything stupid. When I turn around, purple hair dances in the wind, framing Ally's face.

"Take her car home. She'll see you tomorrow." I stated.

Climbing into the backseat, I quickly catch her as she tries to jump out. Throwing her to the other side of the car, her head hits the window with a *thud*. Shutting the door behind me,I give Ally no other thought. Kenna turns towards me claws at the ready to tear me a new one, but I clamp her mouth shut with mine while my hand drags her on my lap by her throat.

"You'll learn not to tempt me."

Breaking our kiss, toss her into the seat beside me, her head smacks into the door, but I don't reach for her. Seeing red is the only thing I focus on. West hops in Kenna's car with

Ally to make sure she doesn't follow us, while Cole slips into the driver seat to take us to the basement. It's time to show her that she's ours. Kenna Kingston thinks she can do what she wants without consequences, but tonight she'll finally see what happens when you step on a snake.

* * *

DEEP HOLLOW SCREAMS bounce off the concrete walls of the basement. A perfect symphony just for us. Cole and West are still getting everything ready while Kenna is currently curled against the opposite wall. She struggles with the battle happening within herself. Trying to wield her eyes to look away, but she's just as much of a viper as I am. Secretly loving the blood that spilled in her name. If she didn't want this, her ass wouldn't have been planted on his dick tonight. Lucky for her, I'm almost done with him. My dick stiffens at the thought of me getting my hands on her.

"Come here, Killer. I want you to see what you do to us." I call over my shoulder.

Cole stands at the man's head, tying his hands to a large wooden post while West does the same to his feet. I can feel her heat before I see her, small hands trembling at her sides, but still she steps forward with her head held high.

"Oh god…" She gasps.

Turning into her, my bloody hands landing on each side of her face, "No. This isn't the work of God. We did this for you. I warned you what would happen if you defied me. Now, he'll watch while I fuck you and it'll be the last thing he sees."

Her eyes widen.

Pushing her fallen strands from her face, "Really it's a gift. To watch you come all over my dick. The look of pure bliss on your face will be the last thing he sees. It's the one thing I can give him before he dies."

Kissing her neck, the taste of her mingles with the sweat that beads across her skin. Licking up the moisture, a groan fights its way out.

"Fuckkkkkk." it comes out low and drawn out as each drop glides over my tongue. "You taste like heaven and hell, a perfect blend for such a sinful little killer."

Something between a moan and a whimper falls from her lips and that fucking sound pushes me over the edge. I drag Kenna to the ring, slipping us both between the ropes. Letting her go once we reach the middle, I step back waiting to see what her next move will be.

Turning fully in a circle, her gaze lands on my blood-stained skin. Her eyes dart around my exposed flesh, tracing the lines and blotches of red that acts as a skin I never want to shed. The quick rise and fall of her chest draws my attention to the swell of her breasts. When our eyes meet again, something causes her pupils to blow wide. Something hidden in the depths of whatever soul remains there. Is it fear? No. It goes deeper than that.

Want.

Need.

Hunger.

She's a snake just like us, but is she ready to strike?

Looking back at my brothers, she hesitates before lunging forward towards the ropes, but I'm faster. Using my leg I shove her backwards. she lands flat on her back, the air forced from her lungs. I don't let her catch her breath as I clasp my hand over her ankle, flipping over. A groan passes through her lips when her head snaps back from the impact. Pressing my dick into her ass to show her how hard I am.

"I can't wait to sink into your tight cunt."

She's breathing heavier now, her chest pressed into the mat, she turns her head to the side for more air. Screams fill the room again from the other side of the ring, where my brothers are playing with their toy.

"Please. Don't." She gasps out.

Sitting up on my heels, I pull her up against my front. My fingers pinch the thin material and with one swift motion, it tears right down the middle. The sound of fabric ripping and the screams trying to drown it, is music to my ears. Whimpers mix with wailing, making my dick leak in excitement.

"That's it, Killer. I bet your cunt is dripping for me."

Skimming my fingers slowly caress the length of her body. Goosebumps following in my wake. In one fluid motion, I flick her button open and slide her zipper down. Exposing just a hint of the material covering her. "He's getting a little sleepy brother." West says, letting me know I need to hurry.

Leaning closer to her ear, "I hate to rush, but we have a point to make. Next time I'll take my time fucking this pussy. It's mine to take. Remember that, Killer."

Tugging her jeans down to the bottom of her thighs, I twist her thong and with a snap, it rips between her legs. Her scream has me almost blacking out from ecstasy. Dragging us both to the edge of the mat, I push her down, leaving her perfect ass in the air. One hand presses between her shoulders keeping her head down, making sure she can see the man bleeding for her. My other hand slides between her thighs, coating my fingers in her slick heat.

"Fuck. You're so wet for me baby." My head drops forward to take in the sight before me.

Unbuttoning my jeans, a deep growl comes from my chest at the sudden relief. I pull my dick free, using my fingers to coat myself in her arousal. Starting from the tip and spreading it down, all nine inches. I guide myself to her entrance, resting my tip against her opening. My other hand snakes into her hair, wrapping it around my fist and pulling her head back at the root.

"This is all for you. He's bleeding just for you."

"Ryker please." She cries.

I slide my dick into her all the way to the hilt. *Fucking hell.* So. Fucking. *Tight.* Her pussy holds my dick prisoner. Clenching so hard around me, I couldn't move if I wanted to.

I never fucking want too.

She shakes with sobs, screaming in pure bliss and agony with how full I make her. Wiping the tears that fall down her face, I add them to the beautiful mess we're creating together. It takes every ounce of control I have to pause, giving her a moment to adjust. At the slight relaxing of her walls, my hips begin to move.

"Eyes on him, little killer. Squeeze my cock while he watches what I do to you."

My hand slides from her hair, only to find a new home around her throat, cutting off her whimpers. Pulling almost all the way out, her walls trying to hold me like a Venus fly trap. Such a needy little bitch. My needy little bitch. Snapping my hips forward, I slam into her. Over, and over, and fucking over. Fucking her in punishing strokes, my nails dig into her hip. Gasping for air, she claws at the hand around her throat, but her hips move back meeting me thrust for thrust. Whimpers turn into moans. Cole and West continue their work of art on the man at our feet while I fuck Kenna into oblivion. Her pussy quivers around my cock with each stroke.

"That's a good girl, you love watching what we do for you. Only you, Kenna."

Thrust. Whimper. Moan. Thrust. Scream.

"Fuck. Your pussy was made for me. You. Are. Mine!" Moaning out the last word, I slam into her again.

"Rye, please." She begs but this time it's for more. Always more. She's a needy little bitch.

The lethal grip I have clasped on both of her hips is unrelenting. Ensuring she'll be bruised tomorrow.

"My little fucking slut. You're such a whore for me. Come on my dick, Kenna. Squeeze my cock like a good girl."

"He's done." Cole calls, not looking this way.

Knowing I couldn't control what would happen if he saw her this way, they both keep their eyes on the dying man on the floor.

"Kenna, eyes on him. I want him to watch you shatter."

"Fuck, yes!" She screams.

Thrusting into her one last time pushes her over the edge. Her cunt pulses around me, milking my dick of every last drop. I fall forward, barely able to keep my weight off of her. It takes us a while to come back down. I don't know how long it's been, seconds or minutes, but Cole and West have already left the room. Leaving the body in here with us, while we lay on the mat. Sliding my dick free, the wet sound of her pussy gripping me one last time echoes around us. Curling my body around her, Kenna shakes against me. I can feel her tremble with each breath, my fingertips tracing circles into her silky flesh, she slowly relaxes into me.

"Good girl, Killer." I whisper against her skin, trailing my lips up her spine.

"Why?" She asks, her voice a low whimper.

Brushing the wet hair from her face, "Because, you belong to me. No one touches what's mine. I warned you."

Nodding her head, she lays in my arms until she drifts off to sleep. "This is just for you." I say, kissing her forehead.

Taking my eyes off of her, they swing to the stranger. Sitting lifeless on the chair with the words *I'll always bleed for you* carved into his toros. It's not until later, when I move us off the mat, I let her see the hard work we did for her.

At her feet, lying on the floor in a pool of blood is the shell of a man who thought he could grab her hips, attempting to claim her skin with his mouth. Only, he's missing a few parts. His dick is missing, shoved up his ass. His balls removed and shoved down his throat, but it's the lack of eyelids that really forced him to watch her come undone by my cock. Spinning away from the mess, she tucks her face into my chest.

"Shhh." My hand rubs her back. "You learned your lesson right, Killer?" I question.

"Ye-yes." Her words are spoken softly.

"You were made only for me, Kenna. I'll slowly stitch us back together after I'm done burning us to the ground."

Walking her out of the basement, we leave the body for G to handle. The little bird lost some feathers today, but her wings are not yet plucked.

CHAPTER TWELVE

KENNA

Wincing at the pressure my thumb applies to the skin around my thigh, I continue to work the area. The worst part about physical therapy for me is stretching the skin while using different massage techniques. It fucking hurts. Add that on top of the massive healing tattoo that now spreads the length of my ankle up to my hip on my left side, and the pain is unbearable. Breathing through the next stretch, my muscles work to release the tension that's built up from how tight I've been lately.

My mind wanders back to the other night after the game. The heated touch of Rykers hands on my body, the feel of him filling me. My chest tightens as the image of the man lying in his own blood flashes in my mind. Guilt settles in the pit of my stomach at the reminder of how mine sang in my veins from Ryker slamming into me from behind. How little a life means when your own is on the line. Denial climbs her way up my rib cage to settle behind my lungs.

The bitch props her feet up against my bones, making it harder to breathe. How can I say the Stone brothers mean nothing to me, when the proof stares back at me every time I look at the dark, swirling black and grey ink on my leg.

Moving to my bed to rest my muscles, I give up on my exercises. Unable to continue with my thoughts muddled around a set of caramel brown eyes. Soreness shoots through me when I plop down on the mattress. I drop my gaze to the box sitting in the middle of my bed, waiting for me to open it. Tempting me with its big red bow, but nerves have prevented me from slipping the ribbon from around the lid.

"Just do it." I tell myself.

Being here at Hawthorne with them has made me retreat back into that scared little girl who spent months in the hospital alone. Learning how to take care of myself and my bandages with no one else's help. But I'm not the hurt teenager anymore. I'm Kenna mother fucking Kingston. This is my castle on the hill.

Inhaling a deep breath, my fingers pinch at the bow, slowly pulling the knot loose. The ribbon falls onto my blanket, the red standing out against the grey and black. Pushing my shoulders back, I use my fingernail to push the lid off. Letting out a slow exhale as the contents stare back at me.

Sitting inside is a piece of small cream colored paper, covering an item underneath. But the scratchy writing is what puts me on edge. Lifting the smooth sheet I trace the scribbled words. Focusing more on how the pen dug grooves into the paper rather than the message staring back at me. Raw emotion bubbles in the pit of my stomach with each letter carved into the thin sheet. I sit there rereading each word until my leg goes numb from me sitting on it.

I'll always own the deepest part of you, my little Princessa. Every part of your pain belongs to me. When you look in the mirror you'll forever see what I gave you. Don't worry, I'll set fire to anyone who stands in my way.

The last sentence sticks with me. My shadow threatens to set the Stone brothers on fire, but he's already burned his touch into my skin, now I just need to remember his face. Folding the small paper into a square, I move to the item sitting in the bottom of the box. My heart thunders in my ears, pulling out something I thought was lost forever in that warehouse. There, in the palm of my hand, sits a gold crest ring with a snake wrapped inside a skull. It's the crest of our families. The skull for Kingston and snake for Stone. Together they were unstoppable.

It was lost in the fire that night. When I woke up in the hospital, I no longer wore the ring on my middle finger. Instead there was an empty space where our families were held. Ironically it represented the loss we all felt that night. How would he have this? Acid fills my mouth at the thought of my father being the shadow who has found his way into my life, but how is that possible? Sliding the ring on my finger, where it's meant to be, I stand heading into my closet to throw on some clothes. It's time to figure some shit out. A ding has me hesitating a second before snatching my phone off the dresser. I'm done hiding from them all.

Did you let him fuck you?

Either tell me who this is or fuck off.

Tempting the one person who could be responsible for both families' pain isn't wise, but I'm done with secrets. The lies scorching their way through this town. It's time I go back to the person it started with. Slipping my phone into my back pocket, I leave the box open on my bed with the note lying beside it. Stepping into the living room looking around for Ally, I notice her door is closed. She's been spending a lot of time online lately, doing god knows what. All I know is when she's not riding West's dick, she's online talking to some guy. The war wages inside me, until I decide it's better to leave her alone. I make my way to the front door, grabbing my keys, and sliding on my vans.

I ensure the door is locked behind me before leaving the dorms. Making my way through the parking lot, I climb into my car, and head to the one place that I haven't been since that first year. One of the hardest places for me to go.

It's mid-afternoon on a Sunday, so the one person I need to see isn't reachable today, so I decide to visit someone who is more deserving. Maybe talking to her will clear my head so I can finally see the missing pieces. Pulling from the massive iron gates, my car speeds down the road heading south along the coastline. Blonde hair whips around my face with my radio blaring. The sunshine brings a small smile to my face, just for a moment. But the feeling of heated eyes on me has my lips falling flat.

Flicking my gaze to the rearview mirror, I spot a car a few paces behind me. Blacked out windows make it impossible to know who sits behind the wheel, but instead of the large SUV I expected it's a sleek silver car. Not seeing the black

Tahoe following me, I relax in my leather seats for the ride, the eyes becoming a distant memory.

The car turns off the road two streets away from my destination. I can't help my deep sigh of relief, knowing it was some random person driving in the same direction. Thoughts linger in the back of my mind, reminding me that the feeling of being followed is still weighing down on me.

Large rows of grass cover yards and yards of space, bigger than three football fields. Del Mar's cemetery is well kept, the grass cut to perfection, flowers on each grave, and the stones cared for. Our dead want for nothing, even in death. I pull the car into an empty slot, shifting into park but leaving it running while I give myself the pep talk of a lifetime. Staring forward, a tall dark shadow steps from behind a weeping willow swaying with the Cali breeze. Turning off the engine and tossing my keys into the center console, I swing my driver door open, letting in the salty air.

Squinting against the sun, my vans plant onto the asphalt, standing to face the shadowed man hiding under the shade of the tree. I charge towards him. Fuck hiding, the answers I need aren't going to find themselves. Pocketing my phone, my legs eat up the distance towards him. Getting closer, I spot differences between the shadowed man and the one in front of me. Where my Shadow appears to be shorter with more bulk, this man is taller, muscles more defined. Built from working out, but not the kind you get from a gym. A few steps closer and an eerie calm falls over me when I get a good look at who's leaning against the rough bark of the willow.

"I thought I told you to stay away." He snaps, ire spilling off of him.

Propping a hand on my hip my eyes roll, "What are you doing following me, Cole?"

Pushing off the tree he crowds me, our chest bumping in the process, coming so close that I find myself looking up to see his face. Emerald green eyes shine back at me, the darkness in them flashing like a beacon warning me of the dangerous man in front of me. Twisted venom drips from his tongue, lashing out at the wounds that he continues to rip open, refusing to let the scabs heal.

"Unless you're here to crawl into the hole I have waiting for you, I'd suggest you fucking leave. It's Sunday. Go home Princess before you find your way into hell."

Soft fabric stretches under my palms, both hands planted on his chest, I shove against him, but he catches my wrist without so much as a shift backwards.

"Don't fucking touch me you poisonous bitch." He snarls.

Cole's hold on me tightens, most likely bruising my skin, forcing me to wince from the bite of pain.

"Let me fucking go Coco."

Using his childhood nickname sets him off, spinning me so fast all I see is a blur of grey headstones, my back slamming into the rough bark. Pinning my wrist above my head, he leans in closer, hot breath tickling my cheek.

"Call me that again and I'll carve this silky skin into a fucking rug for us to walk over. You're not worth the time it'll take to bury you. I won't repeat myself, Kingston. Get the fuck back to campus."

Grinding my skin into the tree, his touch disappears, leaving my arms hanging at my side with a new branding sting in my skin. Walking after him, I decide fast that pushing him for answers is the next best thing since the dead can't speak. Long legs stretch to eat up space in an attempt to distance us, but my need to follow him pushes me faster.

"What do you remember from that night?" I shout after him.

Cole's steps falter for a second before continuing in the direction of the grave we both came to see today. Sunday. He said something about it being Sunday, so I shouldn't be here but what does the day have to do with coming to see her? Ignoring the obvious tension in the air, I keep following until a large grey headstone appears to the right of our path. Avoiding the places where people are buried, I keep on the stone path until it turns onto the row Cole takes. Last thing I need is bad luck on top of all the bullshit going on in Del Mar.

Pausing at the large marble stone, Cole bends at the knee, his head dipped down, mouth moving but his words lost to the wind. Not wanting to interrupt his one-way conversation, I stand a few steps behind him, watching the way his shoulders slump lower with each breath. Reading the name on the headstone has my heart cracking behind my ribs, the grief of it all attempting to swallow me whole.

"Your father snuffed the life out of her. Stealing something so pure from the earth that it weeps with the loss."

Paige Ann Sawyer

Her name dries on the tip of my tongue like chalk. My best friend. Cole's first love. The one life the fire took that hit us the hardest of all. Mr. Stone was like a father to me, so losing him and my father was harder than anything in the world, but Paige? Cole's right, the world lost a light that night.

"What was she doing there, Cole? What were any of us doing there that night?" My words panicked now that I've decided to ask those questions out loud.

He only shakes his head, eyes still staring into the marble.

Pacing. I'm now pacing while talking to myself out loud.

"We never went to meetings at the warehouse. The office? Sure. But why would we be there? And who is the voice in my head that saved me? None of this adds up!" I yell.

Jumping up, Cole turns towards me with a questioning look, "What voice?"

Shrugging my eyes focused on the ground.

"I still have nightmares about the flames. The way it spread over my leg, climbing me like a live wire setting my body on fire. The different voices yelling, screaming in pain, begging for mercy, but over all of the noise there's always *his* voice. The voice that shushes my screams. Promising to take away the pain. Putting out the fire that boiled my skin into nothing but rotten flesh."

Trailing off, my gaze slides back to his, tears pooling in my eyes. Cole just stands there, looking back at me with a mask over his face. Stone cold.

"Whoever it was should have let you die right there beside her. She didn't deserve this, but you do. And I'll make sure you pay, even if Ryker forgets who you are. I'll remind him."

Standing there staring after him, he turns his back and walks away, leaving me with the same answers I had before. None.

CHAPTER THIRTEEN

KENNA

*M*onday. Usually the day everyone despises. But for me, let's just say, it's the one day I don't have to deal with a certain purple haired bombshell sucking face with a Stone brother. The halls of Hawthorne are a madhouse this morning with it being the month of our fundraiser. Every year the college, hosted by the foundation- i.e my family and the other members, throw an extravagant masquerade ball to raise money for charity. Or flaunt their wealth. After all, whoever has the highest donation gets to have a wing of the school named after them. Who wouldn't throw millions at the chance of being a part of that?

It's at the end of the month and the days are flying by way too fast to keep up. Right now, the halls are lined with girls who are hosting different parties, events, and anything in between to have the chance at one of the higher status guys around campus. Me? I'm wearing a denim blue ball cap with my hair down my back, concealing my face. Not that it does any good being who I am, people still stare at me as I pass.

I slam into a body as I turn the corner towards my first class. The move jolts me backwards, but a large hand snatches my arm before I fall on my ass. My gaze travels up the dark black suit, a crisp white button up shirt hugging a large muscular frame. My eyes finally land on striking, cobalt blue eyes that are framed with a thick salt and pepper beard matching his short, thick hair resting on top of his head. .

"My bad, Ms. Kingston." His voice cuts through me, sending chills up my arms.

Something familiar tugs at me, the shape of his face, his bright cold eyes, they almost feel like a distant memory. He releases my arm now that I'm not stumbling backwards and extends his hand to me.

"Um, not a problem Mr.-" I pause, brows dipping down.

Even being a member of the foundation doesn't keep me in the loop of who they hire, but judging by his age, I'd put money on him being a new member of the staff.

"Dean Addington."

He squeezes my hand gently with our hand-shake, but when his thumb caresses the skin on the top of my fingers I pull back with a smile.

"Well, it's nice to meet you. I'm glad we were able to replace the previous Dean this quickly."

His eyes stare back at me, studying me for a brief moment. Not with suspicion or curiosity. Something a little more sinister lurks just under the surface. Flexing my fingers in an attempt to shake the feeling of his skin on mine, we hold eye contact until a throat clears to the left. Inching my attention away from the snake in front of me only to find a viper with their sights set on us.

"Addington." Ryker says, his tone clipped.

Bouncing between the two men before me, my lip twitches at the change in the Dean's demeanor, almost on edge with Ryker near him. Dropping the untaken hand he offered Ryker, Addington steps backwards, putting space between the three of us. His blue eyes never leave the man before him, who is wound tight and ready to strike. Being so close to the two alpha males, who seem to know each other, sets me on edge like a caged animal. I'm getting sick of being cornered like prey when my teeth are just as fucking sharp.

"Well, if you'll excuse me I have class to get to."

Passing a look between the two men, my foot moves one step forward before the Dean has his fingers wrapped around my arm once again. What's with men getting handsy with me on school grounds? I wasn't aware there was a big ass neon sign flashing *please touch me* over my head yet here we were. Moving my shoulder in a roll I make a show of removing his hold on me but Ryker strikes much faster like the venomous bastard he is.

"Addington, I think it'd be best if you kept your hands off the students. It's not a good look for the first week of work. Yeah?" Words dipped in acid drip from Ryker's sharp tongue.

My stare settles on cobalt once again but this time hunger glares back at me, bouncing from the ice in his eyes. Something unsettling forms in my stomach with each passing second, but the moment is broken just as quickly when Ryker replaces the Dean's hand with his own. My feet stumble over each other as I'm pulled away from the man who seems to tug at something darker inside me.

Students move to the side, avoiding the broody bastard dragging me down the long brick hallway. Shadows dance along the walls as we pass, the low lighting in this building is almost unsettling. One particular shadow catches my attention, but the hidden form sinks into the darkness when we pass. Unsure if I'm seeing things, or if my mind is playing tricks on me, my head shakes to clear the unnerving image. Digging my heels into the tile floor, I lean my weight back in an attempt to break his hold or slow him down.

"Keep trying, Killer. I love when you fight back." He tosses over his shoulder.

I let out a grunt, deciding to pick my battles, choosing to follow him to fuck knows where. Turning down the left wing towards the gardens, the opposite direction of my next class, we keep moving through warm bodies with their stares trailing after us. This is going to get back to Ally and the brothers pretty quick. Ally, I'm not worried about unless she wants to push the narrative of Ryker not being the bad guy, but the brothers? Cole made it clear he wanted his older brother to keep his distance from me since "I'm poison to their family". West doesn't give a shit, as long as I don't turn Ally against him now that she's his fuck buddy, even when it kills his brother.

No longer seeing the walls, people, or even Ryker, my thoughts float to Paige. My best friend. The one person who would know what to do and how to do it. If she were still here, she'd smack the boys and tell them they're all fucked in the head with a smile on her beautiful face. My chest rattles with my next breath. Flashes of her smile bright and wide, filled with laughter, and Cole in the background, looking at her as if she was the sun. She was his. My father took her from me. From him. And now he's lost in the void of what could have been.

The picture in my head swims, the edges blurring, until it's all but gone. Leaving nothing but colorful flowers spanning yards ahead of us off a cobblestone path. Still, we storm past the bushes, the roses, purple wildflowers, until we veer right, towards the small circle where a bench sits. The bench is made of stone, perfectly placed in the middle of a large circle of flowers. Not just any flowers. My favorite. Lilies spread in rows and rows of different colors. Oranges, yellows, reds, burnt sunset, even pale pink and white. Some are altered to get colors that don't grow naturally like the section of dark black settled against the back row.

Breaking out of my trance, I scowl at him, "You need to learn to keep your hands off me."

Turning away from him, my hand rubs at the spot his hand just left, soreness evident with a pinch of pain. Another bruise added to the roaster. Heat engulfs my back, his body warming me, pressing closer with each breath. My blood boils the closer he gets, until I can feel him settled against my ass.

"Maybe you need to learn to stay away from the monsters that calls to you." He says.

My chest rises faster, the small path secluded from prying, urging me on. Bravery is a son of bitch but carelessness is her sister.

"Guess I crave the feel of monsters on my skin."

For a moment I wonder if he heard me. My words spoken on an exhale, so soft a breeze would carry it away. Finger-tips touch the side of my neck, sweeping my hair back, revealing smooth skin for the snake to sink his teeth into.

Licking up my neck, he stops at the base below my ear, "What a shame it would be to taint the lilies with your blood. Then again, spill yours and I'll spill mine. I just know we'd make the perfect color to paint the garden the deepest red."

Kissed wet my neck, my body tenses when he nips at my jawline, "I promise to bury us in the lilies, Killer."

Shuttering under his touch, chills spread down my spine, my core clenching with need and I fight it with everything I have.

"Us?" My question falls from trembling lips.

"You bleed, I bleed. But don't worry, baby. I'll make it feel so fucking good for us both."

A warm hand glides up my waist, ghosting over my breast, skating across heated skin, until it lands just over my throat. Hovering mere inches away, he waits to touch me.

"I'm going to show you how soft your skin feels under my touch."

When his hand finally, fucking finally, claims it's home around my throat my pussy weeps with the sensation. Having his strong body behind me while holding my life in his hands has a way of making me come undone.

Kissing up and down my neck his other hand undoes the button on my jeans slowly inching my pants lower. By the time he has my jeans down to my ankles my thighs are soaked. Tears spring to my eyes with his hold on my airway. Dragging in ragged breaths, my heart pounds in my ears, covering any words that are spoken against my skin. Dipping his fingers into my thong I can feel his moan vibrate against my hammering pulse.

"Fuck, you are so soaked for me, my little slut. You never let me down."

He swirls my wetness around my entrance. My eyes slam closed, the overwhelming feelings floods me as he inches a finger in me slowly. Excitement surges through me when his hand clenches around my neck, my pussy dripping for him. Turning my head, my eyes lock with blown out pupils that seem to grow with every passing second.

"Eyes on me, Killer. I want you to see what I do when I touch you."

Nodding, words unable to form on my tongue, I wait for what comes next. Reaching behind him, something snaps but his hand is back between my legs before my next breath. Something cold and soft sends a shudder through me.

"My girl loves lilies, doesn't she?" He asks.

Unable to respond, my head bobs in agreement. His eyes drop to my mouth as I lick my lips. A wicked grin appearing on his. "Good girl. Now fuck my hand and let me see you come undone for me."

Two fingers sink knuckle deep inside me, but cool softness circles my clit. What? Before I can ask anything, my legs are shaking with my building orgasm. His fingers loosen their hold around my throat, letting me lean against his chest so he can see between my legs. Wild, hungry eyes flick from my core to my face over and over.

"Look what only I can do to you." He orders.

Snapping my gaze below I see a green stem sticking from between his fingers, an orange lily pressed against my clit, while his fingers plunge into me over and over again.

Ohhh fukkkk.

My legs shake, so god damn close to the edge, when he twists the flower over my clit, using it to pinch the sensitive spot. My stare jerks to his, our eyes clashing, need drowning me from the inside out. Slamming his mouth to mine he dominates every inch of me.

Teeth, tongue, anger, it all boils over with each plunge of his fingers.

Biting my lip, he breaks the skin, "Fuck, I want a taste."

Pulling his fingers from me, he spins me, guiding me to the stone bench and dropping me down on the cold seat. Falling to his knees, his eyes never leave mine, both of our chest heaving with each breath. Lashing out, he drags my mouth back to his for a bruising kiss, but when he pulls away he takes the soaked lily that he just used to fuck me, and smears it over my lips.

"Open that filthy fucking mouth, Killer."

Not missing a beat my mouth falls open. Shoving the petals in my mouth his eyes dilate with the sight before him. Legs over his shoulders, skin flushed, and a flower stem sticking out of my mouth. What a fucking mess he must see.

Leaning his mouth closer to my core, his hot breath fans across my sensitive skin, "I want to taste what I do." Is all he says before his mouth is on me.

Licking the seam of my pussy sends me to the edge but I still need a push. Sensing how close my body is to letting go, he spears his tongue inside me, using his thumb to rub my clit. It's all too much. The taste of me on my tongue, the soft petals filling my mouth, his tongue inside me, it's all overwhelming.

"That's it, baby. It'll only be me. No one can fuck you this good with their mouth. Even hate can't keep our demons from each other."

My thighs close around his head dragging him closer. My hips lift, rubbing my pussy over his face, riding him harder and harder.

"I bleed, you bleed." I whisper.

Growling at my words he dives in like a man starved. Both hands landing on my thighs gripping so hard I cry out in pain, and fuck, pleasure too. I'm falling. Falling over the edge of pure ecstasy, and all I see when I close my eyes are lilies and Ryker.

Lips brush against my ear causing my eyes to shoot open.

"You're my date for the fundraiser." He says, and I know it's not a question.

CHAPTER FOURTEEN

RYKER

We're surrounded by sleek Armani suits and polished pearls. West sits to my right, Cole sipping his drink on my left while the foundation studies us. To them we're just kids. Three young boys who can be molded and shaped to their rule, but we've been raised to conquer. It's our birthright. There is only one thing standing in our way. One feisty little thing that I can still taste on my tongue from this morning. She's getting under my skin, in a way I wasn't expecting.

"Rye." West says under his breath.

Oh right. Where were we?

"I'll be escorting Kenna Kingtson to the foundation. We'll do it then where we have witnesses that can provide statements of our location that night. We are going to handle this ourselves."

Those last words are meant for the fucker at the end of the table. Ethan Addington, who we brought in as the Dean, and now the foundation. Running money through the town is one thing, but the school? That involves bringing in the head man in charge. Addington only found himself with a seat at the table, because our previous Dean ran out of town without so much as a heads up. Some men aren't built to run things.

"And she'll sign the papers when presented to her? Before this little plan you have?" A perky blonde eyebrow raises in question.

Dropping the smile I held for pleasantries, my mask falls from my face, showing the man our father raised me to be.

"Kenna Kingston is our problem to handle. Trust me, I've got her molded into the perfect chess piece."

Four sets of eyes look at each other before one by one they each settle on us.

"And Mr. Kingston?" A soft raspy voice says.

Cole opens his mouth to speak, but stops short when my hand raises, halting the rest of their questions.

"Kenna and her father are none of your concern. The issue will be handled at the ball and the papers will be signed beforehand. I'll make sure of it myself. Anything else that doesn't involve them or are we going to continue to waste our time?"

Every time Kenna's name leaves my mouth, Addington's lips thin into a malicious smile that has me on edge. Professor Arden pulls me from my thoughts, his next words sure to piss West off.

Black eyes and even darker hair frame his olive skin, white teeth shining at us behind a sneer, "It's time we brought the baseball team into the deal."

West slams his fist down on the table, "We've had this conversation, so forgive me for not wanting to hear your shit, but I won't shut this fucking idea down again. Next time I'll rip your tongue out. Hell, it'll save us from listening to your rambling."

Turning to him, my mouth opens but he keeps speaking.

"We gave you the football team. Use the coaches, athletic department, hell even the god damn players if you need to, but we are not using the baseball team. Ruining the prospect of my team winning anything is out of the question. Bring it up again and I'll kill you myself."

"Assuming any of you have a say in what we do is a privilege we allow you to have. Those greedy fingers may try to grip our throats, but you're too weak. All of you. Next time you want to meet, bring us something fucking useful." I spit.

Cole adds, "I'll be tracking Kenna, so if anyone makes a move before we say jump you'll be the one burning alive in the middle of town for everyone to see."

Pale blue eyes watch us, emotion void from their faces. Those two are fucked in the head, but they keep their mouth shut. Addington however can't seem to sit still in his seat, so I make a mental note to have G look into this fucker. Cole can run his background and put a tracker on his electronics to keep an eye on him.

We shove away from the table at the same time, standing over the four on the opposite side of the table, making sure to cement their place below us.

"The Lawless boys are in town, should that be a concern?" A feminine voice says.

Looking down to meet those startling blue eyes, we hold contact, both trying to get a read on the other. I don't look away. She'll break, they always do. My stare hardens into ice.

"No one in this town is of your concern unless we say so. Until then, do the job we gave you or it'll be your last. Understood?"

If she had a visible Adam's Apple I'd watch her swallow down my threat, but the slender column of her throat bobs all the same. Wood chairs scrap against tile with our leave, but none of us look back to the ones we left sitting there, only hatred left in their penetrating stares. Money and power go hand in hand, yet no matter how much they have, we will always own them. The Professor stays in line... usually. However, with our newest addition you could cut the tension with a knife. The twins are a different story, if they're not kept on a very short leash they become a liability.

"Soon they'll start pushing back. We need those papers signed before we have a fucking mutiny on our hands." Cole barks.

Nodding, we keep moving towards the parking lot. The sun is just about to set in the sky, casting an orange glow on the building. If they know the Lawless brothers are here, then they know about the feud between the two families, yet they chose to say nothing. We need to start getting answers before they do or we'll have no choice but to clean house. Losing our position in Del Mar is unacceptable, but losing family to this business isn't even a fucking option.

Pulling out my phone, I shoot off a text to G.

"He'll meet us at the house." I confirm out-loud.

Working as a unit for so long they don't have to question who I'm talking about, they just know. Reaching our SUV, Cole slides into the backseat without a word, but West stops me on my way to the driver side.

Nodding toward the backseat, "He's drifting again, Rye. We can't have that shit right now. It's a risk with everything going on, but we knew having her near him would bring back old memories. He's pulling away."

Worry laces his words. Sharing a look, my hands grip both shoulders giving them a squeeze.

"We'll take care of it, West. He needs to blow off steam instead of holding himself up in that room playing on his computer talking to fuck knows who."

"He's been smoking again to take the edge off, but I'm fucking worried, Rye. I-"

Tapping on the glass has both of our heads turning towards the window, but the tint hides the face behind it. The feel of Cole's eyes peering into mine makes me pause for a second before turning back to West.

"We'll handle it." I repeat. Those words taste like ash on my tongue with how much I've said them tonight.

The drive back home is silent but short. I thank God for the quiet, allowing me just a few moments of peace to run over the events from this past week. G was able to get rid of the body without issue, not that I had any doubts he would.

One problem solved, a *million* more to go.

. Our moves are being watched, not that we give a shit, but any mistake could change the game for us. I make a mental note to look into Addington. The way he looked at Kens has me thinking, he's bound to be a problem. Thirsty men always are.

* * *

"You sure you'll be able to do what it takes when the time comes?" Cole questions.

My knuckles turn white with my grip on the controller for our gaming system. West and G sit on the other couch watching, while me and Cole play a round of COD. Keeping my eyes on the game doesn't keep their eyes off the side of my face. I let out a long exhale, rubbing my hand down my cheek and over my mouth, my fingernails scrape the growing beard I've forgotten to shave.

"I'll do whatever it takes, Cole." I remind him.

"Now that you've had your fill of her? You think we don't know you've been dipping your fingers into the pie?" West laughs to lighten the mood.

G joins in, "Yeah man, you've licked your fingers clean after that meal." He jokes.

The thud of the controller landing on the coffee table echoes in the room, jumping to my feet, I head for the front door.

"Where you going, Rye?" West asks.

"G, focus on Addington. I want everything you can find on him. I'll be out late tonight."

Shutting the door behind me, I head to the one place that has a tight hold on me. They don't know that I've claimed her as mine, even when she belongs to all of us. In the end I'll be the one to choke out her light, but that doesn't mean I have to keep my hands, or dick, clean before then. Restraint is something I've learned to control over the past few years, so no, they shouldn't be worried.

Yeah, continue to tell yourself that.

Shaking that thought from my head, I decide to walk the two blocks back to campus, making a stop along the way. By the time I reach the dark walkway in front of her dorm the lights in her window are out. Visions of her long golden hair splayed across her bed with her tan skin on display makes my dick grow stiff in my jeans.

It's time to leave her a little message. Our little killer needs to know that her time is limited. *My* killer. Because no matter what needs to be done, she is mine.

Stepping into the stairwell of her building, my shoes squeak against the metal steps leading to her floor. Not worried about someone stopping me, I pull the little silver out of my back pocket. I made a copy, because, well... I'm me. Slipping it into the lock, I twist it slowly, the *click* is music to my ears. The door opens slightly to a dim living room. The smell of her hits me in waves, sliding through my nostrils like the most blissful line I've ever taken. I follow that floral scent that makes my head swim, it leads me to a shut door near the back of the apartment.

Signs of her are shown through the living space, but even in the low light I can see that her roommate, Ally, splashed her bright colors throughout the space as well. Opening the door to her room, the only light she allows is from the window to the right of her bed. The curtains pulled open and the moon peeks in, shining down on the blonde bombshell sleeping in nothing but grey sweats and a black sports bra. My dick has been hard since I turned the key, but seeing her in such a vulnerable state almost makes the pain unmanageable. I set down the surprises I got on my way here, positioning them around her room for her to see when she wakes up, in just a few short hours. But tonight, I want to play a little game.

The foundation wants information? Cole and West want to make sure I'm able to do what's needed? Then maybe I should show them that she doesn't have a hold on me. Not in the way she craves. Not even when her pussy is squeezing my dick with her head thrown back on a scream. My name falling from her lips. Defiance in her eyes. None of that means anything when it comes to her purpose here. So, I'll remind her of that tonight. Stepping to her window, my gaze travels over the campus grounds, landing on a dark shadow a few yards away.

Blinking, my eyes trace the area, but I only see a lamp post. I pull her black out curtains closed, cloaking us in darkness. Starting from the bottom, I kick off my shoes, followed by my pants and shirt. Leaving me naked except for my boxers, which is doing absolutely nothing at hiding my raging hard on. Bending to grab the lighter from my jean pocket I close it in my fist. Excitement builds in my stomach. The need for her tears has my throat drying. Even in the pitch black I can sense where she is on the bed, her heated skin like a beacon, I crawl up her sleeping form until I'm hovering over her.

My lips part getting ready to speak, but I think better of it. Instead I reach over feeling for something to cover her mouth. A smile pulls at my lips when my fingers brush against silky fabric. My imagination runs wild, thoughts of shoving her soaked underwear down her tight throat take over my vision.. Clamping my jaw shut, my molars grind together as I try to stifle a groan threatening to escape. My thumb traces the seam of her lips before pushing them apart.

Leaning into her, I slide my tongue along the shell of her ear as I whisper, "Open up, Killer." I whisper.

Her body tenses for a second before she opens her mouth to scream, giving me the perfect fucking chance to shove the fabric in her mouth. Using the same hand, I move it down to her throat holding her head still, pinching her jaw closed to prevent her from spitting it out. I wait for my eyes to adjust enough to see the outline of her writhing under me.

"That's it baby, keep that little mouth of yours shut."

Struggling against me, she attempts to knee me, her nails scratching at my arms. That's it baby, fucking fighting me. I'm going to fuck the fight right out of her.

"Keep fighting, but you're not going to get anywhere."

Leaning down on my elbow, I use my other hand to flick open the lighter. The orange glow cast light around the two of us, her eyes grow wide with fear, while the look in mine reflects how wild she makes me. The animal that's slowly breaking free around her claws at his cage, howling to sink his teeth into her. Answers. I remind myself why I'm here and it's not to get my dick wet.

Using the lighter, I look around the room in search of something, but when I don't see what I need, my eyes trail down her body. Her chest heaves with each breath, my hand now gone from her throat, but the fabric in her mouth still blocks her airway a little. Moving myself to straddle her waist I make a decision that has her smokey grey eyes watering. My finger burns from the heat of the lighter, but I hold it above us anyway.

"Fight me and I'll fuck you until you can't walk. You'll be so bruised from taking me that you won't be able to forget the feel of my cock inside you. Understand?"

Choking on a sob, she nods her head in jerking movements.

"Lift up." I order.

She lifts as high as she can with me over her, my free hand snatching the bottom of her sports bra, pulling it over her head in one harsh yank. Her tits bounce with the force of them being released, drawing my attention to them. A large bandage covers the skin between her breast and her sternum causing my brows to dip in confusion. I've seen every inch of Kenna and the only place she has burns is her leg so I make a mental note to look later. Right now my hands are busy with something else.

My mouth waters with the urge to pull her rosy nipples between my teeth. Pushing her back down, I use one hand to wrap the black bra around her hands but I need to close the lighter to tie her to the frame. Sending us back into darkness, I can feel her tremble beneath me from the sensation of being tied, in total darkness, with a monster above her. It spurs me on.

Leaning down to her mouth, my tongue traces her soft pillowy lips, "I bet you're so fucking wet for me. Even in fear, you're a sick filthy fucking slut for my dick."

Tying her hands around the railing, my fingers pinch her chin, tipping her head back.

"This is going to feel so goddamn good, Killer."

Licking up her throat, a moan slips free from the sweet taste of her tears rolling down her face. For a second I almost forget what I'm doing here with her trashing under me, but the metal of the lighter in my palm reminds me. Flicking it back open, she stares into my eyes watching for my next move. Looking down, I take in every inch of her creamy skin slick with sweat, her perky tits bouncing with each movement we make, her breathing making the rise faster. And that's when I know where to start.

Spreading my knees, I let my hard dick settle against her core, showing her just how much I want to see her hurt.

"Let's play a game. You bleed, I bleed."

She mumbles around the gag she has in her mouth, but I just smile.

"Who worked with your father to betray mine?" I ask.

Her brows dip, but she shakes her head.

Dropping the lighter lower, I hold it mere inches from her skin. Her hips begin to buck into me, pressing her pussy up against my dick, but not the way I want. Horror fills her eyes. True numbing fear covers her face, tears falling faster, her entire body shaking with every inch the fire comes closer.

"Ahh, so my little fighter here is afraid of something." I rumble.

Sobbing behind the fabric, she tries to scream at me, but no words form.

"Now that I have your attention."

Tracing her torso with my other hand, my fingers trail up, cupping her left breast in my palm. Leaning down, I take her nipple in my mouth, biting down until she throws her head back with a muffled scream.

"What were you and Paige doing there?"

Looking up to see her eyes on me, she clamps her mouth shut, anger replacing the fear. And fuck, my dick leaks at the image in front of me. Kenna Kingston is a fucking goddess laying here, tied and gagged with her half naked body at my mercy. Her hips buck, trying to fight me and the fear that threatens to possess her.

Fuck she consumes me.

Licking my lips, I nod my head.

"Hmmm, fucking hell. I knew you were brave, but this? I can't wait to fuck the defiance out of you."

Bucking against me, she rubs her pussy against me over and over again. This little brat is trying to make a point, but she doesn't know that the monster is so close to breaking free. Snapping the lighter shut, darkness blankets us once more, but this time I don't give her a second to breathe. No, I'm flipping her over and shoving down her sweatpants in one smooth motion. Screaming from the twinge in her arms, I ignore it. My control snaps at the sound of her crying.

Twisting her long hair around my wrist, I pull her up onto her knees, head tips back, resting against my shoulder. Lowering my grip to circle around her slender throat my mouth moves to her ear.

"Let's see how much fight you have left when I'm so fucking deep in this tight little pussy you can taste me in your throat. Or do you want my dick that bad? Do you crave my cock in your pussy?"

Ghosting my fingers down the crease of her ass, my fingers stop just over her hole.

"Or is your need something more primal? Want me to fill your ass, Killer? Is that what you want? Only if you beg." I spit out.

Slapping the exposed skin on her ass hard enough that the sound reverberates through the room. Pulling against the rail, she continues to fight me, fueling me further into the pitch black corners of my soul. She fucking broke the band and now I'm going to claim her in every way. Biting down on the soft skin between her neck and shoulder, I hold her by the throat and teeth. Shoving her thong to the side I don't even check to see if she's wet for me because my girl is always soaked.

Slamming into her, my eyes swim with tears from the feeling of her tight cunt gripping me. Holding her hip still to let myself adjust to her heat, my fingers curl tighter around her throat, my teeth drawing blood. Pulling away, I let her go to grip both sides of her hips.

Slamming my hand down on her ass, "Keep fighting me. Fucking push back."

And fuck me, she does. Meeting me thrust for thrust, she turns her head to look over her shoulder at me. Anger and hate may fill her eyes, but her soaked pussy loves the feel of my dick.

"God, your cunt is only for me. I knew you would be a nasty little slut for me. Even when I own every inch of you."

"Yes." I let out a low moan.

Reaching forward, I pull the fabric from her mouth, "Beg."

Her eyes darken with that one word. Clamping her mouth shut, she sneers at me.

"Fuck you."

Slapping her slick skin, my handprint marks her flesh, pumping faster, my legs shake with my building release. Leaning forward my finger slips between us to rub at her clit, but not enough to send her over the edge. No, I want to grab some of her slick heat to spread somewhere else. She'll beg for it. I want her screaming my name until she wakes everyone in the building.

Pulling her cum from between her legs, I rub it against her asshole, the tense of her muscles has a low chuckle escaping.

"I told you, I own every inch of you. I'm going to fill every fucking hole you have."

Biting her lip, my thumb rubs the rim, my dick twitching inside her with anticipation.

"You don't want to talk? How about scream?" I grunt.

Shoving my thumb into her tight hole she freezes against me, clenching around my finger.

"I'm going to fucking love watching you break beneath me." I remind her.

Using my other hand to untie her, she drops forward before catching herself with her hands. Fucking her harder I drive my finger deeper, her walls quivering around my dick.

"That's it. Take it. Take what you want, all you have to do is beg."

Pulling all the way out, I use my hold on her hip and the hook of my thumb inside her tight little asshole to slam back into her. Stars shoot behind my eyelids, but I keep moving inside her, her wetness spilling down our legs, she's drenched.

"Oh god!" She screams.

"Wrong name, Killer."

Twisting my thumb, I curl it inside, pumping into her cunt at the same time.

"Please. Please." She chants. Her hands fist the metal bars.

Reaching beside my knee, I pick up the lighter and flick it open, shining the orange glow over us both.

"I want to see you scream my name while your pussy soaks my dick."

Using her hold on the bed frame she arches her back, pressing her ass into my palm more, my thumb fully seated inside her hole, her eyes meet mine over her shoulder.

Lifting her ass she drops back down over my dick slow but rough with each movement.

"Ryker, please fuck me." She lets out on a moan.

Her smokey eyes never leave mine. Matching me thrust for thrust, her lips fall open with each move. My balls tighten. I'm so fucking close, but I hold off on finishing because I only want her to come right now. Before she calls my name out again she fucking shocks the hell out of me by slipping forward until my thumb pops out. Turning around so fast my dick plops against my stomach. My hands reach for her, not knowing what she's going to do. The lighter falls on the bed closing us in the dark again, but she's not fighting me anymore. No, my girl wants to play.

Shoving me backwards, her legs cage me in until her pussy hovers over my dick, dripping over me, her warm cunt so close to my cock. My fingers fight to find the lighter, finally they find purchase casting the light on us again, her face is shadowed with need. Lust. Cravings. In one swift move she sits, sinking down on me, riding my dick with so much fucking hatred dancing in her eyes.

"Fuck, Rye. Please." She shouts.

A long low growl builds in my chest at the sight of her head thrown back on her plea. One palm closes over her breast, pinching and twisting her nipple while my eyes stay on her face as she fucks me. My orgasm builds higher when her hand slips between us to flick at her clit. She's playing with herself while using my dick to reach her orgasm. Fuck me, she's fighting back the only way she knows how. And I'd be a liar if I said it didn't make me black out a little when her walls started to twitch around me.

"My turn." I say, dropping us back into darkness to grab her throat. "Ride my dick like a good girl."

"Rye oh god please!"

"Yes, that's it. Soak my cock, Killer. I knew you were a fucking slut."

"Only for you." She moans.

"Good girl."

I lift her hips leaving a little space between us so I can fuck her faster and harder. Her fingers are still playing with her clit.

"Rub your clit harder for me."

She does as I say, sending her over the edge, her body shaking with the force of her orgasm. Her thighs clench around me trying to hold me still through the wave of sensations, but I pull her off before she can clamp around me again. Sliding off the bed, I drag her to me by the throat, my feet landing on the floor, I lean down to her ear.

"Open that pretty mouth wide baby."

Without hesitation she does as she's told and I slip between her lips, the feeling has my head falling back. Both hands frame her face using my hold to fuck her mouth.

"Swallow around my dick. I want you to take all of me."

Working myself deeper I pull her hair back into a messy hold, pumping into her mouth until I fill her to the brim, but still I don't pull out. I want her to swallow down every drop. And she does. Licking up from the base to the tip she cleans the mixture of us from my dick.

"Mmmh." She moans.

"Fuck, Killer." I groan.

In the pitch black room only our breathing can be heard. Her tears come next. And then my belt buckle. Followed by my shoes and shirt. Before I know it my feet are eating up the distance to my apartment. Shit. I need to wash her off me before going home, so I head to the basement. The fights should be over by now, but either way it's the best place for me right now. The whole way to the empty house all I see is grey eyes staring back at me. Kenna Kingston is going to be a problem.

"Hey man, what are you doing here?" G stands just off the steps of the porch.

"I need to clear my head. When did you get here?"

Lighting a cigarette, he offers me one and I gladly take it. The bitterness covers her taste on my tongue. The light from his brightens when he pulls in a long drag.

"I got a call that we had a few guests. Thought I'd come handle it, but since you're here." He shrugs.

Nodding, I follow him into the house, tossing my cigarette on the way in since we decide to keep the filth to a minimum. The house is lit with bright LED bulbs, one single couch, a fridge with drinks and beer, and a stocked medical cabinet. Other than that we keep the house basically vacant. A few beds upstairs if needed as well. The basement door opens and shouts spill through to us. Soundproof. Following G down the light blinding, people falling into place beside me, slapping my back, and making small talk.

Always a scene to make when one of the Stone brothers shows up.

Stepping into the ring I pull my shirt off tossing it to G with a wink. Flipping me the bird, he makes a show of dropping it to the ground. If it were anyone else I'd knock him in the teeth, but G is my boy. Always has been. A brother in his own right. His blue eyes glow with humor, his snake tattoo curling around his neck, the brand of our family. He's just as big as me, built by years of running things for us, and lean from years in the ring with me. West may be the pretty boy, but G has a swag about him that draws in all the barbies.

Shaking my head I lift my arms to hype up the crowd. It's really for me giving myself a chance to scan each and every face. It doesn't take long until my eyes laser in on our target. "My turn?" A voice says from behind me.

Turning slowly to give off a show of indifference my stare connects with dark blue ones.

"Why not." I say.

With a smirk he turns to look at the two men standing just behind him. A girl with striking blue hair is wrapped under their arms, but it's the look on her face that has me stepping back a step. Most would think they were protecting her, but they'd be wrong. That one is a Savage.

"Stryker Lawless." I announce to the crowd.

"The one and only." He laughs before lunging forward.

CHAPTER FIFTEEN

KENNA

Sore. That's the first thought that registers when my eyes open the next morning. My thighs, my core, my fucking wrist, even my throat hurts. I don't need to look in the mirror to know that I'll need makeup to cover fingerprints on my neck. Sitting up, a gasp falls from my lips. A sea of orange covers my room, the smell of Lilies entering my senses. Ryker fucking Stone filled my room with Lilies from the garden. The sudden reminder of what we did causes memories to flash through my mind. Mixing the garden and last night together in one big confusing mess. What is he trying to pull?

Throwing the blanket off me, I stand, my foot stepping on something smooth and soft. My gaze drops to the floor, my breath hitching, seeing an array of lilies. Even after everything he's done to me I still find myself fighting a smile. Beautiful orange and black lilies are littered on the floor. A massive bouquet sits in the center of my dresser. I don't stop the slow smile that spreads across my face.

Ryker has a way of crawling his way inside me. Bending down I pluck one of the flowers off the floor. My heart stutters in my chest when I allow myself to inhale the intoxicating scent. I'm riding a high, or I was, until I saw what was sitting in the center of the bouquet on my dresser. What the actual fuck? In the middle is a single black lily from the garden, but wrapped around it is a snake ring. That's not what has my stomach curling. No, it's the large middle finger that rests on the tip , not able to slide down fully, that has my empty stomach filling with acid. Ryker left me a severed finger, my guess is it's from the bar guy, and has it sitting in the ocean of flowers that fill my room.

"He left me a fucking warning wrapped in a pretty little bow of memories." I say, talking to myself like I've gone insane.

Hell, I might have with the thoughts I was having right before this. If I thought I could outsmart Ryker before I'm rethinking that now. Heading to the bathroom to grab something to clean up his little gift, I got an idea... It's time to give him a taste of his own medicine, but not before a nice hot shower and a road trip. Rykers visit last night finally opened my eyes to what I need to do, it's time I stop hiding behind the school. Today, I'm going to get answers from the man who started this all. My dad.

An hour later I'm pulling into the empty parking lot, my radio blaring *Nightmare* by Halsey. Shifting into park, I swing down my visor. Bright gray eyes take in my reflection, makeup covers the bruises surrounding my neck, my lips still a little swollen from being wrapped around him. I open my center console, my fingers fumble around until they finally grasp the small black tube from where it slipped to the bottom. Looking back to the mirror I thumb off the top and apply the deep red lipstick with a shallow smile.

"Let's get this over with."

Pumping myself up to actually go inside, my shoulders roll with tension, the tink from my tube of lipstick falling back into the console compartment is lost to the music. Rubbing my lips together I snap the visor closed and toss my phone into my purse and slide it under my passenger seat. Looking back up, I spot a large black SUV driving past the entrance to the parking lot. Blinking past the sun in my eyes, I squint to see if it's the Stone brothers, but it's gone far too fucking fast. Shaking my head, my eyes go to my rearview mirror to check behind me, but when all I see is the empty parking lot I roll my eyes at myself.

Keys and wallet in hand I step out into the hot sun. My car sits in the center of the lot with only a few others, more come in slowly now that the somber gray and tan building is open. Walking towards the tall fence that wraps around the entire property, lined with barbed wire at the top. Contrary to what people assume, the main fences in the front don't have barbed wire. It's not every day that someone attempts to climb in or out of this place.

Making my way to the door with two tall sliding glass doors, my black and white Nike shoes squeak across the just mopped tile, opening into a small entryway. Straight ahead is a square office glassed into the center of the hallway, an entrance and exit on each side. Both have metal detectors for you to walk through. Hanging on the wall is a sign with big bold letters that reads,

Rule number one: No phones or outside items.

Rule number two: No touching.

Stepping up to the booth a large burly man stands from his seat, bending to see through the glass slot. Not that my five-foot nine frame is small, but that's just how fucking huge this man is.

"Visiting or picking up?" He asks.

Pick up? This isn't a daycare and I sure as hell won't be taking one of these fuckers home. Huffing out a short laugh, I look up to meet the man's stare.

"Visiting."

through a small slot, he slides a clipboard with a sign in sheet connected to it. He nods to it and asks for my I.D. Signing Kenna Kingston in the rectangle area, my eyes stop on a name that triggers a memory from my childhood. Hank Harlow. It shows that he was here earlier today. My brows dip in confusion, but my attention snaps back to the man, with my I.D. He slides it back through, while taking the clipboard and giving it a once over.

"Step through. Clear your pockets and meet the guard on the other side. Have a nice visit." He eyes me on my way to the tall metal detector.

Standing just on the other side, is a short stocky woman, ebony curls stray free from her low bun and freckles splatter across her face. A bored expression is plastered on her face while she waits for me to step through. Pulling my wallet and keys from my pocket, I toss them in the clear container sitting on a long white table beside the larger machine. She hulk grabs the container, sliding it from one side to the other while I slowly walk through, my gaze straight ahead.

"Ms.?" Her voice is throaty with a smoker's rasp.

"Kingston." I give her my last name only.

Not here to make friends. I keep my face blank, the name alone should signal her not to give me shit. Being the Heir to an empire tends to give you those perks.

Waiving me to a green metal bench bolted to the faded white wall she instructs me to take a seat.

"Remove your shoes for me." She says.

Jerking back, I look at her with what I would assume is a confused as hell expression, but she just holds out her hands for my shoes and waits. Slipping them off, I'm left with only my black socks while she shoves her hands inside my shoe, feeling around looking for anything I could have snuck in. After several minutes of her searching my wallet, shoes, pants, and even having me lift the bottom of my bra and shake, I've finally passed her test. By the end of my shake down I've thought of going home twice and regretted coming at least a dozen times.

Following Helga the guard, she walks me through a few more glass security doors, glass being the main word because security and break-ability go hand in hand here, we make our way to a section with a large D on the wall. Each group is sectioned by letters and then numbers, but visitation is held in a large room with tables, vending machines, and benches clutter the space. Some places are like that, but not here in Del Mar. Prisons are strict when it comes to visiting even down to the clothes you wear.

Nothing that shows your cleavage, no holes in your jeans, no sandals or open toed shoes, nothing too tight, and the list goes on.

It's the reason I'm wearing straight legged jeans paired with my Nike shoes and a plain white tee that hugs my body but is just loose enough that if I wasn't wearing a bra you wouldn't notice. On our walk she goes over a few of the rules, visitation time, and how the payment system works for the vending machines. In order to buy things for the inmates, or yourself, a card has to be loaded with money that you use to purchase things. Adding a whole extra step just to swipe another card.

"He will be sitting at one of the tables or benches. You can hug once, but after that no touching. If either of you want snacks, drinks, or anything from the vending machines, you will need to be the one getting it. Visitation ends in an hour." She says.

Her hand hovers over the curved metal handle to a double door. Looking back at me once more, she tugs the door open, revealing a spacious room. Surrounded by grey walls and black plastic chairs, the room is filled with round cafeteria tables placed throughout the space. Men are seated around the room with family and friends visiting them. She Hulk keeps moving further into the room while my legs drag behind her, giving me time to take in the space around me. Locked in a giant room full of criminals. Fucking great.

A chair scraping loudly across the floor pulls my attention past her to the man now standing near the center of the room. Grey eyes stare back at me with bewilderment, his salt and pepper hair showing his age. Looks like my father was expecting someone else. I wasn't expecting him to jump for joy at the sight of me, not with how he left me for dead, but the look in his eyes isn't one I was expecting.

"Hellcat." He says.

Ice slithers down my spine with his words. That name. His voice. It's all enough to send me back to a time in my life where he was my king and I was nothing more than a little princess. Pausing in front of him, the guard looks to each of us before deciding that our drama isn't the kind that warrants her services. Black boots screech across the floor on her way to the corner of the room. I look away from her retreating bringing my focus back to the turbulent storm brewing in my father's eyes.

Nodding to the chair across from him, he takes a seat without so much as an attempt to embrace his only daughter, the one he tried to kill.

"What are you doing here?" He questions.

His tone is hard, but behind the malice is something softer.

"I'm not here for you. I'm here for me." I state.

Chewing on the inside of my lip, my gaze rolls over the man that raised me to be the person I am today. Only, that man is gone and in his place is a shell of who he once was. Where Kane Kingston was powerful, un-movable, and resilient, this person before me is anything but. A coward is all I see. Betrayal burns the back of my throat just sitting near the man responsible for Paige's death. For the past two years I've claimed him innocent, but looking at how truly dark he is now, I know how wrong I was.

His hand moves, as if to reach out to me, but he hesitates when I flinch away from his touch.

"You shouldn't be here. If they see you've come to visit me it'll be the final piece they need to come after you."

I huff out a short laugh. No amusement can be found in the sound that leaves my chest.

"Come after me? They already have and it's no thanks to you that I've survived this long." I snap, my voice getting louder.

Bodies shuffle around us drowning out my rage, but the true fear that flashes over his face has me sitting back in the hard plastic seat.

"What, you thought they'd let me walk away from what you did to their family. To ours!"

Shaking his head, "The Stone brothers are where you're safest. Do whatever you need to keep your place there." Reaching for my hand he squeezes me roughly, "They'll want to kill you themselves, but they need you alive so they won't. Use that to your advantage because there are snakes at Hawthorne that want you more."

Yanking my hand from his, "I'm not worried about the monster I don't know, it's the one I do. So why don't you tell me what the fuck is going on?" I spit at him.

His eyes darken, "You can't trust anyone there, Hellcat. Keep those boys close at all times, because you're in their veins. Stay away from the Foundation." He warns.

Leaning in closer my voice lowers, "Tell me what the hell is going on, dad." My voice cracks on the last word.

Looking around the room, keeping his eyes off mine, he pauses for a moment.

"I was set up by someone we thought we could trust. You and Paige were never supposed to be there. I'm handling it from inside, but they are pushing for things I can't give them. Once I run out of chips to play with they'll come for you, the only thing left I have to lose, and they will break you. I can't allow that to happen, so you have to listen to me."

Nothing he says is making sense. Who would Alec and my dad trust so much that their judgment was tainted? Alec was never one to let anyone close enough to his family to cause harm, so it didn't make sense.

I'm already shaking my head before he starts speaking again, "No. Alec never trusted anyone with his family. Not his kids or me."

"This person was from our past. Someone we cut out long ago." He says.

Dropping my palms to the table with a thud I shove my chair back, "Then tell me who! If what you're telling me is true then you have no reason to be in prison for arson. For murder!" I'm yelling and attracting attention. Several eyes land on us, some merely annoyed, but a few are curious. I can see my fathers back straighten at the sudden notice from his fellow inmates. Turning back to me a mask drops into place leaving the cold man I saw when I first came in.

"Don't come back, Kenna." He barks. My name feels like daggers to the heart with the way he spits it at me.

Standing from the table, tears threaten to spill, but I refuse to show him weakness. Even with his actions I still want to please the father who loved and cherished me. He must see it on my face because he exhales a breath.

"Stay away from the Foundation. Keep your distance and trust only the brothers."

Nodding my tongue slips out to wet my dry lips. Tasting my lipstick, the reminder has my shoulders pulling back. Standing straighter I ask the last question I have for him knowing he isn't ready to give me more.

"If you're innocent, why are you sitting behind these walls? What happened to the man I grew up thinking you were?"

Two steps forward and he's in my face, "Family. Always." He whispers. Leaning in he keeps his hands at his sides but his lips drop to my forehead as if I was that little five year old girl again. "Don't come back."

And then he's walking away. Leaving me alone again to figure out the mess he left me with and the riddle that now runs on a loop in my head. He said that the Stone brothers are the safest place for me. Does that mean he knows who my Shadow is? He had my ring from the night of the fire so he had to have been in the building. Walking back towards the double doors, I let myself process the information that I got today. What little he did give me because let's face it, I have less than when I got here now that I know he didn't set the fire.

Running over the things I know, I list them off one by one.

First, Ryker may break me, but he'll be my saving grace in the end.

Second, my father isn't the murderer I thought he was, but he just might be a coward all the same.

Third, my Shadow set the fire and he's someone from our families past, so if he's after me then he's also after the brothers.

Only I'm allowed to cut them down by their heels. No one will take that away from me, not even Shadow, even if that means he has to go through me. If they want to break me that's fine. I'll gladly let Ryker's flame consume me, but I'll rise stronger than before when they're by my side. They bleed, I bleed.

CHAPTER SIXTEEN

KENNA

My foot hits the accelerator, pushing my car faster down the winding road towards Hawthorne. My father's words keep repeating in my mind, giving me more to think about when it comes to the brothers. What I don't understand is how they could be the safest place for me when they are the ones I should fear. Not that Ryker doesn't remind me of that every fucking day while he holds my next breath in my lungs. A dark image of the shadowed form in the hallway outside of my class that day pops into my head, reminding me that maybe I've been running from the wrong monster, but what would my dad know about him?

Yanking the wheel right, my tires screech across the asphalt with my speed. Coming up on my turn my foot leaves the gas, but I don't go for the break, instead reaching for the emergency break. Pulling it at the same time as my left hand spinning the wheel, I manage to take the turn at fifty miles an hour, loving the feeling that sinks into my stomach. I can't help the smile that forms on my face with the adrenaline. Up ahead the tall metal gate looms over me, bringing back a sense of foreboding, like my body knows it's not a place of freedom, being trapped behind these bars.

Slowing down, I roll my windows down to let in the breeze. My hair whips around my face, the sun breaking through now that the tint isn't keeping it out. Passing all of the students that linger around campus during the weekend, I pull into the parking spot I've claimed since the first day. Popping the gear shifter into park, I look in my rearview mirror, peering into soft grey eyes, an empty smile looking back at me. I thought today would be different. Not that I expected a warm welcome, but to be turned away after being abandoned? That shit stings no matter how much I've grown and if anyone else expected any different then fuck them. Feelings don't make me weak, it's what I do with them that shows just how strong I am.

Before shutting off the car I roll up the windows and steady myself. *Show no weakness.* The words of Alec Stone pop into my head. It takes more than one deep breath to keep the tears at bay for the man who taught me so much about what it means to be a leader. To own who we are, even down to what makes us the darkest of all. Finally stepping out of the car, my eyes roam the area taking in the large castle-like space, knowing that this is where I should feel most at home. By the time I reach the door to my dorm my body is dragging with exhaustion. Between being woken up last night and the way my day went today, I need a damn nap.

Going to unlock the door, my hand twists the key only to come back surprised that it's already unlocked. Nerves have me hesitating for a split second before I shake it off. Ally must be home, logic tells me. As I push the door open my eyes are met with darkness, fingers feel around for the light switch, flipping it up, shedding light on the open space. Taking stock of my surroundings I spot Ally's door shut, the T.V. off, and my room door slightly ajar. The hair on my arms stands. I know I shut that door. Unease prickles my insides as my mind runs wild with possible threats, but instead of leaving myself to freak out, I urge myself forward towards my room with logic hitting me.

"Ally." I murmur to myself.

I bet she just wanted to borrow something of mine to wear and didn't think to shut my door all the way. Chill out Kens, nothing's going to pop out and bite you and if it does, you'll probably like it. Well, only if it's from a certain snake. Toeing the door open, my gaze takes in the room still covered in lilies that I left in their place. The sweet floral aroma hits me like a ton of bricks, making my core clench from the reminder of the garden. I let out a loud laugh when I find the room empty, but it's cut short when I see a small brown box sitting in the center of my bed. The brown standing out against the grey comforter.

Swallowing, my throat burns from the bile threatening to flood my mouth.

This box is bigger in size, but still no larger than a small shoe box. A thin red ribbon is tied in a neat bow on the top, drawing my eyes to the lid. My teeth sink into my bottom lip, biting down hard enough to draw blood. Numbness coats my skin, preventing the pain from surfacing. Last time I opened a box from Shadow there was a secret hidden with soft threats and promise, but the size of this one brings the vow for more to come.

Trembling hands reach out with nimble fingers, sweat covering my palms, I suck in a deep breath pulling the box to the edge of the bed. Looking behind me to make sure Ally hasn't made her way back in the dorm without me noticing, I steady myself, preparing to come face to face with god knows what. The closer I pull the box the more a rancid smell pools under my nose, making my stomach curl. My chest rises faster with the need to know what's under the lid, so I tug the silky ribbon until it falls flat against the bed, adding the only pop of color against a sea of grey.

The floral smell throughout the room starts to dissipate with the unsealing of the lid, but I keep going. Wetting my lips, I gather up every ounce of Kingston blood that pumps through my veins, and lift the top with one quick move, yanking the metaphoric band-aid off. Revealing a small gold envelope with *Princessa* scribbled in messy handwriting on the front. Tracing the letters I can feel the rushed anger in each letter. It's thick and tapped on the back to hold it closed, but when I lift it black and gold paper covers a second item. Formaldehyde and rotten flesh fill my nose, making me gag from the putrid scent coming from the bottom of the box.

"Oh my god."

I'm going to be sick. Curiosity wars inside me between the smell and the thick items in the envelope. I opt to back away from the bed and slip my fingernail behind the tape. Fuck it. Tugging it open I pour the items into my palm, revealing a stack of photos. Pictures of the garden. Ryker between my legs, my head thrown back in ecstasy, one after the other more and more photos of us. Pictures of me going into Jax's shop, the gym, between classes, with Ally, but it's the last two that have my stomach plummeting. One of them is of me sleeping in my sports bra and boy-shorts, my grey blanket tossed to the side. You can see my tattoo in this photo. A tattoo I know Ryker hasn't yet been able to see fully to know what it is. Not that he'd look since it covers the one thing he refuses to look at.

The last photo is of me this morning walking into the county prison. These are freshly printed and left here which means whoever placed these in my room hasn't been gone long. Chills spread down my spine, fear mixed with anger boils in my blood knowing someone invaded my privacy. Tracking me. Ally could have been here and been hurt. Searching my memory for anything that could point to who followed me this morning nothing comes to mind. Two steps later and I'm back up against the bed, ready to see what else I've been left. Flicking the paper to the side, my stomach rolls at the sight before me.

Dropping the stack of photos in my left hand, my right covers my mouth, running from the room I barrel into the bathroom. Sweat pools at the base of my neck, I barely make it to the toilet in time to puke. My stomach heaves, emptying everything I've had today, leaving me feeling cold and empty. My arms shake on each side of the toilet almost too weak to hold me up. No matter how strong I try to be, I'd never be prepared for what's in that box.

"Ahhhhh!" I scream, throwing my head back with tears falling down my face.

My fingers itch to pull my hair out. It feels like fire and ice cover my body fighting for dominance. This morning Ryker left me flowers and a finger as a threat that I belonged to him, but this? This is fucking sick. Slamming down on my ass the cold tile helps to cool off my heated skin through my jeans. Leaning my head on the bathroom door I let my eyes fall closed, my breathing erratic, but I count to ten in my head to calm myself.

It's all a game, Kenna. He said they would be the safest place for me, but how could they when they try so hard to break me. Trust no one? Never. How do I know who Shadow is if they refuse to show their face? Thudding my head against the door I try to force myself to see something, anything, I could be missing. That's when it hits me. The black SUV that sped past the parking lot this morning. Kicking the bottom of the toilet, I yell one more time before I swallow down my feelings and block it all out. Pushing off the floor I move to stand at the sink, looking at the woman in the mirror.

Hair a mess, eyes red, tears staining my cheeks. Nodding at myself, my hands move automatically. Fixing my hair into a messy bun, my eyes track each movement with no emotion. I've blocked it all out, drinking down everything that's been thrown at me until I feel nothing but numbness in my veins. Washing out my mouth I use my foot to flush the puke down and head back into my room. It's time for me to make a delivery of my own before Ally gets home and has a fucking fit.

Cleaning the flowers off the floor and dresser, I shove them all into a trash bag and toss them in the corner of the room. Keeping the last item in the box I grab the pictures that I dropped and place them on top of the offending item with tears still trying to break through. Placing the lid back on the box, I work to tie the bow as perfect as it was before, but my fingers are still trembling a little from shock I give up and just put the ribbon around it in a knot. Snatching my keys and the box from the bed I storm out of my dorm to my car.

The brown box sits in my passenger seat, my windows down to air out the car, I floor it to the one spot I knew I'd find Ryker. He thinks he knows all my moves, but what he doesn't know is I have my own secrets. His fucked up obsession with beating on people turned into underground fighting, using houses that our families own through business. That turned into building what they call "the basement", but that's not as much of a secret as they'd like to think. Thinking your dad betrayed the only people you've ever loved teaches you to know everyone in your life like the back of your hand. Cole may use tracking software, trackers on cars, and cameras, but I have my ways.

Letting them think they have the upper hand is what's best for them while they deal with the Foundation. With my father out of the picture and theirs dead, the Foundation has to be breathing down their back. Knowing them, they are fighting every move they want to make. Me included. The Foundation has reached out to me a time or two, but I've turned them down.

Turning down the street I glance at the box, making sure it's still in the center of the seat. Shaking my head, I try to understand how they think I'm so blind. They claim my father is the culprit who started the fire, but then why was their dad there? Why was their dad refusing to let mine out of the business? I heard them fighting a few weeks before that meeting about how he wanted me to have a normal life where I could be safe. They were getting their hands too dirty for my father and he wanted out. None of it made sense and some of it still doesn't, but this? The box in my seat? It's all starting to fall into place right in front of me.

They have shown me exactly who they are and I still keep trying to prove them wrong. He said they were my safe place and now I see why. I'm only as safe as I can be when I'm surrounded by the devil himself. It can't hurt me if I can see it coming. That's what my dad was trying to tell me this entire time. Stay close to the Stone brothers so I can see it coming. Stopping at the curb outside a plain tan and brick house, I push my sunglasses up my head and unbuckle. Lifting the little gift they left me, I slide out of the driver's seat. I breathe through my mouth, taking small quick breaths to keep the smell escaping the box from over-whelming me.

It takes effort to calm the raging storm that's building with each step closer. Climbing the stairs to the small house, I kick the door three times, determined to grab their attention.

"Yo girl, what the hell are you doing?"

Some random guy walks around from the side of the house with a cigarette hanging from his lips. Rolling my eyes at him, I turn back to the door, lifting my leg to kick it again. Sighing, his hand lashes out grabbing me. Thick fingers curl around my calf, halting my next move and throwing me off balance. Using my free hand I lean on the rail to keep from falling backwards when my head turns to him slowly.

"Get your fucking hands off me before you lose it." I snap.

Jerking my leg from his hold I slam my foot into the door one last time. It swings open to reveal G standing there with a smirk.

Batting my lashes with a flirty smile I nod my head in the randoms direction, "Tell boss man if his little bitch touches me again he'll be missing some fingers."

Blowing G a kiss I move past him with the box in hand. I can see the moment he smells it because he spins around slinging the door shut and rushes after me.

"He's not downstairs!" He shouts after me.

Stopping on my heel I turn, almost running into him. His throat tattoo bobs with a swallow, a war wages in his eyes. Another whiff floats from the box so he turns with a follow me look. G may be their right hand man, but he's a boss in his own right. They keep him on a short leash because they know he'd run his own if they let him.

"What the hell did you do Princess?" He laughs.

Elbowing him in the ass on the way up a set of stairs, I scoff. "What makes you think this is my doing?"

Peeking at me over his shoulder he shakes his head, "Because they only make a move like this when it comes to you, but I can tell you right now, if you think this was them then you're wrong. It's my job to know what moves around Del Mar."

"Yeah, well I know for a fact I saw the Tahoe following me this morning so maybe they make moves even you don't know about." I quip.

Reaching the top of the stairs I see a door slightly open with voices floating out into the hallway. Ignoring the men's voices I keep walking, stopping short when a raspy female voice reaches my ears. G looks back at me when he grabs the door-knob, his eyes darken when he sees my face.

"Don't you fucking dare."

But it's too late. I'm already shoving the box in his hands and storming into the room only to stop short at the sight before me. West and Cole stand at the back of the room leaning against the window while three masked men surround a little blue haired bitch standing between Rykers legs working on a cut covering his face.

"What the hell?" Cole says, his voice venom.

West lets out an, "Oh shit."

But Ryker just looks at me with a shit eating grin.

Storming over to him I shove blue bitch from between his legs and spin, placing myself between the two coming face to face with emerald green eyes filled with laughter? I step forward and at the same time the air in the room gets sucked out by the three massive bodies that move at once toward the girl in front of me. A low grunt comes from the middle one, setting off the man behind me, his large tattooed arm wrapping around my waist tugging me into his chest.

"G, what the fuck?" Ryker says.

Blue girl just laughs and holds her hand out to me, but all I do is eye it.

"I'm Oakley Erin Savage. If it was one of mine you were between, I'd do the same, so no harm done. I was just patching your boy up after he went a round or two with Stryker over here." She flashes a huge smile at the man in the middle, all three wearing weird skeleton masks covering their faces.

"Kenna Kingston." I grab her hand.

G walks into the room with the box I left with him, everyone turns his way when the smell hits us. The strange three crowd around Oakley like a barrier. Ryker stands stepping into my back, his hold on me tightens, while West and Cole shove off the wall by the window to come stand beside us. We all face G, but I'm the only one not wearing a look of confusion.

"Someone needs to start talking." West says, his nose scrunched up.

His words remind me why I'm here. Pulling away from the warmth of Rykers hold, missing it instantly, I push that thought to the side to turn and face the Stone brothers.

"You three thought it would be smart to fuck with me? Leaving me something this fucking sick?"

Grabbing the box from G's hands I push it into Rykers chest curling my lip at them. Flipping them the middle finger, my ring catches Rykers eyes and I swear they darken into such a deep brown they're almost black. There on my ring finger is the snake jeweled ring he put on the finger he left me. He saw it as a warning but I made it my crown.

"Game fucking on." Storming out the room I leave them to clean up their mess.

The last thing I hear is Oakley laughing while the men gag at the item in the box, and right then and there I make a note not to mess with that crazy bitch.

CHAPTER SEVENTEEN

RYKER

The weight of my head feels heavy in my hands. Cole's voice echoes off the walls of the room, while West tries to calm him down. That fucking stunt my little killer pulled earlier has sparked some shit through the house with Cole and West. Not to mention she came in like a hurricane while we had other guests here, causing a storm all on their own. Stryker had a field day in the ring with me, but his girl Oak just so happened to have her tiny ass planted right between my legs when a certain blonde blew through the door. G should have been able to stop her and he'll have me to answer to later for that little stunt. Holding Cole back from chasing after Kenna has been hard enough. I don't have time to deal with anymore bullshit.

"Looks like your girl is just as much trouble as our Blue." Stryker says, humor in his tone.

Annoyance climbs up my spine. The three Lawless brothers crowd the room, stealing the last bit of space left. A little feisty woman around five foot nothing stands between her three wolves, giving off the appearance of holding them back, but her bite is far worse than theirs and we all know it. She has a reputation all on her own.

"Kenna Kingston is the definition of trouble." I state.

Standing from the bed positioned in the center of the floor, I turn to Cole and West.

"Head home. I want G there by the time I arrive. I have a stop to make before I meet you there."

Turning to address Oak, I speak to her, knowing their dynamic enough to know she's the boss, "You get what you wanted or do you still need to stick around town?" I ask.

Nodding she glances back at Slade, the middle brother with a sly smile, "I think we'll stick around for a little while. I'd love to see how this all plays out with your girl, but we also need to clean up a few things before we head back to Seattle."

Having them in town isn't the best move for us and I make that known.

Spreading my arms wide I put on a smile, "We'd love for you to stay, but having the Lawless and Savage families walking around Del Mar in the middle of a shitstorm of our own could spark some rumors. Maybe it's best if you lay low."

Crossing her arms, Oakley steps backwards, anticipating not one, but all three of her men to step into her back all at once.

"I hear you, Ryker, but it's already been decided. Just think of it as a partnership. If you get in over your head you can call on us. Trust me, we'll be keeping an eye on things here.

Your father was like a brother to mine, but so was Kingston. I have a personal interest in making sure Kenna isn't touched in any way she doesn't want. Keep that in mind, will ya?"

Wiggling her fingers in a fake wave she turns to walk out the room, while the Lawless brothers stand there watching her walk away. Silas looks back over his shoulder, the youngest brother, and pulls up his mask to flash his black lip ring.

"Clean house or we'll have no choice but to step in. You may run things here, but we won't allow your snakes to cross-over into our waters."

West, Cole, and myself stand in the room alone, the door shuts behind them, leaving us in the silence of what just happened. Before Kenna came in here leaving fire in her wake, we were on the path of them leaving town, but after what they saw I knew they would stay. Kenna thinks we left that little gift for her, but she's fucking wrong. So wrong. Cole almost puked from the sight of the decomposed hand. We've seen and done worse shit, but this was personal. Whoever left that box for her to find not only has a way into her dorm, but they also knew how we would react.

"I'm going to kill him." Cole growls through clenched teeth.

"How do you know it's a man?" West asks.

Storming to the wall and back, Cole wears a path into the carpet. "Because there is no way a woman dug up a dead body to remove a two-year-old corpse's hand. That's how the hell I know."

His words are hidden behind rage and grunts, but we understand him just fine. If we don't get him calm soon, things could get ugly.

Pulling out my phone I send off two texts. One to G and one to Ally.

Time to cash in on that favor you owe me.

Apartment. Now.

Knowing not to wait for a reply from G, I keep Ally's text open knowing she's too smart to keep me waiting.

"Get him to the apartment. Don't let him out of your sight until I get there." I snap at West.

"I'm right fucking here asshole." Cole snaps.

Storming up to me, his fist grabs at my shirt, snarling in my face, he presses his forehead into mine. Being the baby of the family means nothing when you're six foot five of pure fucking muscle. Cole may be the quiet tech nerd, but he's far from the tame one.

Gripping the back of his head to pull him closer, our eyes clash, "I've got this brother. Go back home and deal in whatever way you need, but keep your head." Twisting my head I shove against him in a rough headbutt, "Keep your shit together, brother. We need you."

My phone vibrates in my hand so I pull away, but keep my hand on the back of his neck, holding Cole in place. West's eyes are on the side of my face watching for any sign of trouble, because no matter what Kenna thinks, what she gave us today was a threat against all of us.

What do you need?

"I'll handle Kenna. Cole, get home and get some of your tech shit set up to tap her phone. I want tabs on this girl every second of the day."

"You sure it should be you that goes after her?" West says, no humor in his words.

Typing out a text to Ally I pocket my phone and look back up to my brothers. This entire day went to shit so fast.

"Trust me, West. All I need is a night."

Take a look at this

"Fuck."

A text comes in from one of our boys that rolls the streets for us. A photo of a certain little brat leaving the county prison today.

"Looks like our Princess went to go see Kingston."

Showing my brothers the photo they both give me a look that has my fingers twitching. It solidified her place with us. She's meeting with the man who killed our father and dropping boxes that for all we know, she had done all in the same day.

"She was there last Sunday. I ran into her when she was on her way in to see Paige."

Cole throws out that little hook and sinks my ass instantly. Kenna's been playing us this whole time and I've been too busy dipping my dick in her cunt to see it. Well not anymore. Now that I know she's playing her father's game, I'll make sure she drowns in her own blood.

"She just dug her own grave."

Ally text me back with the confirmation I needed.

I'll get it done, but after this we are through. She's my friend Ryker.

Friend. Yeah, but she'll sell her out for money. Ally's family is broke, their status non-existent, no one on the social ladder. If it wasn't for our little loan she wouldn't be here. The little orphan found herself useful being the roommate to a Kingston. If it wasn't for us needing someone to keep tabs on her, she wouldn't be here with a monthly allowance that helps her keep up appearances. So when I call, she answers. When I ask her to keep tabs on my little Killer, she'll follow orders. If I ask her to snatch a phone for me to keep our little princess busy. Well, then she better do as she's told or she'll find herself right back in the gutter she came from.

"Meet me back at the apartment later."

Leaving them in the room I walk out to go see a rotten princess.

* * *

Propped against the stone building, the sun has started to set, the shade hiding me perfectly. A little rat told me my little killjoy should be passing by this way and if she's lucky it'll be soon, I'm getting restless. Rolling the metal bar across the back of my teeth, it clinks against them while I pull out a cigarette. Putting it up against my lips, my lighter cast a low orange light in the growing darkness. I'm taking my third pull from the cigarette when I hear light laughter down the sidewalk headed this way.

Turning my head I let my eyes adjust to the light coming from the sidewalk. Her long legs come into view covered only in thin stockings and a black leather skirt. My dick is instantly hard from the little temptress. Biting my lip, my gaze tracks the way her hips move, the skin-tight white Henley shirt hugging her perfect tits, making my mouth water with the need to pop her nipple in my mouth. Squeezing my lighter, my other hand drops the cigarette to the ground, pressing my foot into the burning ember to snuff it out.

Waiting until she's right up next to me, my arm swings around her chest, pulling her back into me until her ass is planted right against my dick. Flicking the lighter open I watch recognition spark in her eyes, the flames dancing in her grey stare. Pushing her hair to the side to keep from lighting it on fire, I press the flame right up against her skin. The smell of burning hair filling my nose.

"Here kitty kitty." I taunt her.

Struggling in my hold she jerks to the side in an attempt to break free, but I just laugh when her pretty pale flesh catches the fire and she screams. Nipping at her neck, my tongue flattens against her skin, licking up the side of her throat. Pressing the ball of my tongue ring into her pulse point, she trembles under me.

"Mmmhh. Baby, you truly taste like my worst fucking nightmare." I moan in her ear.

Dragging her backwards deeper into the small alley that leads to the groundskeeper shed, my hand moves to her throat to cut off her next scream, making sure we slip inside the unlocked door before anyone sees us. Not that anyone would stop me. I'd fucking rip out their tongue just for looking at my girl getting a taste of her own medicine. Pushing the door closed with my foot I back up against the door, still holding her ass to my front. So *tempting*.

"You little slut. Fuck, Killer. You knew what would happen if you pushed us." I whisper against her ear.

"I did nothing to you." She seethes.

Her anger fuels me. Feeding off the fear that drips from her like rain, I let go of the control I've held for far too long.

"You wanted a monster, well now you have one. On your fucking knees."

Shoving her off me she spins, her stare meeting mine in a battle she'll never win.

Stepping into her, "On your knees, Kenna. Or I'll fuck you so god damn raw you'll beg me to carve out your lungs. Your screams belong to me."

Pressing my hand into her shoulder, I slam her knees into the cold concrete floor, a whimper slipping from her throat.

Turning to the left I light a candle that's off to the side placed here by a ghost that takes orders well for a rat. The orange glow is enough to light the small space in low light, so I close the lighter and the burn on my thumb goes numb.

"Take my dick out." I order.

Steady hands undo my jeans, shoving them down my hips letting my cock spring free. If she's scared she doesn't show it, but she will. I promised them I'd make her hurt for what she did today and that's one I intend to keep.

Taking the hot end of the lighter I press it into the side of her neck. She pulls back, but before she can scream I shove my dick down her throat until she's gagging around my size. Angry eyes peer up at me with tears leaking down the side of her face. My free hand twist her hair around my wrist, allowing me to fully fuck her face without her stopping.

"That's it. Swallow around me baby."

I pump into her mouth over and over, but it's not enough. Not yet. Lighting the lighter I let it burn the metal again. Heating it while she looks at it with wide eyes. Moving on my dick faster she tries to pull me in deeper.

"Oh, Killer. You suck my dick like a goddamn pro, but baby I'm going to sear our souls together. Don't worry I'll join you in the end." Biting my lip I thrust into her mouth deeper.

The sound of her wet mouth gagging around my full cock has my balls tightening. Letting the flame go out on the lighter my fist pulls her hair until her throat is fully open for me.

"Breath through your nose." I order.

Using one hand I hold her head still, while my hips pump into her over and over again, my other hand presses the lighter into her neck burning her skin. She starts to bite down so I yank her hair pulling her mouth open while shoving back in harder, choking her on my dick.

"Be a good girl and fucking swallow me down. You deserve what I give you."

Her tears fall faster now and my dick throbs from the sight before me.

"You earned this. Such a fucking good girl for my dick. You love when I fuck your pretty little mouth like this."

Nodding, her lips touch the base of my dick, swallowing around me fully. Pulling her off me, my hand curls around my throbbing cock, pumping my hand up and down.

"Look at me."

Her grey eyes darken. My other hand drops the lighter next to her knee to grab her throat, tipping her head up towards me.

"I'm going to come all over your face and then I'm going to fuck your tight little pussy while you scream for me."

Squeezing her throat I keep pumping my hand until I spill out all over her face, lips, down her chin, covering her in my come.

"Look at you." I let her go. "So fucking perfect." My finger spreads my come over her lips, shoving my finger into her mouth. "Taste what you do to me."

Curling her tongue around my finger, she licks my finger clean with a moan.

"Turn around."

She follows my direction and turns on her knees, staying on the floor beneath me.

"Pull your skirt up and stockings down under your ass."

I'm going off pure instinct right now. She's in my bones. This woman is the keeper of my soul. A nightmare come to life. Bending down I snatch up the lighter and flick it open.

"Spread your legs."

Her head whips around with wide dark eyes. Part of her is curious, but a bigger part of her is scared. My girl fears fire and I plan on seeing how close I can drag her to the flames before she's begging for more.

"Face forward and put your palms on the floor."

Kenna hesitates for a split second before doing as she's told.

"Lay forward and show me how wet you are for me."

Pressing her chest into the floor, she uses her fingers to reach back and spread herself open for me. She's fucking dripping.

"So drenched for me." I groan.

Pressing the tip up against her entrance, I press the lighter into her inner thigh, at the same time I push all the way into her. Seated deep my eyes roll with how tight she is for me.

"Fuck." I moan. My words are low.

"Oh god." She grunts.

Pulling her head back with my fist in her hair, my other hand takes the lighter and lights the flame again but this time I keep it lit.

"Eyes on me." I demand.

Our gaze clashes, light vs dark, flames biting into my hand, I take the lighter and trail it up her right thigh. The opposite side that's burned. She trembles under my touch, but with each thrust into her, she pushes back against me.

"I'm going to mark this pretty little skin."

"It's already scarred." She snaps.

Moving her shirt up to expose her back, I release her hair to press her further into the floor. Her cries from the pain is music to my ears. Lighting up the flame again I press it into her back, causing a welt to form instantly just below her bra strap.

"Stop!" Her voice is cracked with moisture.

Sobs shake her chest, but my dick hardens inside her. Thrusting harder and faster her cries mix with moans until the lighter presses into her side under her ribs. Her body tenses and a scream erupts.

"Fuck, Ryker please. Please." She chants.

Tears keep falling. My hips pound into her harder. My nails are digging into her waist.

"Fucking hell, Killer. Grip my dick with your tight little cunt."

Lighting the fire again, I press it into her spine at the same time I slam into her again. My fingers dig into her hip drawing blood. She begs me to stop, but her ass presses deeper into me. Riding my dick and the pain at the same time. Deep down she craves this.

"Beg for more."

She screams.

"Beg."

Pressing the hot metal into her flesh, I slam into her again and again.

"Your pussy loves the feel of my fire scorching your skin."

"No. No. No." She repeats.

Yet her pussy grips my dick. Her ass swivels into me. Her thrust meets mine.

"You little fucking liar."

Dropping the lighter I look down at my work. Red welts cover her back. Using both hands I hold her to the floor and fuck her harder. The knees of her stockings rip. Her shirt has burn holes. Her face is soaked with my come and tears. Yet we fuck and fuck until neither of us can kneel on the cold hard concrete. She soaks my dick, dripping down her legs from her pussy, she pulls another orgasm out of me. Chest heaving, black spots fill my vision.

Laying over her back, my mouth presses against her ear.

"Your soul belongs to me, killer. We were forged in the flames of hell and now I'll never let you go."

"I'll kill you." She says. So low she must think I can't hear her.

I let out a low deep laugh. "Even in death I'll be with you. Hell itself couldn't keep me away from you, I'll consume every part of you. In this life and the next."

CHAPTER EIGHTEEN

KENNA

Sliding lower into the ice bath, my muscles relax with the soothing numbness. The pain spreading across my back eases, now that it's been twenty-four hours. I stayed in my room all day yesterday laying in bed claiming to be sick. But today Ally wants to go dress shopping, so I have decided to ice my body before we leave. I'm pissed that a backless dress is out of the question now that my lower back and sides are scarred with burns. My first instinct is to hide the scars he scorched into my flesh but a deeper, darker, part of me craves more.

Have you ever been betrayed by your own body? Your mind craving something you know should be wrong. I have. I've been ignoring my phone, not that it's rang, sitting on my bed dead. Shadow hasn't sent me anything in two days, so I'm guessing he thinks his little message worked and scared me off or made me run far away from the boys, but he'd be wrong. The Stone brothers are family no matter what and family comes first. I'd like to cut them open while stitching them back together, but every family is dysfunctional.

What shocks me most is that they actually fucking believe I dug up a grave. A grave that belongs to my best friend. Only a sick, twisted, fuck would do that. Paige's hand was rotten and decomposed in that box, her snake tattoo on her finger still intact, but it was still her hand. My stomach turns at the mental reminder. Ally has been floating around the apartment for two days in a chipper mood, even though West hasn't been by to waive his dick stick around. When she bounced into my room yesterday begging me to go shopping, it was with the promise of lunch and after shopping ice cream that sold me.

She said that she has a date to the ball, someone that doesn't go by the name West Stone, so this is going to be interesting. After last night I decided that following Rykers rules wasn't an option. My thirst for him may be growing but I know my worth, so I've decided to bring a date of my own. One I know who will be able to hold his own against Ryker if it comes to that. Dipping lower in the water, my lips start to quiver from the ice water now over my chest up to my neck.

"Oooh shit that's cold."

Knowing the health risks of going underwater for too long during an ice bath, I quickly dip under and come back up within five seconds. My left side aches from the muscle spasms, but I plan on stretching before doing anything else today. Pulling the tub stopper out of the drain, I sit there letting my thoughts run wild while watching the water slowly disappear. My father's words mix together with the hate Ryker spewed at me last night. I need to talk to them face to face and get to the bottom of things. We'll never truly figure anything out if we don't talk.

Stepping out of the tub, I grab my large white fluffy towel that wraps fully around me and tie it over the top of my left boob. Letting my hair air dry, I just dab the bottom to keep it from dripping and head into my room to get dressed. Pushing my door shut with the heel of my foot I let the towel drop to the floor. Ditching it to air dry. Double checking to make sure my curtains are closed, I walk to my closet for clothes. After picking out a loose fitted shirt and a pair of black skinny jeans with rips up the thighs, I grab some burn ointment. I manage to get most of them, but the one in the middle of my spine is hard to reach.

It only takes me a good thirty minutes to get ready before Ally is knocking at my door rushing me out the room.

"I'm driving!" She sings.

Rolling my eyes I look over my shoulder with a *'with what'* look.

Holding her hand out, she makes a grabbing motion for my keys.

"Oh no..." I laugh.

"Oh yes." She reaches for my purse, but I dodge her grubby hands and dash for the door. She's gotten faster and manages to grab my arm stopping me.

My mind immediately flashes to my back, the fear of her bumping into me or rubbing against them causes me to drop the keys into her hand. Her perfectly plucked eyebrows raise, assessing me.

Shrugging I smirk, "This just means I have a head start looking at dresses on sale." I say.

Reaching into my purse I search around for my phone, but don't feel it. Propping the tan bag up on my knee, I open it to reveal a missing phone.

"What's wrong Kens?" She asks.

"My phone. I left it on the bed."

Putting her hands on her hips she shakes her head with a smile. "You forget everything. I'm surprised you haven't left the house naked before."

Licking my lips, I nod my head, but still head to check my room anyway. I know it wasn't on the bed when I walked out of the room, but now that I think about it I don't remember seeing it after my ice bath. Pushing my door open my eyes fall to my perfectly made bed only to find it bare of any items. Dropping to my knees I look on the floor, under my bed, around my dresser, and under my bedside table. Ally stands at the door watching me crawl around on my hands and knees with a goofy smile on her face.

"You may not be able to find your phone, but you'd make one hell of a dog." She lets out a loud laugh.

"Hardy har har."

If I roll my eyes one more time they may actually get stuck in the back of my head. Coming up empty, I use the corner of the bed to come to a stand at the edge of my dresser. Catching my reflection out the corner of my eye, I pull down the back of my shirt before Ally catches sight of the burn right below my ribs. Huffing out a sigh my palms smack into my thighs in frustration.

"It was on the bed when I got in the bath."

I'm talking more to myself than Ally at this point. Her powdered nose stuck in her own phone, fingers flying across the screen, she's lost all interest in helping me.

"Well thank you for the help." I state.

Jerking her hazel stare up to mine, "Oh sorry. West." Lifting her phone in the air with a wink she turns and walks away, leaving me standing there confused and phone-less.

"Come on! We can find it later, but I'm starving." She whines out her words.

"You're always hungry."

Scoffing, she looks over her shoulder with mock horror, "What are you trying to say?"

Another eye-roll.

"Don't be dense."

I love this girl, but sometimes she gets on my last nerve. Popping her hip out she smacks her ass while making her way to the door. Her purple locks are down around her shoulders styled with a wet hair look that gives the allusion of being curled. Black fishnet stockings with tiny diamonds down the sides cover her legs and a pink long sleeve crop top that flashes her butterfly belly ring. Ally's a walking, talking, Victoria Secret ad with the attitude to match.

"Where are we going to eat?"

My stomach lets out a loud growl right after the words leave my mouth and we both pause for a second before laughing.

Pulling the door open she steps to the side to let me pass, "I was thinking of the little Cafe on the beach in Newport."

"Seaside?" I ask.

It's an adorable little Cafe off the coast about thirty minutes from here, but it's close to all of the high-end upscale boutiques. Knowing Ally that's where she wants to go shopping, not that I mind, it's not like I don't have the money to blow on a designer dress.

"Yep, that's the one!" She pops the P with a smile.

After locking up and loading our hungry asses into my car, I sit back and watch the cars pass by while Ally nods her head to the radio. Slipping on my sunglasses I let my eyes close for a second. Sleep has been hard to find lately, so I take full advantage as passenger princess and rest on the drive.

Before I know it Ally is hitting the brakes making my head smack against the window with a hard thud.

"Fuck!" I yelp.

Rubbing my temple I look over to Ally, but she's too busy staring out the windshield at a random guy passing by the car.

"Really?"

Shrugging she winks at me with a flirty smile, "What? West doesn't own me."

Snorting, I lean up grabbing my purse, "Let's go, I'm starving."

CHAPTER NINETEEN

KENNA

"Oh-muh-god."

"Really?" Ally laughs, rolling her eyes at me.

My tongue slips out to swipe up the syrup running down my chin, mouth full of warm pancakes, I nod at her. Swallowing down the way too big of a bite, a smile breaks free.

"These pancakes are heaven!"

She nibbles on the sausage link hanging off her fork, rolling the end in sticky syrup before taking another bite, keeping her eyes on the boy at the counter. She amazes me with how fast she can turn her attention around to someone else. Her small hand brushes back vibrant purple strands of hair, she truly is so beautiful, a wild card for sure.

"Got your eye on a new toy?" I joke, nudging her with my foot.

Dropping her head forward she eyes her plate, lips twisted to the side, looking perplexed with the question.

"West is fun, but that's all it is with him. Fun. I know we can sleep together and it'll mean nothing at the end of the day."

"And that's not what you want?"

It's an honest question, but she seems surprised that I'd be so bold.

Holding out my hands I give her a soft look, "It's not always fun playing the short-term game."

Flicking a piece of egg off her fork, her gaze meets mine, "And what if the long game is one I'll never win."

My brows dip, "And why is that?" Her statement taking me by surprise.

Ally is anything but unsure. Most girls would show off their body to cover their insecurities, but she doesn't give a shit. She's herself through and through. Shoveling another massive bite in my mouth I wait for her to respond.

"Let's just say I wouldn't consider myself miss perfect and innocent."

The tink of her metal fork dropping on the table has my eyes dropping to her plate and back up.

"No one is perfect, Ally. Don't be so hard on yourself. I don't know where I would be without you. You've been an amazing friend to me even through all the shit with the Stone brothers."

Squeezing her hand with my clean one, I flash her a smile, because it's true. Ally has kept my head above water more than I'd like to admit. Wrapping my lips around my straw I take a deep pull of the orange juice in my glass. Thank heavens for the tangy taste. Wiping my mouth with a napkin the ding from behind me has my head turning on instinct. Resignation sinks in my stomach at the sight of the middle brother walking in, showcasing a wide grin and enough natural swag to drown any girl's panties.

"Well shit." I mumble under my breath.

Ally's eyes light up, but her smile isn't fully there when she sees him this time. It's more reserved and it has me wondering if West has done or said something to her to mess things up.

"Ally baby! I see you saved a spot for me. Let me slide in." His voice bounces off the wall.

The amount of energy this man carries in one toe could fill my entire body. He doesn't need coffee, he is the coffee. Ally has her eyes glued to him, but she doesn't move. Her hesitation has his smile dropping an inch, but he catches himself. She may not have seen the slight change in his stance, but I know exactly what a Cobra looks like standing tall. She looks from me to him before she realizes that we are both watching her waiting to see if she was going to move for him.

"Sure!" Her voice filled with false excitement.

She starts to slide over giving him space to sit when his large hand engulfs hers, pulling her to him.

"Ally baby, why don't you go to your boy at the counter and order me a slice of apple pie."

It's an order. One she doesn't fail to abide by. She chances a glance at me, we both caught that comment, *her boy,* and the worry in her eyes is evident. She stands and her chest rubs against his with how close he's standing to the booth. His tall frame leans down to whisper in her ear, I can see a shiver roll through her body with his word.

"Don't worry about it, baby. He'll never touch this skin while a Stone owns every inch of you."

"You-"

Grabbing her hair, he pulls her head to the side with a dark laugh, "I never said which brother, doll."

Releasing her, she walks away on shaky legs, but by the time she makes it to the counter her sassy demeanor is back in place. Even West can't keep that girl down for long. These Stone brothers think they can do and say whatever they want and we'll just bow down to them. They need a taste of their own medicine. Sliding into the booth, his bulky frame takes up most of the space, murky brown eyes taking me in.

Reaching in his back pocket he pulls out a red package wrapped in plastic. Tossing it to me, he almost spills my tea all over the table, but I manage to snatch the cup out of the way before it ended up all over my lap.

"What the fuck." I growl, annoyed with our girls' day being ruined.

"What? Disappointed I'm not the other Stone brother?" He raises a thick brow.

Laughing, "You're right. I'd prefer Cole over you any day."

Sarcasm drips from my tongue coating my words. West pulls back with surprise, visibly shocked that out of them all, he's the one I hate the least. Accepting it for what it is he nods to the pack in my hand, making my stare fall to the table. There in my hands is a super-size pack of Twizzlers.

"I'm guessing they are still your favorite?"

He doesn't wait for me to answer before he grabs a pancake from my plate, rolling it up, and shoving the entire thing into his mouth. His jaw works around the food but his eyes never leave mine. He's studying me. This isn't a friendly visit but he's making it seem like one which puts me on edge, my eyes slowly take in the open space around us. A low buzz catches both of our attention at the same time.

UNKNOWN: Princessa.

UNKNOWN: You look ravishing today.

UNKNOWN: I see you got my gift. Have you been a good girl for me? I guess I'll have to see for myself. See you soon.

My palms begin to sweat against the cold table, unable to look away from the lit screen. I read over those last three words twice before the screen goes dark. My gulp is damn near audible with how close West has leaned in to see my phone. Swiping it off the table to slide it in my back pocket I realize something that has me standing from the booth with confusion pumping through me.

"How the hell did you get my phone?" I question.

"Who the fuck was that, Kenna?"

Ally chose that moment to saunter back up with a pie in one hand and a milkshake in the other. Dragging the straw to her mouth she drinks down a few sips before looking between us, noticing the tension in the air. Popping her hip, she presses the plate into his chest, grabbing my wrist, she tugs me back to the table. West stands there watching us both walk away, but my thoughts are not on food anymore.

"Ally, how the hell did my phone end up on the table?" My voice raises in panic.

Nothing is making sense. It was on my bed then it was gone. It wasn't on the table earlier but now it is? I knew trusting the brothers was a bad idea but if not them then who? The only way into my dorm would be through Ally. Ally was in the dorm when I got in the bath. Ally was at the table when West showed up.

Yanking my hand from hers I spin on my heels, turning back to West who has yet to move. Storming back towards him, a smirk lifts at the corner of his mouth with my advance. He can see it in my eyes. The realization that no matter where I go I'm not safe. Not from them, not from Ally, and not from Shadow.

"So now you have Ally working for you? Was the stalker not enough for you that you added the one person I should be able to trust?"

Each word is punctuated with my finger jammed into his chest. The ache of being utterly alone fills my blood.

"You want to win that badly? Do you even know what really happened that night or are you just running around following your new daddy?"

Without thought my hand lashes out, striking him across the face. For a split-second fear washes through me, but then pure rage takes its place. Turning back around I ignore Ally, who has shrunk against the back of the booth. Her small stature is no match for mine. Betrayal is the worst fucking kind pain, but I've been here before. I know exactly how to survive this. Pushing the door open I run right into Cole waiting outside. A cigarette hanging from his lips.

"Looks like you're smarter than we gave you credit for. Not that West wanted to give you any credit at all."

Taking a pull, the red cherry grows brighter, Cole blows the smoke in my direction.

"Smell familiar?" He laughs.

I fucking hate the smell of cigarette smoke.

Curling my lip at him, I go to move past him towards my car when I remember Ally drove us here so she has my keys.

"Fuck." I groan under my breath.

"I think Ryker has that under control. Trust me, he's the only one brave enough to touch poisonous pussy."

"Go to hell."

Cole tosses his still lit cancer stick at me before walking inside, leaving me out here alone.

Forgetting about the car I decide to walk down the beach to the boardwalk. There is no way I'm making myself face them again right now. No. She has my keys, with *my* brothers, absolutely not. I thought I could walk away with my tail tucked between my legs, but I refuse. Never again. Starting now. Ryker may be mine, but so are they. West and Cole hate me and I fucking loathe them, but they're Stone and I'm Kingston. Family. Always. It's the one rule we live and breathe by. It's why I know if they want me dead. Truly want me dead, they would have killed me by now, but they haven't. I refuse to let my mind think that there is another reason for that.

Slamming the door against the wall the glass cracks, not that I give a shit, my legs eat up the space to the booth. Ally sits beside Cole who has slid in where I was seated while West sits in the middle of the opposite side. Flashing them all a wide, almost too wide, smile I lean across the booth to get in Ally's face.

"I'd have your shit out of my dorm before I make it home tonight or you'll find yourself left with only the shirt on your back."

She looks between the two boys before lifting her hand to slap me, but Cole snatches it out of the air in a harsh hold. My eyes flicker to his face before returning to hazel ones. Grabbing a handful of her hair my fist smashes her face into the table. Ally lets out a loud scream, but no one looks our way. This is between us.

Whispering in her ear, "No matter how much you ride their dicks you'll never be me. Remember that the next time you spy on me for them."

Grabbing my keys from her purse I toss the rest of her shit all over the table, letting it roll to the floor. Not giving West or Cole a second thought, I walk out of the Cafe with blood on my shirt and a grin on my face. Sun rays meet my skin as I slip on my sunglasses. I reach for my handle, but before I can, a thick hand pulls it open for me. "See you later, Killer."

Leaving me with those words, Ryker walks away from my car to join his brothers in the Cafe with a bloody faced rat.

Standing on the outside looking in stings, but I'll make my presence known until they have no choice but to accept it. I'm tired of fighting what my dad was trying to tell me. He was right. These boys are my home and it's time they understood exactly what that means.

CHAPTER TWENTY

RYKER

"You had one fucking job."

West tosses the controller down on the table, the words *Game Over* flash across the screen, frustration pouring off him. Our little princess figured out Ally was helping us faster than we thought, but it's the words her filthy little mouth dropped before she left that has us all spiraling. Cole's been tossing back beer after beer since we got home so I doubt he'll be much use, but that's perfect because what we have planned doesn't involve him anyway. We need him for something much easier.

"You hear what she said?" West asks.

Cole laughs wildly behind the glass pressed against his lips.

"And you really think she's little miss innocent?" His words are already slurring.

None of this makes any sense. Kenna claiming us as hers threw us for a loop. If she really is working with her dad then she wouldn't feel the need to mark us as her own.

Reminding Ally where her place is was a power move on Kenna's part, and the little killer did it in front of us for a reason. She's a true Kingston. Not the one her father turned into, but the one her mother was. Loyalty without question.

Cole reaches in his pocket with a loose grin on his face, pulling out a half smoked joint, he holds it up in offering. He knows West and I don't care for that shit. It's a good way to blow off steam, but lately the only thing that calms the demons is a blonde haired nightmare. West stares at me with a look that reminds me of our previous conversation.

"Don't you have a party to be at?" I ask him.

Licking his lips he flashes me his teeth, "I thought I'd bring the party here, brother." Opening his arms in a sweeping motion he calls out to the back of the apartment. "Come on out, Kitty." He taunts.

Cole's eyes darken in warning. He's the one who sent Ally to the back room so he wouldn't have to look at her. He thinks we don't know about his little obsession with the little rat, but it's one of the reasons West fucks with her. Cole's been cold for a while now so West thinks pulling a reaction out of him will break through the ice in his eyes, but he hasn't taken the bait yet. Ally is the perfect pawn.

Stocking covered legs pass me on her way to stand between West's legs, but he taps her thigh, signaling her to spin. Ass-cheeks peek from under her tight skirt, his hand coming down to smack her, the sound loud in the silence.

"Have a seat." His eyes slide from her ass to Cole.

The flick of a lighter has my mind going back to a tempting little brat with a need for punishment. The itch to touch her milky skin has my knee bouncing in response. It won't be long before I'm standing outside her window watching her. Waiting for the perfect time to climb in her bed and forcing her to open up her sweet little cunt for me. Cole putting the flame to the end of his joint and tugging in a puff has my attention coming back to the room.

"Thank fuck." He lets out a sigh with the thick smoke that falls from his mouth.

Ally watches his mouth, biting her lip. She sits on one brother while craving the other and that right there is why she can't be trusted.

"See something you like?" West leans forward speaking in her ear, but making sure we can hear.

He plays this game well, that's for sure. Three hits later and Cole's eyes start to gloss over, his eyes never leaving West hands on Ally's legs. Taking a drink of my beer I check my phone for a text from G. We're waiting for him to let us know when he picks up our package. West trails a finger up Ally's leg, hovering over the crease of her inner thigh. Cole's eyes sharpen at the contact until he's slinging the blunt in the ashtray on the coffee table.

Slamming his beer down with his other hand, the bottom cracks, spilling out the rest of what's left all over the floor, but he doesn't stop there. Turning towards a laughing West, and a confused Ally. Cole jerks her up by her throat with a grunt.

"Let him touch you again, Doll and I'll fucking have you to blame for my brother's missing fingers." He spits.

Flashing a snarl towards West, he drags Ally away, yelling at her to put some clothes on. A few seconds later the sound of a door slamming and a female squealing has both of us laughing.

"You feel better now?"

"It's about fucking time he broke that damn wall down. He's far from being fine, but maybe some wet pussy will snap him back to reality."

West leans forward, picking up Cole's dripping bottle and drinks the last few remaining drops before tossing it to the trash can across the room. Fucking athletes.

"We have a little bit of an issue on our hands. Like we need more bullshit with everything else going on."

West doesn't look at me, so I know it's something that's going to piss me off.

"What is it?"

Propping his arms on his knees, he leans forward looking me dead in the eyes.

"Sit your big ass on that couch and don't go storming off anywhere."

His order rubs raw against my skin, like a knife carving out meat. I'm the oldest. I give the orders. West putting his foot down isn't something he does often, being the carefree brother. Nodding, I wait for him to continue. He looks at me for a minute realizing that I didn't promise a fucking thing.

Pulling out a smoke, he tosses it to me and hands me a lighter.

"Seems our little Princess has gained herself a stalker. Someone she's named Unknown in her phone. I didn't see much, but from her reaction whoever the hell it is has her acting like a scared little mouse."

Blowing the smoke between us, West watches my face. Waiting for the viper to strike.

"What did they say?" My words are low. Possessive.

"From what I saw, the fucker is the same one who left her that box. Or he was talking about a different gift, but either way his final words were '*see you soon*' and that alone had her snatching her phone up."

Kenna Kingston is going to be the downfall to everything we have planned. Pure trouble.

I shift to move from the couch when West grabs my arm, dragging me back down.

"Don't you fucking dare. We have shit to handle tonight. We can send G by the dorm if you feel the need, but really what's the harm? Hurt is hurt no matter who it comes from. Unless you have a soft spot for the Princess?" He lifts a brow.

He's goading me into admitting that she's under my skin, but even that's a lie. She isn't just under my skin. She's in my bones. My soul. She's buried herself so deep into my marrow I couldn't release her if I wanted to. Kenna Kingston is my toy to play with and I'd be damned if anyone else felt the way her pussy feels coming down from a high. Pulling a long drag from my cigarette, my thoughts move from one issue to the next.

"Fucking hell. She's ruining everything."

"My thoughts exactly." Pulling out his cell, the light hits his face. Brown eyes that mirror mine study the words on the screen. "Looks like we caught a fish." Waiving his phone, he stands from the couch. Clapping like a kid in a candy store, excitement lines his face. He enjoys this part way to fucking much. I never said we aren't sick mother fuckers.

Heading towards his room down the hall I say, "We need someone to keep an eye on Ally."

Looking at me over his shoulder, he shrugs, "That's Cole's job now."

G's text comes through in the next second, sending me a photo of a tall tattooed man who is standing far too close to something that's not his.

Where?

My eyes stay on the screen waiting. Another picture comes through, showing me exactly what my little Killer is up to tonight. I hate to crash her party, but well, I crave the type of chaos only she causes.

CHAPTER TWENTY ONE

KENNA

ou know that carefree feeling you get when your day is filled with something that makes you happy? Yeah, I'm drowning in that feeling. Not because I love shopping, or getting pampered, or hell, even getting waited on hand and foot. Because I don't, but I do love this feeling. Bags line the arms of a hired driver that I called last minute. Why drive myself around when I can have someone else do it? I thought using blood money would make me feel gross, sick to my stomach with the guilt. What I didn't see coming was the power it gave me over everything.

Bags filled to the brim with accessories for the Gala. The dress Ally was eyeing at the little boutique she wanted to go to today, hangs over the shoulder of the driver in a white dress bag. That one was personal, seeing how it's far too short for me. My dress is being designed as we speak and will be ready the week of the fundraiser. My phone rings in my purse for the millionth time, but I just keep walking. Only a few more stops to make, but this next one is the most important. The Stone brothers getting their hands on my phone blindsided me. Something I don't plan on letting happen again.

"Just wait in the car for me. Only one more stop to make, but I'm going to step inside here for a moment first." I tell the driver.

He's older, probably mid 50's with a shaved head and a stubby salt and pepper beard. I don't require him to wear the stuffy suit that hugs his body, but he insists. Not one of the rich pricks he may be used to, I flash him a sincere smile on the way into the store. Cal, the driver, walks towards the town car parked off to the side and pops the trunk. Leaving him to take care of the bags, I pull open the door to my next stop. The bell above my head rings and an elderly woman greets me from behind the counter.

"Need help finding anything, Dear?"

Her voice is soft with a low rasp. Walking to the shelf near the front counter I pick up the first box I see and place it in front of her.

"Will this be it?"

"Yes ma'am." I smile.

Her small wrinkle covered hands shake when she reaches out to pick up the small box. Scanning it, she tucks it inside a small bag, and gives me my total. Swiping my black card I ask her about her day and she happily returns the conversation. I doubt many customers give her the time of day, but older people like her just want someone to talk to. I can't imagine getting old alone. Her bare ring finger shows no tan line of a past lover, but that doesn't mean she never had kids.

"Here you go, Dear." She says, her voice cracking on the last word.

Handing me my bag and receipt, she gives me a soft grin and a pat on the top of my hand.

"Have a wonderful day."

Walking out of the store, I see Cal is standing just outside the door for me. Handing him my latest purchase I walk past him down the sidewalk, continuing to window shop until the sun slowly starts to set.

"Ms. Kingston?" A familiar voice calls out to me.

The hairs on the back of my neck stand on end with the way my last name rolls off his tongue.

Spinning around I spot two things at once, the Dean heading right to me, and Cal sitting in the town car a few spaces away looking directly at me.

"Mr. Addington, right?" I ask, even though I remember exactly who he is.

The way his face lights up at my recognition makes my skin crawl. There is something about this man that has me on edge.

"It's always weird running into teachers outside of campus." I joke.

My laugh comes out forced. He steps closer, only leaving a couple feet between us. The heat from his flushed skin brushes against mine with our proximity. Those startling blue eyes explore their way down my body. It's not until he notices the subtle way my body moves away from him that his gaze finds its way back to my face. There is a slight twitch under his eye with irritation at being interrupted with his musings.

"Don't think of me as a teacher. I don't deal much with the students. I'm more of a manager."

He pushes his way forward, invading my space. Putting me on edge. A door opens somewhere behind him, but I can't see past his broad shoulders. A long meaty finger pinches a loose strand of hair, twisting it around the fat digit.

"So pretty." He whispers.

He's so close now that I can smell the hint of whiskey on his breath. A quick chuckle escapes my throat. Wrapping my fingers around his wrist, I pull his hand away from my face.

"I think it's getting late. I'm going to head back to campus. Maybe you should sober up, yeah?"

Dropping his wrist, I pull my hand back before he has a chance to grab me. The Dean's pupils grow wider, covering the cobalt blue of his eyes with pure darkness. There is something wrong with this man and the fact that the Stone brothers allowed the foundation to employ a fucking creep doesn't sit well with me. It's time for a change in control if this is what's going on behind the scenes. Turning sideways I keep my eyes locked on his, a manic smile in place on his face as I scoot past him back towards Cal. Before I'm fully past him, the Dean bends forward, his whiskey-soaked skin so close to mine.

"I'll see you soon."

A shiver runs down my spine with his words. Flashes of the last text sent to my phone comes to mind, but I keep walking. Giving him no signs that I caught what he said my feet pick up speed until I'm damn near running into Cal.

Cal, who is in fact headed this way with a blank stare in place, is holding his right hip. Just what we need.

"I'm fine, Cal. Let's get out of here."

Squeezing his shoulder on my way past, I decide to save the last stop for another day. I need to clean out Ally's shit first anyway. Ally's face from earlier breaks through the wall I put up. My heart pinches at the complete fear in her eyes when she saw me coming. No matter how betrayed I feel for what she did, it still hurts. No one loses a best friend and feels fine the same day. I'm not heartless, but I am vengeful.

Cal opens the back passenger side door for me and I slide against the leather seats, putting on my seatbelt before turning back to him. Before closing the door, he hands me the bag from the last store, I say a quick thank you before I'm left alone. Tinted windows block wandering eyes, so I take this chance to pull out the prepaid cell phone that rests on my lap. I decided it was best to use now since my other one was compromised. I'm not paranoid, I'm smart. Cole Stone is a tech wiz that loves to try out new bugs. I'll be damned if I have not only one stalker, but four. It's bad enough that I don't know who Shadow man is, but I do know how sinister the brothers can be.

During the drive I add one number. One contact. The only person I trust and I just so happen to have an appointment with them later tonight.

* * *

CHANGING from skinny jeans to black stockings and a white cotton skirt gives my tattoo a little more room to breathe. Jax has been working the skin over pretty rough the last few sessions, but he's managed to keep the tattoo intact. The skin hasn't been damaged and I'd like to keep it that way. It took two hours to unpack everything, put the dress in a safe spot, and change the locks. I'll be damned if Ally thinks she can just walk in here after what she did. There's a voice in the back of my mind that tells me maybe she didn't have a choice, but that's pushed aside when I remember all the times I had her back. All the times I trusted her with my secrets. A text comes through as I'm walking out the door.

We need to talk.

Ally's name, with a purple heart emoji, stares back at me on my phone. My thumb hovers over the text, indecision gnawing at me, but I just slip it into my back pocket and keep moving. It's well after dark now and the wind has picked up, giving the illusion of a storm brewing. Living by the ocean means weather changes quickly, you never truly know when it's going to pour. We need a little rain to wash out this fucking town. Stepping from under the patio cover outside our building, my eyes slowly adjust to the darkness. A few of the street lights are on, giving me a decent view of the court yard.

A few students wander around campus between dorms, most likely hanging out with their friends. I've been so lost in everything with my dad and the Stone family that my studies have severely suffered, but I was never here to study anyway. It's not like the college can drop me either way. I'd have this entire place caving in from the inside if they tried. This is my legacy. The foundation wants to point fingers at my father, but they seem to forget that my mother was the true Kingston. A couple around my age sits on the grass, a tree covering them from the impending storm. No worries or responsibilities outside themselves and their studies. So lost in their own reality, they don't notice when I pass. A part of me wishes I could just blend in and not be pulled down by politics, business and power. Living a normal life was my father's dream for me and I'm starting to believe the nightmares playing like a movie in my head every night. The ones where Alec fought with my dad about backing off from the illegal shit and them being in too deep. I have so many questions, but would going to see my dad really be the best plan? Another two blocks and I'm coming closer to the neon light outside the shop. A sense of welcome falls over me at the sight of the open sign still lit. I'm still in my head when the door opens.

"Sweetness, there you are." His low tone and wide smile has me flashing him one of my own.

"As always, you know when I need you."

Winking, I step past him and slide off my shoes, pushing them up against the wall. This place has become my second home. Jax lets me get as comfortable as he handles a few things at the front counter. Walking around the side I place my palms on the counter lifting myself up to sit beside him. Snatching a sucker from the basket to my left, he watches me unwrap it, the root beer flavor exploding in my mouth.

Shaking his head with a laugh, "You always pick the nasty ones."

Twirling the stick, my lips pop around it when I tug it from my mouth, "More for me, I guess."

"What's with the urgent need for new ink?" He wonders, not making eye contact.

My tongue wraps around the candy, I give myself time to think about how to answer that. Jax has always seen me as a little sister and while he is mid-twenties I know he's aware of the bullshit going on around here. He has to be. So, I do worry about sharing too much with him for his safety. Yeah, I mean Jax is fucking huge, but the Stone brothers? They shoot first and ask questions later. Just look at the bar guy with his severed dick up his ass.

Jax doesn't look at my face, it's his way of not forcing me to answer, he's just like that. The lights inside flicker for a second, making me jump. He places a heated palm on my knee with knowing eyes, like he's looking right past the bullshit I throw his way.

"My sweetness, let's get you on the table."

Distracting me with a needle is a weird way to win me over, but it works. Excitement rolls through me at the thought of finishing my chest piece. We only have a little bit of color to do and it's finished.

"I didn't come here for new work, but I'll never turn you down."

Patting the top of his hand, I slide off the counter and toss my sucker into the trash can.

"I'll go get my station ready for you if you want to get everything situated."

Rolling my eyes, I pat the black leather chair at the front of the shop. What's the use in ignoring a perfectly good place to tattoo? Jax is a rule follower when it comes to shop regulations, but this is Del Mar and I'm making the rules tonight.

"Come on. Go get the color and the gun so we can get this party started!" I'm damn near yelling.

Sighing, he does as he's told. He never says no to Kenna Kingston. I pull off my shirt, and unclasp my bra as I turn towards the wall, hiding my tits while I stick on some pasties. Looking down at my handy work, both are crooked and one of my nipples is threatening to escape. An uncontrollable laugh bubbles out of me, not just from the pasties, but from the irony of the events from today.

"What's got you so giggly?" Jax says, walking up behind me.

Spinning around I show him my hard work and he cracks a smile, but it's forced. He jerks his gaze back to my face after acknowledging the joke.

"Lighten up, Jax." I smack his arm.

He's huge, so my hand stings with the hit. Shaking my fingers out he moves over to the one bench in the room dragging a small table with him. Tugging my hair free, I flip my head forward, gathering my blonde locks in one hand, twisting a ponytail holder around it with the other. Flipping back over, my bra free breasts bounce a little, making Jax cough out an awkward sound. High pony in place I make my way over and sit down.

"Can we sit the back up so I'm not laying down this time?"

Grabbing the metal handle he nods his head, "Yeah, lean forward for me."

Doing as he said, I lean towards him, my bare skin inches from his arm, the warmth pouring off him heats my flesh. The back of the chair moves forward so Jax uses his free hand to push my shoulder down, making me lay all the way back.

I roll my eyes, again, because he has a way of pulling that attitude out of me. The chill from the cold leather has goosebumps skating up my arms.

"Holy shit!" I squeal, "Could you warn a girl next time?"

His low deep laugh has my mouth feeling dry, but my core has no reaction. All I hear in that moment is Ryker Stone's raspy chuckle in my ear. Like an ice-cold bucket of water was poured over my head, I snap out of this weird flirty space we're in. He picks up on my sudden change and scoots back to give me space. Prepping his materials he makes small talk, ensuring that I'm comfortable around him and it secures his place in my life even more.

"Wanna go somewhere with me?" I ask, knowing that he's the only person I trust right now.

"And where's that?" He mindlessly moves around doing his thing.

Rolling my lips together, I wait for him to look up at me. When he does I blurt out, "Go to the Gala with me. I need a plus one and you'd look great in a fitted tux."

Winking, I punch his arm.

"It'll be fun. We can talk shit about all the stuck-up rich pricks."

His brows dip, "Aren't you included in that, sweetness?" His face is blank, but his voice gives him away.

"Ha ha ha. So funny. What do you say?" I question, giving him a pleading look.

Shrugging he agrees, "But you owe me dinner and the tux."

Clapping, I flash the biggest smile, "I'll buy you the best steak dinner you've ever had!"

He laughs at that, shaking his head at my excitement. My face hurts from how hard I'm smiling. Being around Jax is so easy. Painless. But my body craves something darker. Someone more sinister. Soft will never be enough for me, knowing what it feels like when Ryker's breaking me. I'll never want anything else. Jax taps my leg, snapping me out of my thoughts.

"Alright, you ready?"

He always makes sure I'm ready because my pain tolerance may be high, but my needle aversion is forever growing stronger.

"Yep. As ready as I'll ever be."

Giving him a thumbs up he rolls his stool closer to the bench, getting into place when the glass door shatters. A scream rips from my throat at the same time Jax jumps up, knocking the black stool over in the process. Jax drops the gun on the table, the needle digging into my thigh, breaking the skin. Tossing a clean white towel over me Jax stands between me and whatever danger just entered the shop.

"Get the fuck out of my way." A familiar voice growls out over the sound of my heart beating in my ears.

Jax has his entire body shielding me, his size alone hiding my exposed body, but it's the haunted voice behind him that has my heart stopping. Ryker stands in the doorway, his shoes crunching the glass below his feet. I don't need to see his face to know it's him, I would know that voice anywhere. It's the one that haunts my nightmares and plagues my dreams. The waves of anger blowing this way can't be my imagination. No, he is literally sucking the air out of the room with his presence.

"Stone, you need to get the fuck out of my shop."

He scoffs at Jax's demand. I can hear him stepping closer. Tapping Jax's shoulder, I motion for him to move.

"It's okay, Jax." I whisper for only him to hear.

Only I thought Ryker was further away.

"Oh, Killer. I don't think you truly believe that. Now do you?"

Jax turns his head to check on me, crystal eyes probing my face, but my stare is locked on the man standing past him. My heart stalls in my chest, because when he does I see the barrel of a gun pointed at the back of his head.

"No!" A scream rips from my throat.

Three things happen at once. My hands shove Jax to the side, a boom shatters in my ears, and pain explodes through my body.

CHAPTER TWENTY TWO

RYKER

"*H*eavy mother fucker."

Grunting, I lift the dead weight off Kenna, who's currently hyperventilating, and drop him to the floor. Blood trickles down the side of his head from the butt of my gun. Stupid. My girl refuses to learn.

"Oh my god!" Her voice cracks, her screams becoming white noise in my ears.

Blood is flowing freely from a wound in her shoulder, the bullet going straight through, but my girl just sits there screaming at me. A mix of pain and fury take turns flashing across her face and I can't help the smile that slips free. She's a sight.

"How fucking insane are you? You shot me, you stupid fucking psycho!"

She tries to strike me in the chest with her foot but misses, hitting my thigh instead. Kicking the bastard lying on the ground in the ribs I make sure to use the toe of my shoe to dig in between the bone. He'll wake up later with a broken rib or two and a concussion.

"How many times do I have to remind you not to let anyone touch what belongs to me?"

Using one hand I yank my shirt over my head and press it into her shoulder. "Hold this here." I snap.

She may be hurt, but I'm pissed. Seeing red and not the liquid crimson flooding the floor below her. She's going to wish I fucking killed her. Or him. Because I'm going to make sure she never defies me again. Leaning down I take her bottom lip in my mouth, biting down until she's crying out. Sucking the pain away, my tongue dives in to swallow down the sweet taste of hell. Fire and brimstone swirl around my mouth when her tongue joins mine in the fight for dominance. Only this time I'm not letting her win.

Using both hands, I drag her down the table until her hips are damn near hanging off the edge.

"I'd keep that hand over your shoulder or you might bleed out."

"Ryker let me go!"

Panic sets in and her grey eyes widen in horror. She's losing blood. Red face and tear-stained cheeks stare back at me. Her chest heaves faster, pulling my attention to her bare skin, my eyes rake over her. She's a temptress laying bare below me, her doe eyes wide, dazed. My heart aches to consume her.

Her normally tan skin grows more ashen as blood pulses from the hole, but it's slowing slightly. My gaze catches on the new ink centered in the middle of her chest. A phoenix, wings spread wide, takes flight between her breasts over her rib cage. The color is unfinished, but the outline is clean and crisp. Flames cover the bird while ash fall from the feathers.

"The phoenix rises from the ashes." I say, my voice low.

Looking back at me, she stares into my eyes without showing an ounce of pain. She says, "I'll burn, but I'll always rise."

Throwing my head back with a low chuckle, "We'll see about that."

Reaching down, I pinch the stickers covering her perfect nipples and rip them off in one move. She bites her lip but doesn't give me the scream I wanted. Stepping between her thighs the tips of my fingers trail up each leg, stopping at the apex of her thigh, her body trembling below me.

"Look how needy you are for me."

"It's the shock." She smarts.

Leaning over her I drag my lips up her neck stopping right by her ear, my breath fans over her heated skin.

"Baby, your pussy is drenched for me and I haven't even touched it yet."

I nip at her earlobe before pulling it into my mouth.

"Rye, please."

"That's it, Killer. Beg."

Pinching the seam that runs between her legs, I pull, ripping the center open. Giving me the perfect opening to her sweet little pussy. She moves her hand away from the shirt, trying to grab my shoulder, but I push her off.

"Keep your hand there or you'll fucking bleed out." I bark.

My other hand comes up to pinch her cheeks together, forcing her to watch me, to see exactly what she does to me.

"Eyes right here, Killer. I want you to see exactly what I have planned for you."

Slipping my hand inside the hole, my thumb rubs her slit through her thong.

"You're always so wet." I groan.

Her hips lift, pushing against my fingers, silently begging for more. I don't want silent. Kenna Kingston is going to scream my name tonight. Pushing the drenched fabric to the side, I slip a finger in and twist. Curing it up to rub that perfect spot.

"Oh god!" Her moan is long and low.

Adding another finger, I put pressure on her clit. Her hand lifts from the shirt, so I slam my free hand down on it and she cries out. That sound makes my dick jump in my pants.

"Fuck, baby. Make that sound again and I'll come all over your needy cunt."

Moving back to her face, my hand cups the back of her head, lifting it off the back of the bench.

"Watch how your pussy swallows my fingers. How hungry you are for me."

Pumping in and out, the sound of her wet cunt sucking me back in over and over has my mouth watering.

"Rye, please. Please."

"I'm just getting started."

I rub her clit with the pad of my thumb while pushing my fingers in and twisting until her legs are clamping around my waist. Letting her climb that high until she's so close her body shakes with the building release. I slide my fingers out of her dripping cunt, and grip her hair, I want her still for this part. Her eyes follow my other hand, watching and waiting. Leaning to the side I grab the tattoo gun and dip it in the black ink that's sitting to the side.

"Tsk tsk." I shake my head. "He should really keep his area clean. Someone could get a fucking infection from open ink."

Turning back to her, I hold up the gun with a feral grin. My teeth are more bared in a snarl than a smile.

"Unbutton my jeans." I order.

Leaning forward as much as she can with her hair twisted around my wrist, she uses one hand to free my button, sliding my pants down my ass.

"What are you doing?" Her voice shakes.

"Grab my dick, Killer."

She swallows. Licking her lips. So fucking needy.

"I want you to guide my dick to your dripping pussy."

"Mmhm." She moans around an exhale.

Moving forward as she pulls me closer, she rubs the head of my cock against her clit, chasing after that high. Pulling backwards she drops me, her grey eyes popping up from between us, she bites her bottom lip again.

"Try again."

This time when she pushes me against her slit I jolt forward and bury myself inside her.

"Ryker!" She screams.

Heat shoots down my spine when her pussy quivers around me. She tries to breathe through the adjustment, her hips lift, dropping down in a slow motion. I let her keep the pace while I force her head back, bending her until her eyes are only on me.

"I told you what would happen if you let someone touch you."

Thrusting harder a moan slips past my gritted teeth. That sound drives her on, her heels dig into my back, using her thighs to grip my waist. With my hold on her hair I flick the tattoo gun on using my toe to press down the button on the floor. She instantly stops as the buzzing sound reaches her ears. I use the hold I have on her and yank, making her head turn back to me.

"Eyes on me."

Looking between us, I spot a smooth patch of skin just above her waist band, near the dip of her hip. With one last look at her wide eyes, I press the needle into her skin. She doesn't flinch away from the pain, she chases it. My dick twitches inside her watching how she takes my dick while I mark her skin.

"Oh fuck. Please Ryker. Please."

"This is what happens when you let other men touch you. Now shut that pretty little mouth and let me finish it."

She's trembling. Sweat covering her skin. Her eyelids lower. I drag the needle through her skin one more time. It's messy and fucking shitty, but it's mine. Looping the last letter, I toss the gun to the floor still buzzing. Looking down at the red jagged line, my chest caves at the letters on her skin. Her movements are slowing. Her eyes connecting at the same spot.

"Ryker. Oh god!" She cries out.

My fingers grip her thighs, lifting her, dried and wet blood covers us both, I walk us backwards until my legs hit the couch. Sitting down, I slam her back down on me. Pushing all the way to the hilt, she takes every inch. Gripping the back of her neck I pull her closer, nipping at her throat, her collar bone, her nipples. Every inch of her skin.

"Fuck me. I want to watch you lose control of that tight little cunt. Soak me down to my balls."

Slapping her ass, she jolts, but does as she's told. My hand snakes to her front, tightening around her throat. Her lips turn purple, her skin already to pale from the blood loss. The shirt already forgotten when it fell to the floor, the blood dried at the wound, but still she rides me. Tattoo bastard is still laid out on the floor unmoving. Using my free hand I pull the band out of her hair, letting her blonde waves cascade down her back like a deadly waterfall. The sight before me has my head falling to the back of the couch.

Her tits bounce, making her phoenix look like it's taking flight. Her chest rising and falling faster, both of us covered in blood, with her riding me. Skin slaps skin, her legs shake, I can feel her pussy pulsing around me. Sliding my hand between her legs, I play with her clit. Pressing and pinching the swollen bundle of nerves between my knuckles while I slip a finger inside her.

"Oh fuck. Yes. Please. So *goddamn* full." She moans.

"You're mine. Say it."

Her head drops forward. Tears leaking from her eyes when she looks back down to her new ink.

"Look at it and say it." I growl out.

"I'm yours." She whimpers.

"Fuck, Killer. You'll only ever be mine."

Lifting my finger I press it to her lips, silently ordering her to open. She does. Wrapping her tongue around the digit and sucks it clean. Using that same hand I press her down on me, my hips thrust up to meet hers. My hand squeezes her shoulder and she screams from the pain, but I'm too far gone to care. Watching my dick disappear inside her while looking at my name carved into her skin has my dick throbbing.

"Come all over my dick. Soak my cock like a good little slut."

Those words mixed with the pressure I'm putting on her shoulder and my hips slamming into her, she finally let's go. My name leaving her mouth on a wail. I slam into her once more, letting her pussy grip me, milking me of my release. Stars fill my vision. Her weight falls over me, her body spent and no longer bleeding. I lift her off of me, letting her settle into my lap.

I tap my hand against her cheek, "Killer."

Her eyes roll back and then she's gone. Her cunt spilling our release down her legs, blood dried to her body, and my name scarring her skin. She looks like the angel of death laying there and my soul cracks at the realization that I've burned her too deep into my thoughts.

Kissing her cheek, "I'll only ever see you. No matter how fast you run or how hard you fight, you'll always belong to me. There's no world in which I don't crave you. No life in which I won't possess every inch of you. Kenna Kingston, I'll burn the world to ashes to keep you now that I've tasted you."

CHAPTER TWENTY THREE

KENNA

Iron hot pain spreads through my right shoulder, jolting me awake. My body is stiff when I stretch out across the soft sheets. My head swims, memories fading in and out, unable to piece them together. Bright white lights blind me as soon as I open my eyes. Waiting for them to adjust, the first thing I note is I'm in my bed, but that doesn't make any sense. Pain echoes through me, a constant reminder of memories that allude me. Pushing off my blanket, a tug against my arm has me halting movement.

"Shit." I mumble.

Looking down, I take stock of my body, finding much more than I expected. In the crease of my elbow, an IV sticks out, feeding me fuck knows what. I sure hope it's something for the unbearable ache on the right side of my body. A white bandage stained with blood is wrapped around my arm, under my armpit, and over my shoulder. Pressing down on the center I beg myself to remember. When my fingers make contact, fire shoots down my arm and flashes of a gun barrel pointing at me runs through my head.

"Oh god!" I jolt at the realization that I was shot.

Without the adrenaline flowing through me the pain hits me full force. Looking around my room to put more pieces together I see a body slumped in a chair against the wall, bundled under a pile of blankets. The person's body slowly rises and falls with shallow breaths. Whoever it is they are passed the fuck out. Turning to check for my phone my breath hitches, my heart skipping a beat at the sight of a vase. My nightstand houses a massive bouquet of orange and black lilies. At the base is a cream-colored slip of paper with *Killer* scribbled across the front. Licking my lips, my eyes close.

Squeezing them tight, I force myself to remember exactly what happened. I was getting my tattoo colored in when Ryker busted through the shop door. Glass flashes in my mind, pictures blending together, blood and screaming.

"Oh god, Jax." I whisper, my fingers covering my lips.

Drawing in a deep breath I keep pushing myself. Ignoring the throb against my skull, I repeat each memory until small pieces start falling into place.

Ryker entering me.

Jax on the floor, blood dripping from his head, his breathing shallow. *So much blood.*

It all blends together in a kaleidoscope of ecstasy. Ryker has a way of bending pain into a weapon that he uses to manipulate my body. Moving my fingers to my temples, I massage the tension until I finally put the final piece together. Tears sting the back of my eyes, ready to fall at the vision, Ryker name carved into my skin.

"No. No. No."

Throwing the blanket on the floor, I free my legs fully and scoot to the edge of the bed. The IV pulls, but I'm numb to the tubing that tries to rip from my flesh. The real agony is in my soul. My pride demolished into a puddle of tears and crimson. My ribs ache, the organ in my chest screams, even when a deep part of myself rejoices. Screaming in victory. Finally.

Pulling the IV towards me I stand, my legs weak, I walk to the nightstand and grab a single flower. Lifting the burnt orange lily to my nose I inhale. Flashes of that day in the garden rush through my head, flying off the tracks crashing into everything. Taking out everyone in its path. We are pure destruction, but the damage is done. Sitting the flower down on the table, my fingers pinch the single piece of paper, turning it over to check the back before slowly opening it and revealing the note.

Remember, even bathed in ashes the phoenix rises.

Rise and show us your fire. My demons will always search out yours.

Take care of what's mine, Killer. See you soon.

Behind the note is a bottle of Ibuprofen and tattoo care cream. He also left me antibacterial soap for the cleaning process. Snatching up the soap I walk around the bed to nudge the sleeping body with my toes. Groaning meets my ears.

"What?" A groggy voice says.

Confusion hits me first, then the voice registers and anger follows after.

"What the fuck are you doing here?" I snap.

Ally's head pops from under the blanket with squinted eyes. My blackout curtains were left open last night, the sun beaming directly into the room.

"Dear god, Kens. Close the fucking curtains." She moans.

She starts to pull the blanket back over her head when I kick the leg of her chair. She snaps her head back my way, hazel eyes glaring into mine.

"What. The. Fuck?" I question.

Making sure to drag out each word my brows raise, waiting for her to explain. I know I changed the damn locks.

Sighing, she rest her forehead against her arm, eyes closed, she shakes her head.

"Kens, you were shot. What did you expect?" Her voice is low.

I can hear the fear and concern in her voice, but I'm not budging. She gave the Stone brothers information about me. Putting those puzzle pieces together finally had it clicking in my head. Why would she always bring West around me knowing our history? Asking so many questions about my past, my father, and even the brothers. She's always been nosey, but now I know why. She was using me to feed them information. She knew my schedule, where I was going, when I would be home. Is that how Ryker always knew how to find me? It had to be.

"Ally, I changed the locks for a reason. Unless you're here to pack up your shit, you've wasted your time."

Moving to walk past her, she reaches out and grabs my wrist. Pausing for a split second her hand falls from my arm.

"Let me explain. There is so much more you don't understand!"

Spinning to fully face her, Ally stands up to meet my stare, her eyes wide.

"You're right! I don't understand how my BEST friend could sell me out. How you could spy on me for the one family that wanted to hurt me? Truly hurt me."

Tears are falling. The physical and mental pain mix together as the events of the last few days flood my mind. Being strong doesn't mean I won't break, it just means I'll stand back up. Right now I'm falling and no one is here to catch me on my way down.

"I've been shot, Ally. I've been..." I trail off.

Swiping angrily at the wetness trailing down my face, I shake my head and storm out the room. The IV pole being drug behind me, my frustration has me yanking it from my arm and flinging it into the wall.

Turning my head I leave her with my last words, "I want you out of here, Ally."

Leaving her in my room, I head to the bathroom to clean myself up. My hair is crusted together with brownish red dried blood. Curling my nose at the sight looking back at me, I get to work cleaning up. It takes almost an hour with one arm, no way to fully shower, and no help, but still I ignore Ally when she steps into the bathroom.

"Kenna, please."

Her words crack, I turn from the bathroom mirror to find her waiting on me, her eyes watering. It feels like I've been lost in a dream for weeks and I'm just waking up. Just seeing the sky for the first time. Attempting to shoulder past her, she pushes her way in front of me, her gaze rolling over me, checking for god knows what.

"What? Hoped he did more damage?"

"You have no idea what you're talking about!" She yells. Tears fully pouring down her face. "I had no choice. You did, but I didn't." She cries out.

Seeing her like this pulls at my heart, but knowing what she was doing right under my nose has me stepping past her. Heading back to my room to search for my phone.

"What are you doing? You need to sit down, Kens."

"You don't know what I need." I snap.

I can feel her stepping closer to me.

"Kens." She whispers.

Dropping my head forward, I look down and spot my phone and skirt on the floor by my bed. Going to bend down a pang shoots through me.

"Shit!" I yelp.

Ally nudges me to the side, bending to grab my phone, she looks me in the eyes. Placing it in my palm she leaves her hand in mine, our fingers resting against each other.

"I had no choice. Let me help you, please. Ask me anything and I'll tell you."

She's practically begging. Offering information that I could use to prove my dad didn't do the crimes he's been accused of. Licking my lip my gaze moves to the window, taking a moment to think it over. She squeezes my fingers.

"Please, Kenna." she pleads.

Pressing the power button on my phone I scroll through all my text and calls, making sure I don't have anything important just sitting there. When I'm done I pull up Jax's contact and hit call.

It rings twice and goes to voicemail. So I try calling again. Same thing. I scream out in frustration.

"He's not going to answer." Ally says, still standing close to me.

Stepping into her, my height giving me an advantage, my hands ball into fist.

"What the hell does that mean?" I ask.

Shrugging her shoulders, she looks away before her eyes connect back to mine, "He's with Ryker and the boys."

My stomach fills with acid at the thought of me causing Jax harm for just doing his job. Scrolling past his name, I search Rykers and hit send.

Same thing. Two rings and the line goes dead.

"I can't deal with this right now." I murmur.

My stomach rumbles at that time, so I leave Ally to follow behind me while I make my way to the kitchen. The ache in my shoulder is a steady throb and I know I should have it looked at, but the IV that was in my arm has me thinking Ryker had that done already. The only thing keeping me from checking the wound is a fear of seeing the damage.

"Since you seem to know so much, where is my car?" I ask Ally.

She's sitting at the counter watching me like I'm going to fall over any second. I can see the worry painted all over her face, but part of me questions if it's all a facade. Getting a bowl, milk, and cereal I make myself something simple and easy. I'd be lying to myself if I thought I felt okay enough to cook.

"It's here. Ryker had Cole bring it back. Ryker got you back here and found your key in your bag. Since you changed the locks."

She pauses for a second, letting me know she must have tried hers and it didn't work. It takes effort not to smirk at that, but I need more information so I play friendly.

"Anyway, West demanded we call a doctor to come here instead of taking you to the hospital. He didn't think it'd look good for a Kingston to go in with a bullet hole in her body escorted by a Stone." She rolls her eyes at that and lets out a scoff. Hmm... Seems like she might not have agreed with that decision.

"So, what? They called a doctor and had them come out to patch me up?" My brows arch in question. "What about Jax? Did you see him?"

Letting my worry slip could cause him more pain, especially if she's still feeding them information. Ryker would kill him if he hasn't already, even if he knew that I cared for him, even if it was as a big brother. There is no place for anyone else in my life when it comes to him. He'll remove anyone who threatens his place in my life and I'm starting to see that no matter how hard I fight him I'll never win.

Shaking her head, "No. They had me come straight here to sit with you. I didn't know you were shot until I got here and saw the doc working on you." Pointing to my shoulder, "He stitched you up pretty good and knocked you out with some pretty heavy shit. You lost so much blood, Kens."

Her waterworks are back and in full force, but I can't find any emotions in me. I'm numb from everything that's happened. Pouring the milk in my bowl, I lift the spoon and take a bite. As soon as I swallow it down my stomach growls again, waking up my system and my hunger picks up ten-fold.

"How long have I been asleep?"

"Only one day, but you were out the whole time so I'm not surprised you're starving."

I take two more bites leaving us in silence. Ally just sits there twiddling her fingers. It's not completely uncomfortable being here with her, the company is nice, but I'm not sure if I want to forgive her no matter what she says.

"Kenna."

She calls my name, pulling my attention away from the cereal floating in my bowl. Chewing through the bite I just took, she waits for me to fully look at her.

"There are things you don't know about me. I don't have money." She looks down to pick at her nails. "I'm only here because of the Stone brothers. They pulled me from a shitty situation and placed me here. I didn't know you or the history between the families. I'm only here to earn a place at the school."

"So they paid you?"

Money. I laugh.

"It's always going to be about money. I should have known that's what this would be about."

Raising her hands she stops me, "It's not like that. I don't have family and I don't come from status or an empire like you do. I don't have a family business like they do."

"And that means you, what, spy for money? Are you for sale? Because fuck, I could use some information of my own." I snap.

I don't need her help and she knows it. It's a statement on who she is and how her loyalty is only tied to what someone can provide for her.

"You have everything you could ever ask for. You will never know what it's like to go hungry!" She yells. "What it's like to watch your mother suffer from working herself to death. Yeah, I accepted money for secrets, but I didn't know you then."

Pulling back, I push my bowl away from me, my appetite gone.

"So you didn't know who I was yesterday?" My head tilts, my question put out there for her to mull over, her eyes growing dim with defeat.

Nodding, "I did. It's too late for me, Kenna. I'm theirs to do with as they please. They bought me and I'll never be able to fully break free from what I owe them. I just know that I'll never be used against you again."

Slapping my palms against the counter I raise my voice, "And how can I know that? Isn't it a little late for that?"

"No. No, Kenna. It's not too late. I'm here now telling you that you can trust me. I'll earn every inch you give me until I'm the one you come to for everything. I'll be here, Kens."

This is too much. My body hurts, my eyes are growing heavy, and now that I'm full my mind moves back to the pain. Reminding me of the wounds that cover my body. I step around the counter, leaving the bowl there without a fuck to give.

"Want to see what happens when someone gets too close to me?" I say.

Ally watches every step I take until I'm no longer blocked from the countertop. Rolling my shorts down, ones that Ryker must have put on me, I flash the jagged red letters on my hip. "This is who I belong to!" She sucks in a breath, eyes wide, her hand covers her mouth. A laugh forces its way up my throat. Leaning closer to her I flash her a wink.

"Don't worry, Ally. I'll claim what belongs to me soon and then no one will stand in my way. You want the Stone brothers to be taken down? You're looking at the wrong Kingston."

It's not direct, but she gets the picture. She may have only done this to see if I could help her, but now she knows that I'll never turn against them. We'll break each other, but our scars are welded together. My burns are theirs and their cuts belong to me. Using me to set her free is where she is mistaken, but I don't let her know my real plans. Ally ruined any trust we had, but maybe I can use her to my advantage.

"We'll never be back to where we were, but we can work on it."

Leaving her to process that I head back to the room to take a nap. Stepping past the IV that's laying across the floor, I make my way to my bed. Without checking the time, my phone, or my wound, I crawl under the sheets. My body melts into the mattress, that short amount of time taking a lot out of me. Before I drift too far, I reach to the side and grab the single lily from the dresser, placing it on the pillow next to me. The aroma floats around me and that's the last thing I notice as I fade into a dreamless sleep.

CHAPTER TWENTY FOUR

RYKER

"Rye, I have a game to get ready for." West whines.

"The game isn't for another three days." I growl through clenched teeth.

My muscles strain, pushing the bar above my chest, the weights heavy in my hands. West and Cole stand near the doorway of The Basement watching me wear myself down by working out. I'm wired, ready to get my hands on someone, my fingers twitching with the need.

"You sure you want to do this? She's going to lose her shit on you."

"Exactly."

West chuckles, but Cole doesn't make a sound even though I can feel the heat of his stare on the side of my face. Slamming the bar into the holder I release it and sit up. Sweat drips down my face, into my eyes, making its way down my shirt.

"Where's G?" I ask.

Cole answers this time. "Probably avoiding us after what happened last night."

Cole's irritation isn't with G, but when you are the head of your team you go down for their mistakes. G's boys had Hank Harlow, but he somehow slipped between their fingers and got away. Now he knows we're looking at him, so he'll be on high alert. Cole is pissed and is looking to pick a fight so I told G to steer clear of The Basement for today. As for our tattoo artist, he's in the middle of the ring, waiting for me to join him. Only, we closed the fights for today, so he's in there alone. Using a small blue towel I wipe the sweat from my beard.

"It's about time for a trim caveman." West jokes.

Tossing the towel to the side, I push to my feet, walking towards my brothers. Cole leans against the wall on his phone, waiting until I get closer to look up from it, while West fakes a jab to my ribs. Dancing on his toes he pretends to try to box me, but I'm focused on Cole.

"You straight, man?" I ask.

Ally is with Kenna, which were my orders not his, so he's on edge. He doesn't trust Kenna not to lose her shit when she does finally wake up. I made sure to leave her a little note and the doctor should be stopping back by for a follow up visit soon. I make a mental note to check in with him about her condition and to see if she needs anything. I'm still fucking fuming at the fact she risked her damn life to save some asshole. Which is why he's here instead of sleeping off his concussion and broken ribs. I'm going to get to the bottom of their relationship real soon.

"I'm fine. Just trying to keep track of a lead that I have."

His thumbs are flying across his screen, his eyes moving from me back to the phone, unable to focus on anything in front of him.

"Why don't you give it a rest?"

Slapping him on the shoulder, West says, "You know little baby brother can't do that. He doesn't know how to have fun. Just ask Ally." West winks at me before looking back to Cole.

Cole's thumbs freeze, his body tensing, yet he doesn't move. West's words roll right off him, but West Nudges Cole's arm, pushing him further.

"I bet she'll be crawling back to me once she figures out the only thing baby brother here can rub the right way is his screen."

Cole's eyes snap forward, the blue growing darker and his expression clouds into rage. Rearing back his arm swings forward, fist connecting with West's jaw. Relief floods my emotions when he starts to laugh. It worked. Even though it came with a punch to the face, it got Cole off his fucking phone and in the present with us.

"Who are you watching anyway?" I ask, trying to probe some information out of him. "I don't know. They seem to be a fucking ghost, but I can see the trail they're leaving and it's a mess." He seethes as we make our way from the weight room to the ring.

Looking at him from the corner of my eye, "Then what makes you think it's got something to do with Del Mar?"

His steps falter, "Because it has something to do with dad's death. The patterns, the names on the accounts, they all point to around the time dad died."

We continue down the stairs, coming up to the closed door. Reaching out I push open the red door to reveal our guest sitting in a single chair in the center of the mat. He's blindfolded and gagged, but from the movement of his hands I can tell he's finally awake.

"Are you going to share with the class?" I ask Cole.

Stopping to face me he tilts his head, "I will when I have more. You have to trust me on this, brother."

Nodding, I clap him on the back and keep moving forward, leaving Cole and West to fan out further into the room. This is my show. They are just here for the fun.

"Well, well. Look who decided to wake up."

Kicking the leg of his chair with a laugh, I don't bother trying to hide my disinterest.

"What the fuck do you want?" His voice is even.

"Most people in your position would be cautious with how they speak to the people who have them tied up." I kick the leg of the chair again, but this time behind him, continuing to circle around him.

"Most people are scared of you and your brothers."

"Let me guess. You're not most people?" I snort, laughing at that.

Shrugging his shoulders he keeps his face blank, which pisses me off even more.

"Let's just say I have a bigger interest in Kenna Kingston and I won't be run off by some little boys trying to run daddy's empire."

In less than two seconds I have him on his back, the chair under him, and my knife to his throat. Using my free hand I snatch off the blindfold so he can see how serious I am.

"I'll carve your tongue out right fucking now for even saying her name."

He doesn't flinch. His eyes connect with mine, showing no fear. Most men aren't afraid of another man until they're given a reason to be, but this is different. Looking in his eyes something settles in the back of my mind.

"Who are you working for? Her dad?"

He doesn't say anything.

Pressing the tip of the knife into his throat, I drag it down his neck. A bead of red follows the blade rolling down his shirt.

"Who has you watching her?"

Nothing.

Rage bubbles in my stomach, pushing me over the edge. Twisting the knife into his skin I flick my wrist, cutting his neck deep enough to have him grunting, but not enough to kill him.

"I can do this all day. It's a gift of mine honestly."

My voice light, I smile, letting him see just how far I'm willing to go.

"So, tell me. Was it her piece of shit father that hired you?"

"Go fuck yourself." He spits.

There's no anger in his tone, just a matter of fact attitude, as if his employer could somehow protect him from being the next gift I give my little Killer.

Leaning down, "I'm going to slice you into little pieces and send you to my girl. Every time she gets a chunk of you, I'll pop into her head. She'll only ever think of me when she sees you."

Not giving him a chance to respond, I drag the knife across his arm, ripping a chunk of skin off.

"Oh shit. I really fucked up that tattoo. I hope that didn't cost too much money."

His jaw is clenched so tight I can hear his teeth cracking. Blood flows from the cut, his flesh split wide open, down to the muscle.

"You should have seen how much of a fighter she was." I taunt, "She saved your pathetic life and in turn got herself shot." Waiving the knife around, red splatters around us with each hand movement. "So, I guess that means I owe you a bullet. Lucky for you, I only have this knife."

Looking at the tip, I bring it closer to my face, judging the sharpness of its point. Without warning I rare back and plunge the blade into his shoulder, in the same spot where Killer took a bullet for this fucker.

He is a tough mother fucker, but he still lets a scream slip through his teeth. It's like music to my ears.

"Now, it's not my best work..." I trail off with a laugh.

"You're going to regret that." He spits.

He breathes through the pain like a trained fighter moving through the punches.

"The only thing I regret is not moving my girl out of the way before pulling the trigger."

He laughs.

"When they find out you shot Kenna Kingston your entire little kingdom is going to come crashing down."

His words cut through me. I'm sick of listening to this bullshit. He's refusing to answer and I'm getting nowhere. Images of my girl waking up without me there fill my head. Tapping his face with a sneer, I kneel into his chest.

"I'm going to go give my girl a visit. Sit here and wait for me will ya?" Pressing into his chest where his broken ribs are, "I'll try to remember to send in the doctor to patch up this shoulder."

Digging my hand into his shoulder I pull the knife out, the only thing that was stopping the blood, and stand. Ignoring his cussing from the pain, I turn to see my brothers watching me. No judgment, just acceptance. I haven't admitted it yet, but they know I'll never let anyone else have her. Traitor or not, Kenna Kingston isn't going anywhere. We'll deal with the foundation our way.

I'm halfway to the door when he calls out, only he's not asking for help. He's dropping a name of who hired him. While I'm not surprised, I am starting to wonder what Kenna has to do with the Savage family. I look at my brothers seeing the confusion on their faces. We're all wondering what the fuck is going on. What the hell is Kenna doing in the middle of three families?

CHAPTER TWENTY FIVE

KENNA

It's been seven days since Ally betrayed me. A week since a bullet went through my shoulder. Six days since Ally came home with excuses begging for forgiveness. A week seems so short, but the last one hundred and sixty-eight hours have been hell on me. The only bright side that has come from the past week, is my shadow is nowhere to be seen. He made his last threat, then radio silence. The unknown makes me hesitant, but a part of me feels victorious at the small win. I've been a ball of nerves since Ryker carved his name into my flesh, marking me as his. Now when I look at the tattoo on my leg, I know it was the right choice. Not that I've shown it to him, even though he's inside me every chance he gets. Possessing me.

"You almost done?" Ally says, tapping on the open bathroom door.

Looking at her through the mirror, our eyes connect. A knowing look crosses over her face when she sees my back through my sheer black shirt. Her mouth opens and closes a few times before she clamps her lips together.

I spread bright red lipstick over my lips, my eyes track the movement as I try to not look at the traitor standing behind me. I lean back and rub my lips together, admiring how the color pops against my outfit. A white lacy bra peeks through the sheer of my shirt, matching my milk white jeans.

"I don't want to talk about it." Is all I say.

I wipe off a small smudge of lipstick from the corner of my mouth as my eyes meet Ally's in the mirror for a split second. Giving myself one more once over, I turn around looking at a spot just above her head. Needing to get the fuck out of this suffocating bathroom, I head for the door. Before exiting, I place my hands on her shoulders, digging my fingers into her skin. Leaving a trail of crescent moons embedded where my fingernails sit. . She winces but doesn't make a move to pull away, which makes me smile.

Flashing her a wide toothy grin, "I let you come back, but don't mistake that for trust. You have to earn that back and you better fucking try hard. If I find out you're still playing games, I'll do more than ruin your pretty little face." With a wink I slide past her.

Leaving her standing there in shock I make my way to my room. Giving her a second chance doesn't mean I have to make it easy on her. We can laugh and have fun tonight, but at the end of the day Ally can't be trusted right now, so being next to me is the best place for her. I can't let my love for her get in the way again. Sitting on my bed to put my shoes on, I make sure my phone is still sitting on the dresser where I left it. Standing, I move to slip my phone in my back pocket along with my keys, when my eye catches on something outside.

"Ally." I call out.

She comes bouncing into the room with a smile. She brushes my jabs off quickly and that's one thing that's made this easier to deal with. I don't think I could deal with her sulking every day.

"What's up, Kens?"

I don't let her see me wince at her nickname. Motioning slightly with my head I say, "Do you see anything strange outside? Don't make it too obvious."

Stepping up beside me, she pretends to be fixing the back of my shirt. I can feel the cool touch of her fingers tracing down my back while her stare aims out the window. The figure shifts slightly under the light from my room.

"Who is that?" She whispers.

Her breath skates down my neck, making me shiver adding to the eerie situation. Shaking my head in response, we just stand there passing meaningless words between each other while watching the shadow standing below us. A knock at the front door makes both of us jump. We both turn towards the open doorway, our hands clasped together. Looking back over my shoulder, my eyes fall to the space below the window that's now empty.

"He's gone." I whisper.

Knock. Knock. Knock.

Ally shoves my shoulder, pushing me in front of her, a nervous laugh leaving her.

"Go see who it is." she tries to whisper, but it comes out way louder than she intended it too.

I slap her hand away with an eye roll, her dramatics are ridiculous. She should be the one checking to get back into my good graces. I tiptoe across the apartment until I'm standing in front of the door. My hand hovers over the doorknob. The fucker bangs on the door like he's a fucking FBI agent, making me jump and a giggle pass through my lips. Why the hell am I acting scared when all I really want to do is run downstairs and confront the bastard stalking me.

Yanking the door open with more force than the person on the other side expected, their head snaps back in surprise. Deep brown eyes connect with mine and a slow smile follows.

"Wow, Princess. You clean up nice." West says, adding a wink for punctuation.

He can't help but flirt with everyone he comes in contact with and it's that playboy smile that wins over the girls on campus. Shaking my head with a sign, I open the door wider and step to the side without a word. No use in pretending like I'm not going to let him in when I know it's a lie.

"What are you doing here?"

That question comes from Ally. She's standing at the back of the couch, her nose scrunched up with her hands on her hips. Pure sass. West throws a wink at me before sauntering over to Ally. He stretches his arms out wide and sweeps her off her feet. Literally. He swings her around, a deep throaty laugh falling from his lips. She's dazed and taken by surprise, which was his plan, because he flashes a smirk at me over her shoulder. We share the same one. He sets her on the balls of her feet, patting her head, but she swats him away. Pressing her hair back into place, she spins towards me with a finger pointed in my direction.

"You need to be ready in five minutes or I'm leaving your tall lanky ass here." Her tone doesn't match the bossy words she spits.

She's hiding a smile when she turns back to West, smacking his chest with the back of her hand. He jerks left and right, pretending to box with her before stepping around her and jogging towards me. I'm still standing in the same spot, staring at the two of them playing like best friends. It's more than the face sucking they normally do and it sets me on edge, taking me back to last week when I found out she was spilling information to them. West sees the moment my thoughts float back there and halts to a stop just a foot away.

"She's done, Princess. Don't worry, she picked you over us so you win this time."

Curling my lip, our pleasantries long gone, "And what exactly were we playing? What part of I'm done playing these games do you not understand?"

He raises his eyebrows at me. Not in confusion, instead he looks down almost daring me, not that I need the permission he's granting me. One step forward and I'm at his chest. My height gives me the advantage of being able to look him fully in the eye.

"I'll do whatever it takes to prove my father is innocent. Don't ever take my kindness for weakness. Your *brothers*." I make sure to spit that term, "Seem to forget that I grew up both a Kingston and Stone. Family, always." Looking away, my eye catches on Ally standing behind him watching the entire thing. I wet my lips, bringing my eyes back to him, making sure he sees me when I say, "My hate for you and your brothers runs deep. Even after everything you've put me through for unfounded reasons. But I'm just as much a Stone as I am a Kingston and I'll spend forever forcing you guys to see that."

Our stare holds a few seconds longer before I shoulder check him on my way to my room. Grabbing my things, I check my reflection before meeting them at the front door. Tonight we have a baseball game, which is why I wasn't expecting the middle brother at our door, but I'm preparing myself for anything. I haven't seen Ryker since he signed his name in ink and blood. My core clenches at the image of his name on my skin and it sets my blood on *fire*. Loving the way his mark on me feels is one of the reasons I want to avoid the bastard.

The roar from the crowd vibrates the metal of the bleachers. Me and Ally are on our feet, stomping with the rest of our classmates. I haven't seen Ryker or Cole yet, but West has made it a mission to search us out from the field. Wind blows my hair around whipping me in the face, but my smile doesn't drop. Tonight has been just what I needed. Patching things up with Ally has started off smooth and spending time together at the game has been so much fun.

"Wooohooo!" Ally tosses her hands over her head with a wide grin plastered on her face.

We both stand at the same time when West throws the last pitch of the game, striking out the other team's batter. The entire stadium goes wild with excitement. Our school rushes to the field while the other teams school tosses hats, jackets, drinks, and food to the ground. Our clean up crew is going to have a field day with this one. Bodies slam into me and Ally, shuffling us along the bleachers, my feet tripping over steps. My foot catches on the corner of the last step, my weight falling forward, but two large hands catch me.

"Easy, Killer."

Rykers mouth is only inches from my ear, his closeness sends chills down my arms. My body hums with his presence and I know he can sense the excitement pouring off me when he trails his lips up the slope of my neck.

"There's my needy little brat." He nips my earlobe.

The noise around us drowns out the low moan that bubbles at the base of my throat. Pure need shooting through me with the feel of his mouth on my skin. A reminder of what it feels like to have his tongue gliding inside me has my thighs instantly slick. Leaning back against his chest, Ryker makes sure we're touching with each step forward.

"Cole." I nod pressing my lips together.

Cole hasn't acknowledged me up until this point, but this time I don't give him a choice.

"I see you caught you a fish." I wiggle my brows at him.

Both of the boys share a look before Ryker bends down to kiss my jawline. It's not in a way your boyfriend would show you he cares. It's in the possessive ownership he's showing everyone around us and even though I belong to no one, it still lights me on fire inside.

"Doll!" West screams over the noise.

Bouncing on his toes he spots us over the crowd, with the help of Ryker and Cole's height, and the fact that people avoid touching the Elite bastards. Ally on the other hand is hidden in the sea of bodies so West is calling for someone he can't quite see. Sweat drips from his thick dark hair, brown eyes shining with pride, West's face glows bright red from the long game. Ally turns to look at me when she spots Cole. Her smile dips slightly before she snaps out of it and bounds towards him. The broody fucker opens his arms for her, but only to stop her short.

Both hands grip her arms, "I thought I told you to stay away from West." Cole says.

Ryker chuckles from behind me, "Sounds familiar."

Leaning to the side, I turn my head so I can see his stare, "What's with you Stone men thinking you own everyone." I snap.

Dragging me closer by my throat, he yanks me forward fast and hard. Teeth gnashing at my bottom lip. Biting down hard enough to break the skin, blood drips onto my tongue.

"Watch that pretty little mouth." He growls.

Pulling away my tongue traces the inside of my lip, gliding over the broken skin. Our eyes stay glued on each other as the world around us pauses, the death grip he has on my soul makes it impossible to move. West has made it to us by now, his sweaty uniform drips over my arm when he shoves past us, reaching for Ally. A look passes between Ryker and Cole, right before he turns around and sees West... who gave Ally a wink and slapped her on the ass. Ryker's already shaking his head when Cole lashes forward. Cole's fist swings past me, slamming into the side of his West's face. Blood flies from his mouth, spraying my shirt.

"What the fuck!" I shout.

A warm hand clasp over my mouth, silencing my scream.

"No one gets to hear you sound like that but me, Killer."

Ally shoves West to the side, bumping chests with Cole.

"What the hell is your problem?" She demands.

Her tiny hand smacks him across the face. Cole's pupils blow wide, looking hungry and wild. He bares his teeth before his hand lashes out. Dragging her forward by her throat, people start to give us space, the onlookers are openly staring at this point. He pulls her so close, they're nose to nose. Her body begins to visibly tense from the lack of oxygen, right before she passes out he crashes his mouth down on hers in a brutal kiss.

"Does my girl like watching?" Ryker whispers in my ear.

Tilting my head to the side I don't respond. West nods his head at Ryker before rushing off to toss a cheerleader over his shoulder. Heading to the team's dugout he disappears behind the wall. Scoffing, I spin in Rykers hold.

"He pushed Cole on purpose." I state.

It's not a question, but an observation. West knew that Cole would stake his claim on Ally, but he wanted him to. He knew that his brother had a thing for the girl he was fucking. My nose scrunches up at that thought.

"It's more complicated than that." Ryker says, reading my thoughts.

Shrugging, I make a move to step out of his hold, but he tightens his arms around me.

"Excuse me. Are you Kenna Kingston?" A soft voice says from my right.

We both look at the same time to see a meek little girl holding an item behind her back. Smiling, I lower down to height, forcing Ryker to loosen his hold. I smile at the girl, ignoring the rumble coming from his chest. .

"I sure am."

Bouncing in place she pulls a box from behind her back.

"I have to give this to you. It's a surprise."

Placing a small brown box in my hand, my stomach plummets. There around the square cardboard is a red bow. Matching all the others that I still have in my room. Swallowing, I try to push back the feeling of being watched.

"Thank you." I murmur.

I know she barely heard me when her eyes fall to my lips to see the words form on my lips., I stand abruptly, turning and leaving the young girl there to fend for herself. I don't have it in me to make sure she's okay or that she gets back to her family. I can't feel my fingers. My head swims with warning. This one feels different than the rest. Hands grab me, but my body fights them off on instinct. Sucking in a deep breath, my chest heaves through each one.

"Kens." Ally's voice breaks through the noise.

Snapping my head to the side, I see three sets of eyes watching me with different expressions. Ally's hazel eyes peer at me with confusion and worry, while Ryker's caramel brown ones reflect aggression. Cole stares blankly at me with indifference that chills me to the bone.

"Who is that from?" Ally ask.

Ryker steps closer, so close we inhale the same. Shaking it off, I force out a laugh through my weak smile.

"It's just a secret admirer that I've had for a while."

I can feel the piercing gaze coming from Ryker. Ignoring him, I grab Ally's hand in fake excitement.

"Are you ready for the Gala?" I gush.

Ally squeals out her delight and that seems to have Cole and Ryker backing away. I know it won't keep Ryker off my back for long, but I'm okay with the immediate space he offers. Cole and Ryker keep tossing looks over their shoulders while we all head towards our cars. He hasn't said it yet, but Ryker is starting to blur the lines of hate and its sending mixed signals that I can't seem to read.

CHAPTER TWENTY SIX

KENNA

The past two days have been a blur of school, exams, and preparing myself for my appointment with Jax tonight. My hands begin to shake every time I think of going into the shop, only to find that Jax isn't there. He's always there. I haven't heard from him and that has my heart pinching at the thought. Images flood my head of possible reasons he hasn't returned my calls or text. The only reason I haven't been by the shop is because I've let myself drift too far behind in school.

Rolling over, my stare floats to the ceiling. Taking a deep breath, my nose fills with the scent of Lilies as their aroma floats around me. Clenching my legs together, I try to push those thoughts of Ryker from my head. Instead I allow another memory to consume me.

My alarm starts to go off, reminding me that my first class of the day starts in an hour. Rolling off the bed, with little to no enthusiasm for the day, I make my way to the bathroom for my morning shower. Taking out a big fluffy white towel I set it on the rack. My fingers close over the cold metal handle to turn on the water. I let it heat up while I make sure the door is locked, and my phone still rests on the counter.

After school today I plan on going to see my dad again, hopefully I'll be able to pull more information out of him. My father and Alec Stone were best friends, but as of recently I found out there was a third. Rowan Savage. The father of none other than Oakley Savage aka Blue. That connection doesn't sit right with me. Why would their family be sniffing around our stomping rounds two years after Alec's death? Something isn't adding up, and I intend to find out what it is. . My plan is to toss out the family name, see how he reacts and hopefully it will lead me somewhere because I'm running out of clues.

Rubbing my sponge down my stomach, my hand pauses over my tattoo. The lines are jagged and angry, but it's beautiful. I fight the way my body reacts to the memory of Ryker above me. Moving past it I wash my scarred leg, rubbing the healed parts of my tattoo that spans from my upper hip down to my ankle. The skin loosens with each swipe down, the hot water making it easy for my muscles to relax. I beat myself up for not making more time for my stretches and therapy exercises. Letting the water fall down my back for a few minutes, it takes me a while to force myself out of the shower and into the real world.

After drying off, I get dressed for class in a white button-down shirt and tight school skirt with my signature black tights underneath. Throwing my hair in a messy french-braid, I grab my bag and slip my phone in the side pocket. The walk is peaceful thanks to the nice weather. The brown box locked in my closet keeps pressing its way to the front of my mind, but I shove it back where it belongs. I haven't opened it yet in fear of it being another body part. By the time I reach the east building my legs burn from the walk. This campus is massive with so many different buildings that expand a three block radius.

"Kenna!" I hear my name being yelled out from behind me.

Turning, I look around to see if I can spot who it was, but I come up short. Continuing up the stairs of the massive entrance, the double doors swing open revealing the packed hallways. I step inside the darkened halls, kicking myself for not leaving sooner. The dark brick walls suck the light from the building, leaving it feeling more historic and castle-like. Making my way to the third floor, I pass by several classrooms before purple hair catches my eye. Ally stands there with a small smile on her face, her hair tied in a short low ponytail with her foot propped against the door behind her.

She looks up at a figure standing in the shadows and my heart starts to pound behind my ribs. The sound of blood pumping through my body fills my ears. Looking around, I move towards the classroom but keep to the other side of the hall, trying to hide behind the students that pass me. Licking my lips I try to swallow, but my throat is dry. She leans away from the doorway to walk towards the man standing above her by at least a foot. Not that it helps when she walks into the shadows to join him, but at least I know he's around my height if not an inch or two taller.

"Kenna."

Romero steps beside me, breathing heavily and pulling my attention from Ally and the mystery man. My gaze keeps tethering back to see if he steps into the light.

"What do you want, Romero?" I quip.

Not in the mood to deal with his bullshit, I shift to the side to make sure I have a full view of the two people across the hall from me.

"I haven't seen you around lately. I just wanted to apologize for what happened between us."

Looking back at him, I can see the truth of his words. Sighing, I look back to Ally before turning to face Romero.

"No hard feelings. You got dealt a shitty hand, but we were never going to be anything in the end. I'm not looking for something serious and I have a feeling you just needed some fun."

Giving him a smile, I pat his shoulder and start to walk across the hall towards Ally when and the shadowed figure steps into the light fully, his salt and pepper hair giving away who he is. Addington leans forward to kiss Ally on the cheek, but that's not what has my blood running cold. It's the second figure stepping from beside the Dean into view. Professor Arden walks towards Ally, but she shrinks back slightly. Addington catches the movement and stops Arden with a hand to his chest. Pressing my back into the wall near the door I breath in deep, trying to calm myself. Ally Adler has been caught talking to two members of the foundation.

Ally finally pops out from the classroom and turns the corner, going in the opposite direction. Waiting a few seconds, I go to step past the doorway when I hear my name being called again.

"Ms. Kingston." Addington calls.

Stopping in my tracks my eyes roll to the ceilings. What more could go wrong. *Don't push your luck Kenna,* My inner bitch snarks at me. Turning towards the empty classroom I step inside, but the door shutting behind me has my muscles tensing. Professor Arden raises his hands to show that he isn't going to try anything. The foundation wouldn't make a move on me so boldly, so I push the anxiety to the back and decide to focus on what the hell is going on.

"Addington. Arden." I nod at both of them.

Standing straight, I don't let them see me hesitate at being alone with them. Fear is the worst thing to give men like them. Wiping down my skirt I pretend to be slightly nervous to give them a sense of security around me, but I'm anything but nervous. If anything, my nerves are only bad because I just saw Addington kiss Ally's face. Not only is he too old for her, but with the history we have of not being able to trust her, this doesn't look good.

"Are you ready for the Fundraiser?" Arden asks.

Popping a hip, I flash him an open smile.

"I am. We haven't had a big ball like this in a long time, so I can't wait to see what our community can do when we all come together."

I roll my eyes inwardly with my political answer. Taught well with handing questions like that, it has me holding back a laugh. Straightening my shirt, my nails tap on the buttons to distract them. The more men think they'll get see of a woman's body, the more their mouths run, spilling information.

"The foundation noticed the trouble the Stone family has given you so we wanted to check in to see how you were adjusting." That's from Addington.

"We would hate it if they made you feel uncomfortable to attend the meetings." That's Arden.

Biting the inside of my cheek, I contemplate my next response.

Lifting a brow, my smile widens, "I appreciate you all for worrying about me. The Stone family has been less than welcoming, but I'll manage. I'll try to make the next meeting so I can catch up on all the things I've missed."

They share a look. Something flashes over Arden's face, but I can't quite place it.

"We were under the impression that you might need a little help with the brothers. If that's ever the case, feel free to come to the foundation." Addington says.

Stepping towards him I can see his eyes trail down to my chest. Placing my palm against his chest, I bat my lashes at him.

"I was under the impression that the Stone family was in charge here, not the foundation, however the Kingston family may need to step in to clean things up, yeah?" My eyes flit from the Dean to the Professor.

Professor Arden crowds me closer to Addington, both men hovering over me, but I don't fear them. They are just puppets we use to do our dirty work.

"Maybe that's for the best. The Stone name has been ahead for far too long. You may just be what we need to take back Del Mar."

My expression almost falls, but I catch myself before they seem to notice. Stepping away from Addington, my hand falls between us. Nodding at them both I move to the door, resting my hand on the doorknob. Looking out the small rectangle window to see if anyone is standing outside the classroom waiting to get in I look back over my shoulder.

"I'll keep that in mind."

Letting the door shut behind me, I make my way to the end of the hall, but instead of turning towards my classroom I keep moving towards the exit doors. I have a destination in mind and it's not class. I take the stairs two at a time, my legs burning with the stretch, until I come to the glass doors on the main level. Swinging them open, they bounce against the wall and I'm surprised the glass didn't shatter. As soon as I step outside my eyes fall closed and I drag in a deep breath filled with that familiar floral scent.

"It seems we both crave the lilies today. It'll be so fucking beautiful when taint them with the color of us.

Blonde hair and rosy cheeks burst through the door and my dick jumps in response to her presence. She doesn't see me standing to the side; she's too busy barging in like a hurricane set for destruction. Leaning against the wall, I watch her for a minute before revealing myself. The way her head falls back, her eyes drifting closed, the smell of flowers filling her senses. She came here to be reminded of me, even if she doesn't want to admit that to herself. I'll make sure she feels my presence.

"It seems that we both crave the lilies today. It'll be so fucking beautiful when taint them with the color of us." I rasp.

She doesn't jump, not even a flinch, instead a cautious smile spreads across her face. Her red lips, that I ache to have wrapped around my cock, pull my attention to her mouth.

"Ryker fucking Stone." She laughs.

It's a little unhinged and it has me moving forward to crowd her space. Her scent engulfs me, filling my lungs with lilies and vanilla. I step behind her, running the tip of my finger up and down the smooth skin of her arms.

"You look a little lost." Turning her with one hand, I use the other to pinch her chin, "Let me help you figure out where you belong."

Using my free hand I push her down by her shoulders until her stocking covered knees are on the cold ground. She's covered by rows of flowers, so when people look in the garden all they see is me standing in the middle of the stone path looking down. What a sight they'll miss.

"On my knees?" She quirks a brow.

She doesn't deny her place at my feet, nor does she try to fight my hold on her. Instead her gaze drifts to the bulk in my jeans with dark eyes.

Her tongue rolls over her lips to wet them, the hungry look in her eyes growing when my hand moves to my belt.

"No." I state.

Cocking her head to the side watching my movements. "No?" She asks.

Pushing her head back to force her eyes to mine, I repeat her words. "On your knees."

Rolling those grey eyes she motions with her hands, as if to remind me where she is, "I am on my knees."

"Yet, that's not where you belong." I say.

My words come out matter of factly. A mixture of surprise and confusion wars in her eyes. The thirst she's fighting shines through with the sight of my belt sliding off. Leaving it hanging open, my fingers move to the button of my jeans.

"And where exactly do I belong, Stone."

The way she calls me Stone instead of Ryker shouldn't feed the fire brewing in my veins, but it does. Yanking my zipper down, she sees the moment my hunger for her boils over the edge. Her grin stretches her mouth wide, taunting me. Twisting her hair in my hand, I step closer, bringing her head level with my dick.

"Pull out my cock, Killer." I order.

Biting her bottom lip, she does as she's told. The sun beats down on my back, but it's nothing compared to the heat pouring off my skin. Her hands are cool on my skin, the chill has me fighting back a shiver, so I drop my mask and let her see exactly what she does to me. Her eyes scan the space around us to see if anyone's lurking, but I tighten my hold on her hair, forcing her to see only me.

"Open that pretty little mouth. I want to feel your lips wrapped around my dick."

She wets her lips before opening her mouth peering up at me through long thick lashes. Her grey eyes darken as she inches down my cock slowly, eyes roll to the back of my head when her lips hit the base of my cock. But when she swallows around me, hollowing out her cheeks and my tip hits the back of her throat, I almost drop to my fucking knees.

"That's it. Good girl, always so fucking filthy for me."

I grip both sides of her face, using my hold to start pumping in and out of her mouth. Shoving myself farther down her throat with each thrust, she gags with each inch I give her. Tears spring from the corners of her eyes, but she never moves her stare from mine. We hold each other's gaze, my hips picking up speed, her throat squeezing around my dick.

"Fuck, Killer. You suck my dick so goddamn good." I moan.

I'm letting her see me come undone, but I don't fucking care. She's open and ready to take all of me and I'm going to take my time with her.

"You on your knees taking my dick so good is where I want you right now. Your place is anywhere my cock is ready and waiting for you."

Her tongue circles my dick, her lips pulling back while I slam forward, causing my legs to shake. I fuck her mouth harder, like she's on death row and I'm giving her, her last meal.

"Your mouth was made for me. I'm going to fuck your face and then I'm going to bend you over and fuck that tight little cunt until everyone in Hawthorne hears you screaming my name."

A moan vibrates up my dick, embedding itself into my veins. My girl likes the sound of that. Her hand glides up my leg, meeting the edge of my pants where she dips in to cup my balls. Twisting and squeezing them while I shove her mouth down over and over, I thrust one more time spilling down her throat. Her red lips smile around a mouthful of my cum dripping out of her perfect, swollen lips. Cleaning me with her tongue, she releases me with a wet plop.

Taking my thumb I catch a drop of my cum from the corner of her mouth and raise an eyebrow. Without a word she opens up and takes my thumb into her mouth, sucking it clean. Standing, she grips my dick with a rough fist pulling on it while looking me dead in my eyes with a smile.

Her other hand grabs the back of my head, yanking me forward, bringing us nose to nose.

"You taste like brimstone and nightmares." She whispers.

Slamming her mouth down on mine, she kisses me with possessive claiming and I fucking let her. I give her everything she wants and more. She bites down on my lip, sucking it into her mouth, a groan leaves my throat. Stepping back, she makes a show of turning slowly, hips swaying, she rolls her skirt up above her hips so I can see her bare ass.

"Fucking hell." I grunt.

Kenna Kingston is a wet fucking dream come to life. Standing in front of me with her fuck me eyes looking at me over her shoulder. Those stockings she wears have been cut to only go up to her thighs, leaving only her ass and pussy on display. She's fucking bare for me. With a wink she bends forward and spreads her legs open, giving me a perfect view of her dripping cunt.

My dick jumps to life with the sight before me.

"I guess it's a good thing my place is anywhere your dick is out and ready for me." She smarts.

Her fucking smartass mouth. Kenna watches me hesitate, my hand twisting around my dick, my feet carrying me closer to her.

"Want me to fuck your needy little pussy?"

She eyes me before nodding her head in a jerky move.

"Ask me."

She curls her lip in defiance, but she knows I won't give in before she does. My girl can fight it all she wants, but she needs this just as much as I do. Plucking a lily from beside me, I twist and twirl it between my fingers while she stares at me.

"Ask me and I'll let you come all over my cock while I fuck you with this." I lift the orange lily.

We can hear students passing by the garden, but neither of us move. The silence between us is deafening. The little killer thinks she's slick, her hand disappearing between her legs, searching for something to ease the ache.

"Aht Aht." I say, pinching the back of her thigh.

Moving forward, I run the head of dick through her slick pussy. Dipping forward to press up against her entrance she sways slightly. Using one foot I tap the inside of her ankle, signaling her to spread wider for me. Taking the flower I smear her cum over the petals and wait for her to bring those smokey eyes to me. Her mouth parts on an inhale when I take the petals and lick them clean.

"Fuck, Killer." I groan.

"Please, Rye." She whines.

My fingers dig into her hip, holding her in place. Slamming forward, I enter her in one move.

"Ryker!" She screams.

"That's it, Killer. Let everyone know who owns your body."

With one hand on her shoulder and the other slipping from her hip between the front of her legs. Allowing her to adjust to my size gives me a chance to press the lily against her clit, circling, teasing. Pushing her ass into me, she urges me faster.

"More. Please. Ryker please."

Her words come out between breaths. Leaning over her so I can see her tits bounce with each thrust, my fingers twist the soft wet petals against her swollen clit. Her legs begin to shake and I start trailing kisses over her shoulder, sinking my teeth into the soft flesh of her neck.

"Ryker! Oh god." She's mumbling and breathing harder. Her knees buckle, but I move my hand from her shoulder to hold her up at the waist.

Kissing below her ear, my warm breath fans across her skin, "That's it baby, let go. Scream for me."

Rubbing the petal faster, I slam into her at the same time, sending her over the edge. I swear the ground fucking shakes with my name falling from her red swollen lips.

"Ryker!"

Grunting, I continue to fuck her harder and faster, dropping the flower to the ground and gripping both hips. My nails cut into her skin, my thighs smack into hers, but I don't ease up. Throwing my head back, I swear my fucking eyes roll to the back of my head with how tight her cunt grips me.

"Fuck, Kenna!" I moan out long and slow.

She's trembling as I slowly pull out. Leaving her to clean up, I slip myself back into my pants and put the mask back up over my face. Making sure my clothes are put back together, I wait until she turns around with that sassy look she gives me every time I make her cum. She crunches her nose at me, trying to hide her smile.

"Looks like everyone knows who owns Ryker Stone now too."

Patting my chest she backs away waiving her fingers like a fucking brat. Once she's out of view, I bend down and pluck the soaked lily from the ground and slip it in my back pocket.

CHAPTER TWENTY EIGHT

KENNA

My nerves have been bad since yesterday. Running into two foundation members isn't what has my hands shaking. No, it's knowing that Ally is not only hiding something from me, but from the brothers as well. They may have had her spying on me to get information on my father, but I know for a fact that they wouldn't trust anyone to get close to the foundation outside of their circle. Not even G would get that job. So, I've been running through different scenarios over and over since yesterday. The Gala is mere hours away, yet here I am distracted. I'm pissed that I missed my chance to get answers from my dad but I've been too busy babysitting Ally.

Now, I finally have an opening to do something about it. Ally left to pick up last minute things, or that's her story, and she left me here to get ready for the fundraiser. My dress was delivered by a driver an hour ago, but I haven't had the nerve to open the garment bag. Strumming my french-manicure I got done this morning against the granite countertop, my eyes flit to Ally's room door.

"Fuck it." I grunt under my breath.

Shoving away from the counter I move towards her bedroom, looking back to the front door before twisting the handle. I'm cloaked in darkness as soon as I step into the room, so I pull my phone out to shine light throughout the dark space. Paranoia has me avoiding her window like the plague. I'm not even sure what to look for, but anything that gives me a clue on her working with Addington and Arden would be perfect. I never thought I'd have to search through Ally's room, but here we were. You truly can't trust anyone.

I go for her closet first knowing that it's the most common place for people to hide their skeletons. She's like Pandora's box filled to the brim full of deceit and secrets, but I'll cut each one from her mouth if I have to. Pausing to listen for the front door, I open her closet and turn on the small light hanging from the ceiling. Her clothes are color coded and in order of style. Typical Ally. Dropping to my knees I move my hands around on the floor under the hanging clothes, searching for anything I can find. Moving to the far wall I manage to cover the entire space and come up empty.

"Where would I hide all my secrets?"

I crawl from the closet and sit back on my heels. Looking over her dark room, lifting my phone for more light, my gaze falls to her bed. If I were trying to keep my darkest secrets close to me, I wouldn't put them under my bed like a teen hiding their dads Playboy, so I keep looking. Letting out a deep sigh my lips press together in thought.

"Come on Kenna." I whisper.

Turning to her dresser I scoff, there's no way she thinks that is the safest place, but the image of a certain brown box pops into my head. If I thought that little surprise was safe in my sock drawer, what would Ally hide in hers? Pushing off the floor to stand I lean out the door checking the living room before moving to her dresser. Blowing out a breath, my heart pounds in my chest. At some point, I stopped hoping I wouldn't find anything and started thinking about what I'm going to do *when* I do find something. It's weird, losing hope in someone you love, having no trust in the one person you live with. Yet, I feel nothing with that thought.

Pulling the first drawer open my hands feel for anything other than fabric, but come up with nothing. Moving my hand through socks and underwear in her top drawer I worry if I'll find something I don't want to. Laughing to myself I keep searching despite not finding anything. After the third try I start to think I really am going crazy, but then the tip of my finger is pricked by a sharp edge.

"Shit."

Yanking my finger back, I shine my light on the sore spot to see a small bead of blood. Paper cut. My brows dip as I stick the finger in my mouth, sucking the blood off filling my mouth with the taste of copper. Must be some strong ass paper to cut me from just a poke. Opening up the drawer further I gently move the shorts she has folded to grab a small stack of paper. The sound of someone laughing has sweat building at the base of my neck. Slamming the wooden drawer closed, I click off my light and dash out of the room.

"Shit. Shit. Shit." I chant.

I'm not going to make it to my room to hide the papers, so I shove them in the back of my sweatpants and sit on the couch. The door swings open revealing Ally and Jax talking and laughing.

"Jax?"

I force myself not to jump up and run to him. Ally looks at me with wide eyes, her mouth falling open, and for a second I think she's on to me.

"Oh my god! Kenna, it's almost eight!" She's yelling, but I tune her out.

My attention is on Jax, who has fully stepped into our living room, wearing a full suit and tie. Dressed in a fitted Armani black and white suit with a tie that's perfectly in place, my mouth dries at the man before me. He smiles at me, jarring me out of my daze and right into rage.

"Where the hell have you been?" I snap.

He holds his hands up in defense, but it's too late. I'm leaning forward on the couch ready to rip him a new one when Ally steps between us.

"Kenna Kingston it's almost eight and the fundraiser is tonight. Get your ass in your room and start getting ready. I'll go put my dress on. Your date is here, be happy about that." Her last comment is made with snark.

"Is Cole picking you up later?"

Huffing, she spins to walk backward to her room, "Apparently he needs me to meet him there so I'm stuck riding an Uber."

Biting the inside of my cheek I decide it's better to have your enemies close, so I offer her a ride in my limo. When she accepts with nothing less than a squeal I let her disappear behind her door when it hits me. I left her closet light on. Shrugging it off, I stand and turn to Jax who hasn't taken his eyes off me.

"You have some explaining to do."

Nodding, he walks around the back of the couch to sit across from me with his hands on his thighs.

"First, you need to get dressed. I can explain before we leave, but we need to be there on time if you want to use me to make a statement." He smirks.

I open my mouth to tell him how wrong he is, but with one look I know he wouldn't believe my lies anyway. We both laugh. Smacking his shoulder on my way past, I head to my room to get changed. I've already had my nails done so all that's left is my makeup and hair. Letting the door shut behind me, I lean against it letting my thoughts settle from the past hour. Pulling the paper from the back of my pants, I hold in a laugh at the image that must've been. Walking to the dresser I open my sock drawer and pull out the small box. How do I choose which one to open first? I slide them both away from me, deciding on neither. Well... at least until I'm in my dress.

The garment bag is laid across my bed calling to me. I haven't laid eyes on it since it was delivered, so I have no idea if it's what I designed, but here goes nothing. Pulling down the zipper, the sides fall open along with my mouth.

"Holy shit." I breathe.

The most beautiful black floor length gown lies before me. The front dips down and opens to show my cleavage, the tip stopping a few inches below my breast-bone.

My tattoo will be on full display. Sliding it off the hanger, I let my clothes fall to the floor, opting to go completely bare under the dress. Silky fabric slides over my skin, sending chills down my arms. The sides split all the way up to my upper hip, showing off my long, toned legs. Including my tattoo. Scars hidden by ink, fully exposed to everyone. My heart beats faster, the anxiety of that climbing up my throat, my palms sweating. Turning to see the back my breath catches at the sight, erasing any feeling other than pure excitement.

* * *

ALLY HASN'T STOPPED side eyeing me since we got in the limo. Her fingers pick at her nails, showing how nervous she is. Can she tell I know her secret? I've managed to hide the fact that I saw those papers before I left, but I don't know how much longer I'll be able to lie to myself or the brothers. We may have an image to uphold tonight, but that won't keep me from telling them exactly who she is.

"Kenna." Jax whispers, his thumb rubbing the top of my hand.

Jerking away from him, my eyes meet his reluctantly. Before we left, he let me in on his little surprise as well. Hired by none other than Oakley 'blue' Savage to keep an eye on me and make sure I'm safe here in Del Mar. Apparently her dad has history with our families, so she felt the need to make sure things didn't get out of hand. Too bad she didn't stop Ryker from sticking his dick in me.

Shut the fuck up. You liked it, and you damn well know it..

I shove my inner bitch back into place. Jax sighs and moves his gaze back to the window. The limo comes to a stop outside the venue where a long red carpet is rolled out, cameras flanking on each side. Perfect.

"Time to put on a show." I plaster on a smile.

The driver opens the door, letting Jax out first and when he steps to the side holding his hand out for me lights start flashing. Blinded, I use his hand to guide me from the leather seats until my feet find their footing on the walkway. Heels may not have been the best choice. Jax leads me to the entrance, not letting my hand go until we cross through the doorway into a massive grand entryway. Marble floors and white walls open the space, chandeliers hang from the ceiling and Matching hawk statues stand on either side of me. This place is insane.

"The rich really do go all out." Jax murmurs.

"Ms. Kingston." I'm greeted by two women who mirror each other.

Pale eyes observe me, spotting the hand that rests on my lower back. My body goes on high alert, but it's not from their unwanted stares. I can feel him before I see him. My eyes roam the room, looking for the heated stare on my skin, but he isn't anywhere in the room.

"Excuse me." I tell Jax.

He goes to follow me, but I shake my head and move further into the room. Looking around to make sure no one is paying attention, I slip into the hallway to my right. A hand covers my mouth, dragging me into a dark room. I wait for the panic to set in, but the familiar smell of Ryker has my body relaxing instead.

"You really do want me to carve him into tiny pieces don't you, Killer?" Ryker whispers into my neck.

He inhales my scent, breathing me in.

"You smell divine little minx." His tongue rolls over the veins in my neck.

Pressing the ball of his piercing into my skin, he drags it down to my shoulder and back up. The light in the room flicks on, he presses himself into me. I'm held hostage between the wall and his lethal fucking body. Brown eyes take in my dress, so I straighten letting him see it in full effect, knowing he's about to see my tattoo. Dragging the back of his knuckle down the front, he circles my nipple on the way down, taking his time drinking me in.

"You truly are a nightmare come to life." He rasps.

When he reaches the split of my dress he pauses, his breath catching in his throat, and I know he sees it.

"Killer." He breathes.

"Ryker."

Pushing the slit open further, he lifts my leg to hook on his hip, his fingers tracing the lines, feeling every dip of my scar. Instead of flinching away from his touch, I find myself leaning into it. The coil of a black viper wraps around my leg, from my ankle all the way to my hip where the mouth opens at the edge of my hip bone.

His thumb rubs the head of the snake, "Why?" is all he asks.

Pressing into him to get his attention, I wait for those dark eyes to reach mine.

"Because even in our darkest moments my loyalty has been with you."

CHAPTER TWENTY NINE

RYKER

Cole and West pace the room with the information I gave them, but all I can think about is a certain blonde that's currently downstairs with her roommate. One that, according to Kenna, can't be trusted. Not that she gave me much more than that with my hand between her legs when my brothers barged into the room, demanding my attention.

"How do you know?" West asks.

Cole spins on him with a feral look painted across his face. "You doubting me now, brother?"

West backs up a step with his hands up, "I'm just making sure. So, if Hank Harlow is in the wind after we let him loose and Kenna has dirt on Ally, it's safe to say that tonight needs to be moved forward."

They both look at me, but I don't meet their eyes.

"It's not that simple." I say.

Cole scoffs under his breath, but I still catch it. Stepping forward towards him West blocks my path in one move. Bracing me against the wall with one hand he looks over his shoulder to Cole, giving him a look I can't read from my position.

"Then what do you suggest we do?" He growls.

Before I can respond the door bursts open and two figures step inside, the room instantly gets smaller with their presence. Addington and Arden walk to the middle of the room, letting the door slowly fall shut behind them.

"Boys."

"Don't fucking speak to us like we're kids. Remember your *fucking* place." I spit.

We may have been at each other's throat a second ago, but we all move into place beside each other facing the two men in front of us. Both dressed to the nines in their best suits, they play the part well. My brothers relax next to me knowing that these two are no match for us.

"I see Ms. Kingston is still mingling downstairs. Alive and well." Addington says.

"I suppose they still have time." Arden offers.

They speak to each other instead of us and that pisses me off. Taking two steps towards them, Arden pulls his hand from his coat and the glint of metal catches my eye when I'm staring down the barrel of a gun. I pause.

"I see that got your attention."

My fist clench, "I see you just signed your death sentence." I feel no fear.

Cole and West step forward meeting me shoulder to shoulder. There's one thing we were taught young and that's to look death in the face and say fuck you. We've been trained for this, so if they thought we would break down and beg they were wrong. The only puzzle piece I can't seem to make fit is the why. If we die there is no company. Of course they could make their own business here in Del Mar, but all of our money and assets go to charities that we have our hands in, so this doesn't make sense. Unless we're too close to something they want to keep hidden.

"You won't make it out of here tonight, Stone." Addington spits. "I've already made arrangements to take good care of Ms. Kingston, so don't worry about her."

The look in his eyes makes me lunge forward, my hands closing around his throat. I don't see Arden swinging the butt of the gun until it's too late, but West is right there on top of him knocking it from his hands. My fist slam into Addington's face over and over until Cole shouts my name. Looking up I see Cole cornered by Arden, who has the gun aimed at his head. My eyes search for West where I find him lying on the floor with blood running down the side of his hairline.

"Give up boys. Your dad made a mistake trusting three young kids with such a big job."

"The mistake you made is thinking they were alone."

Her soft voice echoes off the walls, pistol in hand, she presses it up to Arden's head. Cole's eyes meet hers over the professor's shoulder. They hold each other's attention when she pulls the trigger without hesitating. Blood sprays across Cole's white shirt, covering his face. I feel the thud of

Arden's body falling to the floor through the soles of my feet. No one moves. Addington groans below me, blood spilling from his mouth, both eyes swollen. Leaving him on the ground, I look to my little killer. Kenna drops the gun to her side, hand shaking. I kneel beside her and take the weapon.

"Kenna, baby, look at me."

Standing, my finger tips her chin back, forcing her to look at me. Cole pushes me out of the way, taking Kenna into his arms, he whispers something into her ear. My hand itches watching my brother hold my girl against his body, but I give him a moment with her, knowing he just watched the woman he hates save his life. Releasing her, he steps back nodding his head at her before storming from the room.

"Wait." She calls out, but he's already gone.

"Let him be, he needs to clear his head." I tell her.

Looking to West, I motion for him to follow Cole. Hopefully he can keep an eye on him. Knowing that he's struggling with it being Kenna who saved his life, and not the fact that he could have been the one with a hole in his head. Pulling out my phone I dial G's number, telling him to send a crew to clean up. Thankfully the music pouring into the room from downstairs seems to keep the guest in the dark about what's going on one floor above them. Kenna's hand trembles at her side.

Leaning down, my mouth hovers over hers, "Where did you get the gun, Killer?" I ask.

Moving the slit on her right leg to the side, she reveals a black holster strapped to her upper thigh where the gun must have been resting.

"It was a gift."

Her tone is bitter, but she smiles up at me anyway. Her long lashes fan across her cheeks with each blink. She's breathtaking. So fucking magnificent and beautiful, like a Phoenix rising from the ashes. A pile of ashes we tried to bury her in.

"Come with me." I state.

It's not a question, yet not a demand either. G's crew will be here in minutes so I decide to leave the fucker on the floor with the dead body beside him. Squeezing her hand I guide her from the room, but after a few steps she snaps out of whatever trance she was in to pull away from me.

"Ally." She barks.

Raising an eyebrow, "What about Ally?"

"Her last name isn't Adler."

Not understanding the urgency, she plants both hands on my chest, looking at me fiercely.

"Have them meet us somewhere so I can explain everything and this time I'm going to make you all listen." She says, her words final.

She storms off, her long legs move too fast heading to the center of the party. The silver snake holding the back of her dress together damn near has me falling to my knees. Ready to kneel at the feet of a temptress. Instead I trail behind her. Loud boisterous laughing mixes with the low hum of music that's playing throughout the party. Keeping my eyes on the top of Kenna's head, my body follows her through the room like she's pulling me by my balls. I'm so lost inside this woman all I can see is her. Fueled by raw adrenaline she storms up to Ally, who's dancing with an older man, and drags her off to the side.

"We're leaving."

Ally looks between us with a confused stare, "but."

"I'll meet you back at the dorm later." Kenna looks at me over her shoulder before turning back to Ally with a small smile. "It might be tomorrow." She gives her a shy look.

My girl is anything but shy so I know it's only for show. Ally does some sort of girlie shimmy on her toes, purple curls bouncing with the move. Ally shoots a wink at Kenna, ignoring the fact that I'm standing right here, and bounces away to who the fuck knows where.

"Well, that was weird." I chuckle.

Leaning down, my lips hover over the soft dip between her shoulder, "Now what?"

"Now we head back to your place to meet your brothers."

She tries to hide the way I affect her, but the slight hitch in her tone gives her away. Kissing and nipping up her neck I whisper in her ear.

"Tell me, Killer. Was your pussy wet when you pulled the trigger?"

Her whole body shakes with the force of her shiver. A moan slips past her soft pink lips.

"Yeah, baby. I think you're still dripping right now." My teeth nip at her earlobe, "Why don't I see how soaked you are in front of all these people."

Dropping her head back to rest on my shoulder, she sways her ass against me, "We can't."

"Then tell me to stop."

My hand rubs down her side, squeezing her hip, my fingers dip into the side of her dress. Drawing circles on her skin, my hand lowers until I can feel the heat between her thighs.

"Please Rye." She groans.

"Please what? Stop?" I taunt.

Turning us in a circle we sway back and forth. Slipping further down, the tip of my fingers spread her pussy open, meeting slick skin. She's dripping.

"Fuck, Killer. You're so fucking ready for me."

My other hand grips her hip, pressing her ass into my stiff cock. The ache is almost too much, but when my finger slides inside her tight cunt I almost bend her over and fuck her right here.

Her head thrashes, "Please. Please Ryker." Her words are urgent.

"Tell me what you want."

Curling my finger inside her, I rub the spot that drives her closer to the edge, adding another finger to fill her. She still needs more.

"So fucking needy. Such a slut for me, baby." My tongue licks up the side of her neck.

"Yes. Only for you."

Pinching her clit, my fingers thrust slowly in and out, dragging her closer, but not enough to push her over the edge. When her walls start to pulse around my fingers, I slide them out leaving her to hover right at the peak.

"Next time I see another man hanging off your arm, I'll rip it from his body and fuck you with it. Understand?"

Smacking her ass I pull her from the room fuming and unsatisfied.

CHAPTER THIRTY

KENNA

Ryker stands near the window looking out at the dark sky, his hand curled around a sheet of paper. The one I found. The one that says *Alice Addington.* The daughter of Ethan Addington himself. My shoes wear a path in the carpet, pacing is the only thing keeping me from storming back to the dorm where Ally is. She has no idea that we know her little secret.

Forgiving her for taking money from the guys to spy on me? It was hard, but we made it through that. This? She'll be lucky if I don't rip out her throat with my teeth. So many questions are left hanging in the air that none of us can focus on because we are missing someone. A piece of us. The ache of having one of us hurting so bad that they go off the grid is unbearable.

"Killer, sit that pretty little ass down or be still. You're driving me crazy."

Ryker doesn't look away from the night sky outside, but he doesn't have to. I can feel his pain as if it were my own, because it is. The anger at being betrayed after taking someone in.

"What's the plan, brother?" West asks.

"We go pick up a rat." I say answering for Ryker.

Ryker turns, caramel eyes connecting with mine. A wicked promise gleaming in their depths. Moving away from the window he takes long slow strides to me, giving me time to run, but I don't. I wait for him with anticipation. Crowding me against the back of the couch, my head tips back to hold eye contact. Grabbing me by the back of my neck he pulls me in, his nose running up the column of my throat, inhaling the scent that drives him mad.

"Yeah, little killer, let's go pick us up a rat." Nipping at my neck he sends a shiver through me.

A groan slips past my lips, "Ryker."

Growling, his teeth sink into my bottom lip, pulling and sucking. He dives in taking my mouth in a brutal kiss that leaves me aching for air. My heart is pounding behind my ribcage.

"If we're going to catch Ally at the dorm we need to leave now. Come on fuckers let's do this."

West slaps the top of the couch on his way to the door, but Ryker keeps his mouth hovering over mine. Our breath mixes together in a heady combination of need and dominance. Stretching forward my tongue peeks out, running it across his bottom lip.

"Killer." He warns.

Kissing the edge of his mouth, I flash him a wink and dash around him to join West at the door. All I hear behind me is the subtle flick of a lighter, his threat hanging in the air. My core clenches with the prospect.

"Promises, promises." I murmur under my breath.

Wrapping both arms around my waist he drags me backwards back into the apartment. He moves one hand to my throat and the other to my center.

"I don't make promises I can't keep, baby."

Rubbing two fingers into the center of my leggings, he waits for my legs to drift open before he releases me and moves around me to open the door that West is standing at. They walk out laughing at my frustration. It's approaching seven at night by the time we pull up outside the dorms. We park away from my building to make sure she doesn't see us coming. We don't want the little bitch to go running. Cole's been MIA for two days while Ally has been holed up in the dorm upset that he hasn't talked to her. She can play it off as stress from finals, but I know better.

What I don't understand is why would her dad send her here to be my roommate, yet not tell her about the fire? If he knows as much as she claims he does then what's his plan? Alice Addington. I repeat that name over and over, reminding myself that there is no coming back from this. Having a hand in the foundations games? Being related by blood to the one fucking person that's caused us the most pain? How long has she known? During her little story time she mentioned that there was a behind the scenes play that we don't suspect and that has worry pulling at me.

"Are we taking her to The Basement?" I ask.

West looks at me in the rearview mirror, I chose the back-seat against Rykers demands, so that I could have space to process my thoughts. I've proved my dad had nothing to do with the fire. I just haven't had time to tell the brothers. Not with Cole gone and Ally being discovered as an inside man for her father. Who seems to have a vendetta against not only the Stone family, but also the Kingston family. For all I know, he could be my fucking shadow. Fucker wears so many masks, but we're about to rip each one off that trai-torous face.

"Let's get this shit over with." West swings his door open.

We step out into the darkness that covers the dark SUV under the broken streetlight. The school has avoided fixing this light at the request of one extremely possessive asshole. The same one who just pushed my hair back to kiss the side of my neck. We make our way into the building and head up to my floor. It's quiet on campus tonight, almost eerie. Pulling out my key I move to open the door, but Ryker beats me to it with a key he has on his keychain.

"Are you fucking kidding me?" I grit.

Looking over his shoulder with a look of a sly kid who stole money from his mom's purse, "You think I'd let you change the locks without making my own?" He says.

West ignores our exchange, his leg bouncing, waiting for the lock to disengage. Opening the door we come face to face with Ally, who is sitting on the couch bundled under her fluffy pink blanket with a bowl of popcorn.

"You almost missed movie night."

"Sorry, I guess I've been a shitty friend lately." I shrug.

Stepping inside I move to the left letting both brothers in and shutting the door. Ally looks over at the boys and then looks back at me with a brow raised.

"I didn't realize we were having company."

Her tone is polite, but she's obviously confused and rightfully so. To her, Ryker is enemy number one and West is just an ex she sees when she has to. But having them both here? And invited by me? It's not something she would ever see coming and that's what I'm going for. Deciding to drag this out to see what we can get from her, I walk over to the couch and sit down. Propping my hands on my knees I lean forward keeping my eyes on her.

"What's going on?" She laughs but it's shaky.

"Have you heard from Cole?" West asks.

Her stare moves from mine to his before she looks back at me. Ignoring the man she used as a fuck buddy to get closer to us.

"Not since he ghosted me yesterday. I've text him a few times, but figured he was busy or just didn't want to see me."

She rolls her eyes with a shrug, popping a handful of buttery popcorn in her mouth, she looks at each of us. Her demeanor changes when she looks at Ryker. He doesn't hide how he feels, so she picks up his hostile energy immediately. I go to speak, but my phone rings. Pulling it from my pocket my eyes widened at the name on the screen. I don't ever remember saving it. Cole's name flashes at me.

"Cole?"

West and Ryker move towards me, but my hand flying up halts them. Well, one of them. Ryker steps into me attempting to listen.

"Kenna?" His words are slurred and unsure.

Ally hasn't moved from the couch, but I don't give her the comfort of hearing our conversation so I motion to West. Signaling for him to keep an eye on her, Ryker follows me into my bedroom. Ryker walks over to my bed, pulling me with him. My ass settles over his lap.

"Where are you?"

"That doesn't matter. I need to talk to you, are you alone?"

Looking over my shoulder, brown eyes crash against my grey ones. Closing my eyes I lie.

"I am."

"Liar. Ryker is with you isn't he?"

Sighing, "Cole, please. Where are you?"

"I need to tell you I'm sorry. Blaming you for Paige and my dad. You were right, Kenna. It wasn't your dad."

He sounds defeated and broken. His voice is low, but his words are drawn out by the alcohol he must have had.

"Have you been drinking?"

He doesn't respond and a part of me wonders if in his stupor he nodded his head instead of speaking.

"I'm sorry, Kenna. You need to understand that your dad didn't do this. We were all betrayed. They just keep piling up."

Ryker looks at me with his eyebrows raised. I wish I could tell him what I know, but first I need to see what Cole found.

"Tell me where you are and I can come to you. We can talk alone if that's what you want."

Silence.

"Cole."

Heavy breathing.

"Please, Cole." I beg.

"I can't take the secrets anymore. I've found so much more than we thought. We turned our backs on you."

"It's okay, I promise. Just let me come to you and you can tell me face to face how sorry you are."

His broken words has tears rolling down my face. Feeling his pain through the phone has the oxygen in the room thinning. My lungs try to drag in a gulp of air. My skin itches with awareness.

"Cole, tell me where you are right now."

"It'll break them. What I've found."

"What did you find?" I ask.

Ryker rubs my knee, his worry for Cole leaking from him in waves.

Cole sighs into the phone. "Do you ever wish you didn't find the things you have? What if we were better off not knowing the truth?" He says, talking more to himself than to me. "I'm sorry."

The line goes dead. Jumping from the bed my blood runs cold. A numb fear nagging at the back of my head. The way he spoke, his words, the distant way he said sorry. No. No. Dear god.

"We need to find him now!"

Ryker grabs me by my arms. "What is it?"

Shaking my head, tears fall down my cheeks. Shoving him off me I burst out the bedroom to find West standing over Ally who is playing on her phone.

"Track him." I snap.

West looks up at me in confusion, "I would if I knew his location."

"I wasn't talking to you."

Ally looks up from her phone with nervous eyes. She knows that I'm aware of her tracking equipment. It takes her a few seconds before she puts the pieces together, answers that have her jumping from the couch, her palm held out in front of her.

"I don't give a shit, Addington." I use her real last name to confirm her thoughts.

"Kens."

Stepping forward a few feet, I let her see every ounce of pure emotion on my face.

"I don't give a fuck who you are, I know you can track him, so do what the hell I said. We'll deal with your lies later."

She nods, "Okay, okay."

She rushes past West to her bedroom. Two minutes later she's back with a prepaid phone that has a map pulled up on it. A flashing blue dot is lit up along the west side of town near the beach. Grabbing her phone I pull it closer trying to see if anything there looks familiar. Showing it to Ryker, recognition flickers across his face.

"We have a house out that way. We don't use it often but it's up against the beach."

"How long will it take us to get there?" I ask.

My stomach sinks with each second that passes.

"Ten minutes if I'm driving." Ryker says.

"Let's go."

Keeping Ally's phone in hand we all move towards the door.

Spinning on my heels I put a finger in Ally's face, "Don't go anywhere. We haven't forgotten anything."

She looks at me with an offended expression, "I don't give a fuck about running because I'm coming with you."

"The hell you are." West yells.

He makes a move to push past me, but I stop him with a hand on his chest. One that Ryker snatches off the second it touches him.

"Killer." He warns.

"Now isn't the time. If we want to keep an eye on her she might as well come with us. Especially if this thing stops working." I waive the phone in the air.

Without Cole, Ally is the only tech geek we have, and I won't take that risk. Shoving past a brooding West, I rush down the stairs to the car.

"You better not be playing us." I say, turning around in my seat so I can see Ally.

* * *

RYKER CALLED G to meet us at the house so we pull up at the same time. Throwing into park we all step out of the SUV. I tried calling Cole a few times on the way here but he never picked up the phone. The way this small beach house is set up, the driveway is around the back of the house so we have to walk around the yard in the dark to get to the front door. Complaining about the layout of the property, I pick up my pace. Almost tripping on the stairs that lead up the front porch Ryker grabs my arm holding me steady.

"Easy."

It's all he says. All of us on edge praying we find him here. My hand closes over the doorknob when my phone rings. Cole's name is on the screen but this time my finger hesitates. Darkness clouds over me in a weird sensation of foreboding.

"Cole?" I ask.

"Don't. Just give me a minute to pull myself together."

Ice cold numbness fills my chest. His words are off. Cole's voice is void and distant. My phone goes black, the call ending, and my stomach drops. I can't explain the feeling building. Have you ever felt a storm rolling in despite the sun shining on your face? That feeling enters me like a freight train. Yanking the door open I run through the house flipping lights on along the way. Ryker calls out after me but nothing stops me from barreling through each room looking for him.

The last door on the right has a small orange glow coming from the bottom of the door. The only room in the house that hasn't been checked. Beer bottles and joints litter the floors of the house. Brown hardwood floors and grey walls stretch out ahead of me. Fear consumes me like a fire spreading. Growing until it takes over everything in its path. My legs are shaking. Opening the door my mouth falls open to release a silent scream.

I don't see anything but him. My eyes zero in on Cole. I see his face and the way his eyes bore into mine. My hands tremble, my knees slamming into the floor, I see nothing but Cole.

CHAPTER THIRTY ONE

RYKER

Shoving past Kenna who is now on the floor I see my little brother. The baby of the family. Cole's crystal blue eyes look past me with utter fear reflecting in them. Jumping into action I shout for West to help me. I'm screaming for Cole but he isn't hearing me. His body is still. Too fucking still. Looking past me, his eyes forward, stuck on Kenna. Forever looking into my girl's eyes. I use my right shoulder to lift him above me, using every ounce of sheer strength I can find. West fumbles with the cord, releasing Cole, letting his weight drop on top of me once he's free.

"G!" I shout.

G and Ally bust through the door at the same time. Ally screams, the sound hollow and empty. A harrowing scream that comes from soul deep pain. Her small frame begins to tremble, her voice ringing through the room, echoing against the walls. That sound breaks Kenna from the darkness but I can't see them. All I can see is Cole.

"Rye." West calls out. His words are a plea.

Once we have Cole free from the strand of cords hanging from the ceiling we lower him to the floor. I don't need to say anything else, G already has his phone out, and is calling 911. G is dragging a screaming Ally on his way out.

"Get her the fuck out of here before I kill her!" Kenna wails, her sobs rattling her entire body.

Kneeling next to Cole I check for a pulse but my head falls to his chest when I don't find one. West rests his forehead on my shoulder, pressing his palm into Cole's chest, Kenna joins us on the floor.

"Do something!" She cries.

The bruising around his neck is deep and looks like it damages his windpipe. West presses his palm into his chest again and again now using both hands. Wrapping my hand around the back of his neck I drag Cole to my chest. My baby brother.

Kenna crawls over me to press her mouth to his, West working his chest, me holding his head. We work in tandem pleading with each other to fight harder. Begging him to stay with us. West pushes air into his lungs, Kenna breathes for him, and I support him.

"Don't leave me." I whisper.

Kenna sobs into his neck on the last breath. Her entire body is shaking with the force of her sorrow. West punches the floor near Coles' head, his own tears falling to the ground. I hold him closer. Pulling him up against me I whisper pleas to him praying that he can hear me somehow.

"They're here!" G yells, running into the room.

Laying him down on his back I beg him to wake up.

"Come back to us. We need you."

"I can't do this without you." West says, his head resting on Cole's chest.

"Kenna keep blowing air in his mouth." She's almost moving on instinct, each move timed, she's completely numb to the noise around her. It's only a few seconds later when people start to fill the room. My hands pull Kenna back but she shoves me off moving back to keep going.

"They need to help him, Kenna." I say.

"No. No. I can't leave him. He needs me. He needs us!" She yells.

Spinning she shoves me in the chest, her face red and swollen, her fist slams into me.

"We can't leave him! I won't leave him. Please don't let him leave us."

She falls into my chest, my arms engulf her. I sit there and hold her while she breaks. Two EMT workers lift Cole's body onto a board but I can see it in their faces. No matter how much air she gave him he isn't coming back.

"Rye." West looks at me. Completely lost and shattered.

Cole's hand falls from the stretcher, his fingers limp. West stands to lift Kenna from my lap so I can get up. Grabbing her from him, we follow them outside to the truck. Leaving the extension cord hanging from the ceiling as we walk out. G is holding Ally to the side of the house, keeping her away from us, but she manages to break free. Sprinting to the ambulance she grabs the hand that's hanging off the side and brings it to her face. Bending down she says something in his ear but I'm too far to hear. Kenna drenches my shirt with her tears but I set her to her feet anyway.

"I need to be with my brother." Lifting her chin I wait for her grey eyes to meet mine. "I need you to be strong for me, Killer."

Nodding she swipes at the wetness on her face.

"Ryker!" West calls out.

Rushing to his side we climb into the ambulance with the team of EMT's hauling us. Ally is moved to the side by G who is looking at us with a broken expression. Cole is his brother too. A young guy climbs in the back with us to check over Cole. They haven't pulled the sheet over him so I allow myself to hope. Hope is a dangerous thing. It's almost like fire. It builds and grows until you're filled with it.

"Please don't leave us, brother. We still need you here with us."

He's too still. A chill falls over me. I drop my head and pray for the first time since my father died. I can't lose my baby brother. I won't be able to survive this. I'm not strong enough. Looking out the open door, grey eyes meet mine. With a nod of her head she watches as the doors close, shutting us off from each other.

CHAPTER THIRTY TWO

KENNA

The flashing lights start to fade when G steps up beside me.

"Ally's waiting in the car around back. I'll pull it around for you so you can have a moment to yourself."

His voice cracks. Reaching for his hand I squeeze it before letting him go. It's a silent comfort that I can offer him when I have nothing else to give. He walks away, leaving me standing in darkness, feeling like I did two years ago when I lost Paige and Alec. Only this time I'll be losing so much more. Ryker will never be the same. I've lost a brother and the man who dug himself deep into my soul. Planting himself between my ribs making a home in my heart.

Hearing tires approach, I go to step forward when a hand closes over my mouth. Fighting against the hold my lungs scream at me. Unable to pull in a full breath, my head swims. My vision starts to fade, my nose burning with the smell of chemicals, I can feel my eyes drifting.

"I told you I'd see you soon, Princessa."

That voice. It's the one from my nightmares. My lips part to scream but I realize it's too late when my body gives out and darkness consumes me.

The End

EPILOGUE

GIO

Two week later

"Where the fuck are you?" The voice on the other line snaps at me.

Pulling my phone away from my ear, my eyes fall to the screen, where the unknown number stares back at me.

"I'm already taking a chance by calling you. If the brothers knew I was reaching out for anything at all I'd be dead."

The soft voice on the other end laughs. "I thought you were their little pet."

Continuing my pacing around the beach house, I can feel my hand shaking around the phone.

"Me being family means this call is even more risky than if I were just another hands man. Letting someone know what's going on behind the scenes?" I scoff.

Shaking my head, my toe digs a hole into the dirt, trying to calm my racing heart. Everything has went to shit the last two weeks. Cole... I don't think I can process everything that's happened with my brother. A brother in every sense of the word.

"Then why did you call me?" She says, relaxed.

My body coils tight at her lazy tone.

"Kenna Kingston."

It's the only name that will pull her from whatever the fuck she's doing. Ryker can't know I called her or anyone else for that matter, but it's all hands on fucking deck. I've had my own reasons for what I've done in the past, but Kenna has always been safe with me. It's the one reason Ryker and the others never gave me the call to put hands on her. They knew what the answer would be. A big fuck you and fuck no. What people seem to forget is the Stone brothers were raised to know loyalty and respect, so me standing my ground means something to them. It's why I can tell them to fuck off and still have my tongue in my mouth.

"Talk to me."

I almost forget she's still on the line, my attention on the black SUV heading this way, speeding through the small street.

"I've got company."

"Kenna-"

Cutting her off, "Find her." It's all I give her before I'm slipping the phone in my pocket.

Replacing it with a cigarette. My muscles relax with the first pull, smoke filling my lungs, calm coating me. The SUV whips into the driveway damn near taking out the mailbox but he doesn't care. I don't try to squint against the sun to see who's driving because I already know. West hasn't been able to come back here, but Ryker? I can barely peel his ass away. We've walked every inch of this property looking for some sign of Kenna or who may have taken her. Even though I have a guess.

The door swings open to reveal a pissed off Ryker. Storming towards me I brace for what I know is coming. Without blinking he rears back and slams his fist into the side of my face. A deep growl passes his lips with the hit. I think me being able to take one of his punches pisses him off even more, but it shouldn't. We've been training together since we were kids so he knows more than anyone that I could take anything he throws my way. Being able to take him down is a different story, but it's been done before. Ryker Stone is a brick fucking wall but I've managed to chip away a few pieces.

Spitting out blood, my eyes stay on the ground.

"Feel better yet?" I ask, he knows what I mean but it still fuels his anger.

He steps towards me, my gaze finally meets his, and he looks like hell. Dark black circles shadow his eyes, his hair is a greasy mess, and his fist. They're bruised and some even broken. He's been in the Basement every night the past two weeks. When he's not out looking for Kenna and causing chaos, he's in the ring damn near killing people. West stopped showing up to control his raging older brother so I'm left to do it.

"Anything yet?"

Every word that comes out his mouth is warped by grunts and growls. He's less man and more demon each second she's gone. Ally's lucky she has a pussy. Lucky that I've taken every hit meant for her. She's lucky in every way that matters except one. Cole. Not that West is letting her forget. For as much as Ryker is giving me everything he has, West is doing the same with Ally.

"I have everyone on our roster on the streets looking for her. We're going to get her back, Rye."

Ryker's face darkens, "I want her location by the end of today or I'll cut out your tongue."

He looks over my shoulder at the house one last time before he turns and heads back to the SUV.

"I'll set fire to this entire town if Kenna Kingston isn't in my hands by the end of the day. Send out a national fucking message if you need to. I don't give a shit. If she isn't back before midnight I'll start slitting throats."

Climbing back in the blacked out SUV, he jerks it into gear, backing out and taking out the mailbox across the street. I bend down to grab the cigarette I dropped when he punched me and slip it between my lips. Before I head around back to my car, I make one last phone call. I know she'll have better luck with Ryker than I've had.

"G." She states my name like we speak everyday which takes me by surprise.

"How-"

Her raspy laugh hits my ears, "I keep tabs on everyone. Now, I'm a little busy with my guys so what can I do for you?"

Rolling my eyes, "I think this would interest you more than whatever fun you have planned."

I can hear rustling around and complaints from the other end of the line before her voice comes through, "Talk."

Not one to waste words she cuts through the bullshit. It's what I like about her.

"Kenna Kingston is missing. She was taken two weeks ago."

Silence. I pull the phone back to make sure the call wasn't dropped or she didn't hang up.

"Where are you?"

My eyebrows dip, "Del Mar. A little beach house that we own."

"By we, you mean the Stone family?" She questions.

I nod before I think better of it, "Yea."

"Hmmm."

She says something to someone in the background before she comes back to the phone.

"I'll be there shortly. Where is Jax?"

Jax is a tattoo artist that befriended Kenna but also works for the Savage family. Seems he hasn't been checking in with his boss.

Laughing I fill her in, "Looks like Jax disappeared right along with Kenna. We've tried tracking him down but it looks like he vanished into thin air."

Silence.

"I'll be there soon. Don't fucking move."

"I don't take orders from you, girl."

A male voice tries to cut in but she silences him, "If you want to keep your heart in your chest I suggest you do. You called me for help, remember?"

"I thought you had an interest in the Kingston family. Keeping Kenna safe was a big project of yours right?"

"I see my motives weren't clear. Let me put it this way, G." She spits my name. "If a hair on her head is out of place I'll wipe out the entire Stone family. Is that understood?"

Gritting my teeth, I swallow down the words I want to say, and chose to break the silence with something else instead.

"You should know that the Stone brothers don't know I'm calling you. They have other-" I pause looking for the right word. "Priorities on their hands."

A door shuts in the background, the sound of a bike starting follows, but still she doesn't speak.

"I know about Cole. That's the last text I got from Jax."

She knew, yet she's still sitting back on her ass not making a move. Not until a Kingston is missing and that's where her loyalty lies. With the wrong family. I clamp my mouth shut.

"There was nothing I could do for them. Stay there, I'm only an hour out."

The line goes dead. We have a missing Kingston. A man who vanished the same night. A rat with purple hair. And a foundation member's body in the ground. It took Kenna Kingston one semester at Hawthorne to set fire to an entire empire.

WHERE TO FIND ME

C.M Nyx Reader Group: https://www.facebook.com/groups/245651841806224

Website: https://covenandcopublishing.squarespace.com/

TikTok: https://www.tiktok.com/@c.m.nyx_author?lang=en

ACKNOWLEDGMENTS

Thank you to my amazing PA, Erin Smith, who has always stood by me. Kept me in line even when my brain tried to drag me all over the place. I love you. I love your face. And I love that Oakley represents everything I know you are!

Thank you to my loyal Alpha readers! You have been so good to me. No matter what I send your way you eat it up and ask for more. I don't think I could do this without any of you.

Bailey and Danielle, thank you for keeping me in line. Dani, you loved Ryker from the start and I love that for you! I will continue to fight you for him but in the end I'm a Cole girlie through and through. Thank you for joining my team you both are the best PR duo.

Brit. Brittney. My editor. My friend. My FaceTime buddy. Our FaceTime calls lasted over 5 hours every time you dove in to edit my story. There was never a dull moment. You brighten my day and I promise to always LEAN on you my PRETTY GIRL. You are the best! You dove in when I needed an editor for this story and really helped me bring it to life. I love you Bunches.